THE TYRANNY OF DENIAL

or

Brexit - the Thriller

The first political thriller about Britain's EU Referendum

By
RICHARD SIMON

Copyright © Richard Simon 2017
This book is sold subject to the condition that it shall not, by way of trade or otherwise, be lent, resold, hired out, or otherwise circulated without the publisher's prior consent in any form of binding or cover other than that in which it is published and without a similar condition including this condition being imposed on the subsequent publisher.
The moral right of Richard Simon has been asserted.
ISBN-13: 978-1546424246
ISBN-10: 1546424245

To my dear fellow Brexiteers John and Nessa... Brexit forever!

DEDICATION

To my dear wife and sister... and all those dedicated Brexiteers who have strived – and are still striving – to give Britain back its sovereignty and freedom.

Much love,

Simon   11th August 2018

Simon Holder
aka
Richard Simon

CONTENTS

PREFACE 1

PART ONE: BETRAYAL 10
- *Chapter One* *10*
- *Chapter Two* *18*
- *Chapter Three* *24*
- *Chapter Four* *31*
- *Chapter Five* *37*
- *Chapter Six* *41*
- *Chapter Seven* *47*
- *Chapter Eight* *57*
- *Chapter Nine* *67*

PART TWO: REVENGE 71
- *Chapter Ten* *71*
- *Chapter Eleven* *82*
- *Chapter Twelve* *93*
- *Chapter Thirteen* *99*
- *Chapter Fourteen* *107*
- *Chapter Fifteen* *113*
- *Chapter Sixteen* *122*
- *Chapter Seventeen* *125*
- *Chapter Eighteen* *133*
- *Chapter Nineteen* *142*
- *Chapter Twenty* *147*
- *Chapter Twenty-One* *150*
- *Chapter Twenty-Two* *157*
- *Chapter Twenty-Three* *162*

Chapter Twenty-Four.. *167*
Chapter Twenty-Five... *171*
Chapter Twenty-Six... *179*
Chapter Twenty-Seven.. *185*
Chapter Twenty-Eight *193*
Chapter Twenty-Nine *203*
Chapter Thirty... *209*
Chapter Thirty-One *215*
Chapter Thirty-Two *225*
Chapter Thirty-Three.. *228*
Chapter Thirty-Four *231*
Chapter Thirty-Five... *238*
Chapter Thirty-Six *246*
Chapter Thirty-Seven *251*

PART THREE: AFTERMATH 259

Chapter Thirty-Eight... *259*
Chapter Thirty-Nine... *264*
Chapter Forty *272*
Chapter Forty-One.. *277*
Chapter Forty-Two *282*
Chapter Forty-Three *291*
Chapter Forty-Four *296*

EPILOGUE 299

AUTHOR BIOGRAPHY... 303

This is a work of fiction. Names, characters, businesses, organizations, places, events and incidents either are the product of the author's imagination or are used fictitiously. Any resemblance to actual persons, living or dead, events, or locales is entirely coincidental.

PREFACE

It was an earthquake. Not the geographical kind, but the emotional one, where the foundations of life become changed forever, and everything that was planned and expected suddenly falls away, is destroyed, and is never the same again. Like the realisation that a nightmare in the depths of slumber is actually the reality of daylight.

Such was the case with Kate and Michael, when a seismic external event caused shockwaves so unexpected and profound, so devastating and immutable, that it exposed rifts never known of or contemplated. It created an abyss of distrust and darkness between two blissfully happy, successful people which could never have been envisaged… And whilst some upheavals are salvageable with time, patience and hard work, some are not.

The couple had each lived a gilded life, orchestrated at regular intervals by the progress of middle-class expectation: due to determined rather than influential parents and good university degrees, neither had ever been tested in the furnace of life, where accepted views and sets of grouped ideals perpetrated by comfortable peer groups would ever have caused more than a ripple: the good life would just happen, just 'be'.

Michael had progressed with a double first from Oxford in politics and economics; Kate a double first at Cambridge in journalism and media studies. Both were set fair to have the expected life of comfort, wealth and plenty. Kate had managed to get into the BBC at an early age, working in the newsroom at Television Centre in West London; she soon progressed to junior producer and researcher, then producer, and then senior producer. Working on stories, news bulletins and the odd in-vision interview, gaining a name for herself in the industry for her attractive looks and trenchant, piercing interrogative style, the archetypal iron fist in a velvet glove from which interviewees seldom escaped unscathed. Michael had gone the literary route and had had his first novel on the ethics of power and subversion published when he was just twenty-three; he frequently wrote articles for major newspapers and was becoming moderately well-known amongst intellectuals in the land.

After meeting at a party after the Oxford-Cambridge boat race in Putney in 1998, they had married soon after but decided to wait a while for children until their careers had become settled. Yet as soon as they had achieved this happy state, they found that there had been neither the time nor desire to forego their happy existence for them, and each subsequently concluded that this was the best thing they had never done. Likewise, both thinking that politics was somehow a distraction and somewhat beneath their intellectual strata, neither had really had any political discussions: like children, it was something that they did not need or desire; their two votes would change nothing. So they were ambivalent, if not disdainful, of political processes and felt happier not being influenced by, or part of, the fray below them.

Nonetheless, soon after this realisation – or, perhaps, because of it - Michael had found himself venturing into politics, and was soon being chased by the three major parties, each who wanted him in their teams to help form and arrange their policies and presentations. It had been difficult for him to formulate any political views because his father and mother, too, had generally thought politics beneath them, a constant squabble of ideas being perpetrated by people who had too much power and thought too much of themselves anyway. Yet it was this that Michael had suddenly found attractive: he realised he had a talent for espousing any view – whether he believed it or not – and creating such persuasive arguments that his polemic almost always won the debate; and even the most hard-bitten politicos had to admit that his ability was extraordinary, even if they resented what he had said. So he stayed in and around the fringes, not allowing any party to claim him for their own and creating much speculation on his alliances depending on his latest paper or argument. He wrote for magazines on each side, too, yet always had the uncanny knack of making his conclusions vital yet ambivalent. In short, he was potentially hot property for anyone who could nail him down for long enough to claim him as their own.

And so it was that, in late 2015, with UKIP breathing down the necks of the Conservatives, and Labour having found themselves with a leader espousing divisive views and in potential hock to an ascendant Scottish National Party with enough seats to swing an election, that the Conservative Prime Minister had promised a binding Referendum on whether to Remain in, or Leave, the European Union if he won the next election… To him, the pundits, the elites and the polls, it always seemed less than likely that he would win this and, thus, any Referendum. Indeed, the Labour party was resolutely against such a plebiscite: but he gambled on the chance that it would silence the debate on Britain's place in Europe forever. Either way, then, it seemed likely that Britain's continuing supplication to Europe would almost inevitably, therefore, continue.

Yet earthquakes are seldom predictable, and the election result proved to be the first tremor in an event of far greater seismic relevance.

*

One Friday morning six weeks later, Michael came down the stairs in his dressing-gown and switched on the news; it was immediately apparent that – against all expectations – the Conservatives had won the election overall with a slender majority of 13. Inside, he could not help but find himself feeling slightly pleased; he had been concerned at what a Labour-SNP coalition might have done to his beloved United Kingdom and felt faintly relieved that the status quo had prevailed. Unusually for him, he was unable to articulate why: he just knew he was pleased, and that was that. Neither of them had voted, as usual; yet for the first time he suddenly wished he had – and he was annoyed with himself for not having partaken of the political process. After all, with his knowledge of the political landscape, he should have been able to decide which party to vote for quite easily if he had put his mind to it.

At that moment, Kate came down the stairs; she immediately sussed the situation and screwed her mouth into a twist of apparent disdain – or was it just disappointment?

"Well, well," she just said, and went into the kitchen to put the coffee on. Yet Michael was suddenly enthralled by the process, as suddenly the cameras cut to the Labour party headquarters where senior figures there were in various degrees of discombobulated denial. He smiled, then he shouted to Kate: "Darling, what are you going to make of this when you get to the BBC?"

"They won't like it," she rejoined, somewhat casually, then: "It'll be heavy going there for a few days. They'll be in a state of resentment. Their in-built hatred of all things not left-wing will colour their bulletins for ages, I'm sure."

"Then you must ensure that yours aren't," he chuckled.

"Some chance. I want to keep my job." She came in with a coffee in one hand and a dripping piece of toast in the other. She gave him a quick peck on the cheek and said she would soon be off.

"I've got an article to write," he said, and put the TV off just as the Labour leader appeared, looking haggard, distraught... and very angry.

After Kate had left, Michael wrote his article, sent it off and then started pondering the ramifications of the election result. So now there really would be a Referendum on Britain's EU membership, and he felt glad that the issue would soon be resolved once and for all. In his gut, he felt the urge to leave, yet he suspected his wife – always under the thumb of the institutionalised liberal groupthink at the BBC - would argue for staying in. It was something they had never discussed: their lives had always been so easy, benign and successful that they would never have imagined any resistance to the status quo. And yet… he felt some sympathy with the idea of not being part of an unrepresentative bloc where democracy was an afterthought, if ever taken much notice of. Yes, people were elected to show some sort of connection with the people, but it had become aware to him that all the major decisions – despite five presidents – were taken in camera, with no vote and no full recourse to the European parliament, rubber-stamping decisions rather in the manner of the old USSR. He smiled as he surprised himself by concurring with why the EU had, indeed, been nicknamed the EUSSR; and although it had never really bothered him before because he and Kate were above all that and doing so well, he had increasingly realised he could not help feeling that something was wrong somewhere.

He put these thoughts out of his mind until Kate came back that evening, by which time the Prime Minister had announced he would be travelling to Europe over the next months to try to get a good deal for Britain which he would put to the country in June. Michael was pleased, but it became apparent that

Kate thought the whole thing a waste of time. "We won't vote to leave the EU," she said slightly arrogantly, "there's too much money, influence and vested interest at stake. We'll stay, whatever the prime minister comes back with."

"But that's surely why it should be challenged and revealed," Michael ventured. "Should we actually subsume our laws, will and democratic sovereignty to an unelected cabal of foreign bureaucrats? I'm not necessarily saying I don't agree with you, but I think it's worth a debate, don't you?"

"No. As I say, I think it's a waste of time and will only cause rancour and dissent. Do we really want that?"

"Not of itself, no. But there are many people who think that the EU is unrepresentative of their views, aspirations and the vast amounts we pay into it."

"They're just stupid," she blurted, with an uncharacteristic spite which he had not witnessed before. "It's only stupid, racist, bigoted, old, poor working-class people who think like that."

"They should still have a voice."

"Well, I certainly don't agree with that if their voice is not worth listening to."

"Darling, that's a terrible thing to say. They're our fellow-country-people. You can't just block them out."

"If they're not wise enough to have a sensible view, then they should be denied it. I thought that's what you thought, too."

"No, not necessarily. And that's disingenuous and

not the point. You're talking like the old aristocracy were reputed to do, keeping the masses in their place and throwing them a few crumbs every so often to make them feel grateful."

"I'm not elite," she blurted, "my father was the son of a postman."

"Yes, working-class – and he worked hard to better himself, for which he was – and you should be – justly proud." He waited a moment to make her realise her contradiction and saw her frame wince with annoyance, and then continued. "People like you – us - have become the symbolic middle-class replacement of the so-called elites – the toffs, even. But you can't have the elites patronising people just by keeping them in the dark and lecturing them, working-class or not. You have to take them with you or there'd be revolution."

"I suppose that's rather my point," she said briskly. "And anyway, that's the predominant BBC view, too," she added, as if that would seal the conversation. But Michael was aware he had reached a conclusion in his life, a standpoint which he had not considered before. Prior to that moment, he was unsure what his feelings about the Referendum had been – either about the result or the reasons for it. He felt good about actually having a view, rather than arguing all around a point to satisfy winning an argument for its own sake. It was gratifying, even if it had caused a minor upset with Kate; after all, he consoled himself, it was only the second time he could ever remember a chill in their usually mutually-shared opinions. Yet it still troubled him. He remembered the other occasion, which, he realised, had been on a similar point: a year or two before, one of Kate's friends was around at the time they were having their loft converted. Michael had recounted a story one of the workmen had told him when they were discussing issues quite unconnected with the necessary building requirements. "You don't *talk* to your workmen, do you?" she had asked with a scornful incredulity. Astonished, Michael had chided her with, "Xenia, you are a socialist, presumably so you can have a clear social conscience, but at the same time you demean the very same working-class people who put you in power, then milk them with high taxes to keep them down, and then use those taxes to pay for your continuing privileged lifestyle." His coup de grace, which had left Kate furious, was that he then angrily charged Xenia with the words, "You socialists only care about other people helping other people: you speak the language of compassion but wish to employ armies of others you never wish to speak to just to absolve your conscience. I will talk to anyone, whatever their class."

Xenia would not speak to Michael ever again; and, as women occasionally do, Kate apparently forgot the exchange… only for it to surface again many months later.

PART ONE

BETRAYAL

Chapter One

It was June 23rd. Michael and Kate had been wary of each other throughout the Referendum campaign. Both their stances had hardened, which had not been helped by Kate often having been assigned to Brussels as an EU commentator, while Michael had thrown his support behind the Leave campaign. Whilst Kate had not actively espoused Remain, her thoughts were fully complicit with it, as she had been expected to be by the BBC. On the night before, with polls all predicting at least a 10% lead for Remain, her demeanour had been smirky, cocky and slightly patronising, while Michael had been cautiously optimistic of an upset and was not that secretly hoping for it. But by 4 a.m., when the result became obvious, tensions in their house reached breaking-point.

"It's a disaster – mad and bad," she wailed, almost in tears induced by an indignant anger.

Michael was relieved, happy and quiet – he did not

wish to throw petrol on the fire. "It'll all work out wonderfully," he just said softly.

"No, it won't," she screamed. "It'll have to be overturned. It's not democratic." He calmly pointed out that it most certainly was – 52% to 48% was a complete majority and, anyway, a proper democratic result, being taken on a pure count as an answer to one specific issue, rather than a tally of seats representing a myriad of political parties, priorities and topics.

"Well, I'm going to work," she snapped. "And go and talk to some enlightened, intelligent, un-bigoted, non-racist people at the BBC."

Michael raised his eyebrows – no chance of much balance there, he thought. "At Television Centre?" he enquired.

"No, Brussels." And she walked out.

Michael did not see his wife for a number of days as she consumed herself in Brussels with the aftermath of the vote. In doing so, she became quite a household name and - although her implicit views were detectable - he admired her for doing a good job. By the time he did see her again, though, the changed political and emotional circumstances would be substantial.

After the Referendum, the current Prime Minister – who, despite returning from Brussels with a 'deal' derided as 'thin gruel' by opponents had campaigned heavily for a 'Remain' vote – resigned. Having used millions of pounds of taxpayers' money on a one-sided campaign dubbed 'Project Fear', citing hysterical claims of apocalyptic, biblical-style disasters if Leave won - and backed up by a booklet sent to every home in the country based on the same dubious predictions - he knew his continuation as Prime Minister was untenable. He was also quoted as saying he did not wish to try to 'sort out all that shit'. Michael was critical of this tone: he was still a statesman and, just because he lost, should have retained his dignity by not implicitly criticising the people he represented. Yet that was subtle compared to the abuse which was already emanating from Brussels, and Michael believed that this only underlined his emerging views: that Britain had been a supplicant nation to a bloc of people who saw themselves as the righteous few against the wishes of the people. He did not like it – and increasingly felt he had made the right choice.

After many shenanigans, a new Prime Minister was installed, who had been nominally on the Remain side but – in true democratic and traditionally British fashion – had pledged all her energies into delivering the will of the people and invoking Article 50 to depart from the bloc after she had assessed all the arguments on how best to do so. But she would have a hard time: within hours, senior figures from the EU were spitefully talking of how they could patronise, humiliate and punish Britain for having the temerity to threaten their power - and would brook no compromise in any negotiations both before or after the triggering of Article 50. What was more surprising – and remarkably un-British – was the resolve of politicians in both the Upper and Lower houses to try to negate, hinder, or even scupper the result; and even two ex-Prime Ministers had oddly claimed that it was more patriotic to have voted to stay in the EU and be subjugated by its laws, excesses and annihilation of sovereignty than to be guided by Britain's own democratic Parliament and accountability.

By this time, Michael had already realised that the anti-democratic clamour of those outside Parliament who had lost would try anything to buy back the result by supporting calls for another Referendum or – even – for the result to be scrapped altogether. Worryingly to him, they were vocally supported and funded by many wealthy bankers, industrialists, celebrities and opinion-formers. Michael had thus found himself becoming far more vocal in the press against such people. It was little surprise, then, when he was subsequently approached by a leading Tory Leave MP with some UKIP sympathies to help the government deliver the democratic result. Her name was Jemima Grice. She and Michael had instantly got on and, were it not for his love for Kate, he would have allowed himself to be consumed by her: but that was not on the agenda, and there was plenty more that was.

He had not seen Kate for nearly three weeks and, whereas they had normally corresponded several times a day via various means, she was becoming somewhat elusive. She had rented a flat in the centre of Brussels and he had visited her there. Once, though, enjoying an evening together in one of its best restaurants, he was aware that she was creating a following amongst the Brussels elite for her reports for the BBC. They were interrupted on several occasions during the meal by MEPs and pillars of the EU hierarchy, which was the only time she had seemed her usual, witty and sparkling self. Yet when she had introduced Michael to them by name, she omitted to say he was her husband: instantly, there appeared to be a covert frosty realisation of who he was and that he was 'on the other side'. After they had gone, he noticed that she reverted to being a defensive and prickly being.

Once back in London, he had seen her most nights on television, and could easily detect the usual predisposition of the state broadcaster seeping through: it was insidious, doubtful, questioning, and always ended with the implication that anything espoused by any Leave supporter was not quite what it seemed. In one sense, it made him smile, in another, its relentlessness was starting to annoy him. On the increasingly rare occasions he did speak to Kate, she began to sound distant and dismissive of him, and when he questioned her duty of supposed media impartiality, she would just retort that she was being "objective."

In contrast, his dealings with Jemima went from strength to strength. Michael had become a trusted analyst and interpreter of both sides of the argument and found himself fêted by a growing number of MPs across the House, even including the Labour ones who had been for Remain, as he had the knack of assessing points quickly and with a concise clarity which confounded many. In short, he had the trust of many members and found himself being used as a sounding-board across the political spectrum.

One day, in the Members' Tea Room, he had been in conversation with a researcher who had just returned from Brussels and said he had met Kate what's-her-name from the BBC there, and how nice she was.

"Kate Hope?"

"Yes – that's her." Michael smiled inwardly, and would have left it at that, but the man continued with an observation that was neither what he had expected nor wished to hear. "She seems very close to that top EU commissioner German politician guy; you know, the one who can't keep his nose out of other people's affairs. Great for inside information, though… eh?"

"Do you mean Guifford Neveu?"

"That's the one. Not very attractive, is he? Just proves that men go for sex and women go for power. If there was ever - "

"What – you mean - ? Are you absolutely sure?"

"Well, it would seem so. Looks quite serious."

"Really?" asked Michael. "How serious?"

"Well, they came in together… left together… just seemed, well, close. Winks, looks, the odd touch on the arm… You know what I mean."

"I do."

"Saw them a few times together in various parts of Berlaymont… Pretty girl. Not a bad reporter, either."

"Mm, I know. She's my wife."

His jaw dropped. "Oh," he just said. Then: "Of course, I mean, er, well, I don't *know* if…"

"Anything's going on?"

"Exactly. But I'm sure there isn't; I mean, she'd be mad, being a high profile BBC journalist and all that … She'd compromise her impartiality, wouldn't she?"

"That I don't know. But thanks for the tip-off. I think I might just get the next train to Brussels." And with that, he informed Jemima Grice that he might be away for a night or two and went home, packed, and was soon on the Eurostar to Belgium.

When he arrived at Central Station, he hailed a taxi and told the driver to head for a street in the Marolles area; when he was within a mile of her flat, he phoned her.

"Hello, darling," he said: "Surprise!"

"What's that?"

"I'll be with you in ten minutes." There was a silence on the other end. All he could hear was the sound of rustling and, in the distance, a door being opened. "Darling? Are you there?"

"Oh, yes, yes. Sorry, I was in bed... didn't sleep well last night. You might have let me know. I mean, I've got an early interview with the President of the European Commission in the morning."

"Trausch?"

"Yes."

"Never mind, I can meet you for lunch afterwards, perhaps." He then heard the sound of a further door closing.

After a moment, she said, "Yes. Look, let me get the flat tidied up and I'll see you in a few minutes. Need to spruce up for you. Bye."

As she said this, Michael's taxi was just turning the final corner into Rue de Vigny, about a hundred yards from her flat. He asked the taxi-driver to stop there and paid him inside the cab, all the while keeping an eye on the steps that led to the flats' front door. Outside this, a black limousine purred. A few moments later, the front door opened and out came the very minister his researcher had mentioned, his gaunt and bony looks trapped behind the trademark dark thick glasses and straight, curtain-like hair - completely distinctive despite his somewhat hasty descent whilst putting on his coat. He was also trying to hold a briefcase whilst struggling with his tie. He jumped into the car as Michael heard him shouting at the driver to get away as soon as possible; the door was still being slammed shut as the limo sped off into the night. It was all too obvious. The researcher had been right: his wife was having an affair with the very socialist and very outspoken EU negotiator in Brexit talks with the UK. And he was married, too.

Chapter Two

At that moment, back in London, Jemima Grice was perplexed to find that she had not known Michael was in Brussels. A Tory MP had suddenly resigned on the grounds that she did not like the way the government was handling the embryonic Parliamentary negotiations for quitting the EU and deemed the new Prime Minister should have called a vote on triggering Article 50, which the new PM, Tessa Lewis, had firmly resisted. In fact, the real reason for the resignation was well known - the MP had not been promoted in the re-shuffle following the Referendum vote and it was sour grapes. However, she was a Remain-supporting MP in a heavily Leave constituency, and Jemima felt that Michael had made such an impression already in the House that she wanted to suggest him for the now-vacant seat. She dialled his number, the phone ringing just as Michael was nervously walking up the steps to his wife's flat. He stopped to answer it, almost glad of being able to delay entry into his wife's presence for a moment - especially when the display showed who it was.

"Hello, Jemima."

"Michael, hi. I thought you ought to know that

Angela Boulbard has just resigned and her seat of Benwith and Skelling in Lincolnshire has come up for grabs. I wondered – as it's a Leave-supporting constituency and you're a Leave-supporting man – whether you might like to have a crack at it."

Despite being in the middle of a huge city, on the cusp of having a confrontation with his wife for what seemed obvious betrayal, and the chill air making his breath still on the breeze, Michael momentarily felt as if he was the only man in the universe – as if time had stood still. "Er... well," he eventually managed to rasp. "Well, am I up to it? I mean, surely there are people better qualified?"

"On paper, perhaps: but you've caught the eye of many people, including the PM, and you'd be so good at articulating our strategy – you've been doing that brilliantly already. You might even manage to make your wife a bit more politically balanced." The gag, well-intentioned but untimely, struck Michael. In an instant, everything fell into place and he knew what he must do, and that was to accept her recommendation if she really thought he was worthy of the challenge. She did, and said she'd see what she could do. And, by the way, where was he?

"In Brussels," he replied.

"Ah, well – won't hold you up, then. Say hello to Kate for me. I'll keep you up to date. Bye." She rang off. Michael stood there, looking at the screen of his mobile which eventually faded to black as he pondered his next move. The call had come at exactly the right moment: if he managed to win the seat and get into Parliament, he could help get Britain out of the EU faster. And his wife's situation added a piquancy to that, he felt, as she was obviously having an affair with one of the EU's highest-ranking officials – and this could be useful to him if he could pretend he did not know anything about it. He surmised he was in a very good position to squeeze far more information out of her – and also, by association, the fleeing minister who had just left her bed. He suddenly felt strangely empowered and optimistic: he would not confront her now; that could wait until he could get the most out of it. He then had a thought that made him shudder: he realised he was already thinking like a politician.

He slipped the phone into his pocket and rang his wife's doorbell.

*

By the next morning, Jemima Grice had got the support of many Tory Leave MPs – she ignored the Remain ones as being too stubborn, intransigent and dismissive - and had been in touch with the local constituency. They mostly already knew about Michael and agreed he would be a huge draw for them: he was classless, charming, polite, good-looking, articulate, and slightly known around the country due to his journalism and occasional appearances on *Newsnight*. And he was a Leaver, unlike the incumbent.

*

Kate's nerves had dissipated the second that Michael arrived in her flat: he obviously knew nothing about her affair, even if his sudden arrival had seemed unusual, and she soon managed to settle into their normal way of talking and arranging things. As for

Michael, he said nothing about his call with Jemima and just said he had missed his darling wife and wanted to be with her for a while 'on an impulse'. This had not only been true - before the revelation, at least - but he wanted to make her feel comfortable so that he could use the situation to his advantage. After all, what if her liaison was just a flash in the pan? If it got too hot, Neveu would be off, and that would probably mean his wife would be out of a job and she would need him back. He felt he had the advantage of possibly having all the cards... if he played them correctly.

So after she had completed her interview and report for the BBC News, they passed a pleasant afternoon walking around the city and topped it with a very good lunch at a Grande Place restaurant before Michael caught the Eurostar home. He had noticed that Kate had received a number of texts, which she furtively glanced at, then came over all sweet and wifely again. Michael was discreet enough to go to the loo after a few had arrived so she could catch up, but the realisation was now growing upon him that perhaps their idyllic past had been less so than he had thought. There were moments during the meal when a comment, which may have previously been taken as a joke or disregarded, now seemed to hark back to a slight bitterness which had seldom been obvious before. Perhaps their very similarities had covered a gulf in their true understanding of one another, their expectations of success subduing any possibility of discussion. And finding themselves suddenly so diametrically opposed politically had once again surprised him. Once, it would have been an excuse for healthy debate, but never rancorous or divisive;

now it had become the catalyst to be so.

All these thoughts were spinning in his head as he passed under the Channel, and he wondered whether Kate was already back in Neveu's arms or whether he had gone back to his wife. Strangely, it did not upset or embitter him as much as he would have expected, and he found himself yearning more strongly for the distraction he hoped he would now have to work harder to achieve – to win the nomination for the Lincolnshire seat which he would then compel himself to win. And so it was that, when the train came up in England at Folkestone, his phone alerted him to a message from Jemima. It was looking good, and he had been asked to attend an interview for the parliamentary seat in two days' time.

*

After Michael had left, Kate called Guifford and told him it was all OK and her husband had not suspected a thing. The relief at the other end was palpable. They agreed that they had henceforward to be more discreet, but neither wished to stop or compromise their relationship; they arranged to meet the next day in a flat which had been paid for by a grateful MEP whom Guifford had smoothed a promotion for - which had then been discreetly purloined by Commission funds. Kate had realised this sort of behaviour early on in her BBC appointment in Brussels and had mentioned its widespread acceptance to her London News Editor; but he had told her to keep quiet about its prevalence. After all, it was something that was best kept from Leave aficionados. And, of course, she might be in a position to benefit from it at some stage whilst she was there and would be grateful, so best not to rock the boat. And here she was, enjoying just that already. Well, if everybody else in Brussels was doing it, why shouldn't she? And her liaison with Guifford would ensure that her innate feeling of entitlement to life's riches would not only continue but be enhanced for the betterment of her future.

Whilst she absolved her conscience on this issue, her phone rang and she was off to film a breaking story about the Commission demanding £500 million from every member state to pay for a fleet of private cars and helicopters to keep Eurocrats safe from terrorists' harm. This was as a result of attacks in Paris, Nice and Berlin: yet the relief and excitement at her expectation of a gilded future blinded her to any former sense of investigative honour. She had gone native, and she was loving it.

Chapter Three

In the Commons, the Government was having a difficult time. Despite the date of serving Brexit having been set, a number of Remain-supporting MPs - who would have delighted in having a binding Parliamentary vote allowing the Referendum result to stand when they thought they would win it - had inconveniently started to argue vociferously against direct and absolute democracy and were trying to thwart it now they had lost: an ex-Prime Minister even called it "the tyranny of the majority". Michael had really balked at this in particular; surely a majority was the whole point of democracy? This same Prime Minister had secured the biggest majority in history in terms of the number of people who had voted for him, yet now he disagreed with the result, it was a tyranny. How could he square that with either his conscience or his earlier success? It was the day before Michael's interview for the Benwith and Skelling seat and he found himself writing a brilliantly-constructed speech for Jemima to deliver, counteracting this argument, and she delivered it perfectly. It had gone down very well and Jemima made sure that everyone knew Michael had penned it to help his chances. Not only that, but he found himself debating that point persuasively on *Newsnight* that evening, which set him up well for his meeting the next morning.

Kate, in her lover's flat in Brussels, saw the interview and was both proud but horrified: his arguments were impeccable – but she could never be seen to agree with any of its substance for fear of compromising her own future or that of Guifford. In Brussels, as was being shown in London, democracy was handy when politicians wanted to sound honourable and grandiose: but when it got in the way, it could be all too easily subverted.

As an illustration of this, some weeks before, an ex-model and a hairdresser had managed to bring a case to the High Court demanding that the Prime Minister's right to trigger Article 50 to start Brexit proceedings without Parliament's consent (using the Royal Prerogative) was unlawful. This caused fury in the country, as that consent had been voted on in Parliament prior to the Referendum with a six-to-one majority, where the winner would have that right if necessary. Yet, because Remain had expected to win - and saw the Referendum as a waste of time - once they lost, honour was forgotten as they tried to argue it was 'only advisory' or – as one MP branded it, 'an opinion poll'. To compound this insult and anti-democratic behaviour, the High Court Judges had delved back into any constitutional arguments they could draw on to prove this point. Using a law from 1972 – passed before Britain had even entered the forerunner of the EU, the European Economic Community – they ruled that it would overturn the

British Constitution and so quoted it as justification to uphold the challenge. It did not escape the press and the public that nearly all were vocal Remain supporters, so were possibly compromised by their views. One judge had even helped draft the Article 50 legislation in Brussels. Newspapers branded them 'The Enemies of the People': by supposedly upholding the Constitution they had therefore been perceived as trying to destroy it. And so it was that, on the morning before Michael travelled to Lincoln, the government announced an Appeal to the Supreme Court. Yet the mood in the country was turning ugly, and Michael surmised that the power and influence of the elites – augmented by a direct denial of the Referendum result – would aggravate the restlessness of the people. At that moment, he did not realise how prescient his thoughts would be…

*

Guifford had just left for the office and Kate was still in bed in his flat. After phoning Michael the night before, she had looked at his smiling picture on the screen and for the first time wondered if she was doing the right thing. His face was so enchanting, calm and friendly. It had haunted her all night and now she felt compelled to look at it again. She held the phone for several seconds, contemplating again that his picture had been taken only a few months ago when none of this had happened. And now she was unfaithful, at odds with him politically and on the cusp of making herself a name in the European Union in Brussels, with all the perks, handouts, expenses and frills that came with it. Guifford had promised her a plum position as one of his assistants

– no, his main assistant – in the Spinelli building, named after a communist founder of the EU. She was glad the EU had not become fully communist, yet even within the short time she had been there had begun to realise that many of its dark and anti-democratic influences were prominent in its daily business. Yes, there were referenda, there was a parliament... but even a sympathiser such as her could see these were just fig-leaves for the greater ambition of total coercion and control. Referendum reversals had happened in France and Holland with the Maastricht Treaty in 2005: this referendum, to enact the European Constitution, had been rejected by larger majorities than the Brexit vote, yet the EU was determined to enforce it for the goal of 'ever-closer union'. So it was re-drafted as the Lisbon Treaty, with the contentious bits ostensibly left out but subtly included so few would notice. But the canny Irish were immediately aware of the subterfuge, and their government offered a referendum on it, despite much teeth-gnashing by the EU elites. The Irish followed the Dutch and the French in rejecting it, meaning that it could still not be passed into EU law. So the EU claimed it was not the 'right' result, and the Irish were bribed with their own money to have another referendum – and another – until they were so confused or bored with all the threats and insults that they fell into line. The Treaty was then enacted: this was the EU version of democracy.

Kate had been aware of all this at the time, but somehow, back then, it did not seem so important; yet now it was, and here she lay in the bed owned by a man who had helped to push those votes through. It troubled her, for it gave the impression that the EU did not embrace the true spirit of democracy. More worryingly, this was a situation now being tried in Britain by influential hardline Remainers who stood to lose money and the power to lobby and manipulate. Terry Cash, the ex-Prime Minister, was one of them. With this man involved, it made her ponder whether it was being done by even more underhand means in Britain just in case the people noticed: she was by now aware that Europeans seemed to care less about politics generally – if it was good for one country then it must be good for all the others - and they accepted it without demur. Except in Britain, of course, an island nation, where freedom of the press was so much more prevalent and respected. She felt glad that her BBC objectivity was coming through; despite being all for the European Project, deep down she still felt proud to be British because they – she – could dispute authority, and it continued to thrill her, even if she was using it to challenge the will of the British people. Yet that was what made her 'objective': for example, she supported the Supreme Court's decision, but not the means they used to justify it. She sighed with satisfaction, feeling fortunate to be able to see both sides of an argument so clearly – it was a gift from heaven. For now, though, here she was in Brussels, implicitly agreeing with it all for the sake of her future, if not all of her beliefs. Yet she had been dealt a wonderful opportunity and if she were to advance, then she could compromise on principles now and return to them when she was well set-up if necessary.

She focussed back on Michael's face, which had become a blur as she reflected on all this. Perhaps he had been right, and the episode with her friend Xenia came into her mind: so many of these people *were* patronising and dismissive – and perhaps Michael had been right to chastise her for her condescending opinions. Then the phone rang and Michael's face was replaced by Guifford's, cutting through her inner polemic. She was back in reality. How lucky she was that an institution so short on accountability was awash with accounts which could afford her every dream she wanted. They would soon be going out to lunch and European taxpayers were footing the bill, bless them.

*

On the train to Lincoln, Michael immersed himself in a selection of newspapers: some mentioned his *Newsnight* appearance and any comments split inevitably down the usual divide: The Telegraph, Mail, Express and Sun were supportive, and the Mirror, the FT and the Guardian almost dismissively contrary. While he was mulling over the critiques, his phone rang: it was his wife, wishing him luck, although he knew very well she did not mean it. She had rung a couple of nights ago and the Shakespearian quotation, "Methinks she protests too much" entered his head. But he kept up the act – as he was becoming used to – and asked when she might be home for a few days. Not unsurprisingly, she said she was far too busy at the moment and, what with all the furore and stories surrounding Brexit, she would find it difficult for some time. And it was great for their bank balance. She seemed happy, at least and, after they rang off, he contemplated how he would play the situation out over time. Forgive her, if or when it all collapsed with Guifford? Well, whatever the outcome of that, he felt it was over – all he must do was extract the best political and financial capital from it. He shuddered: he realised he was being brutal and scheming – Machiavellian, even. This had never been in his script for advancement – if there had been a script at all – as life would just be a success. And he – and Kate, of course – had accepted this blindly. But now he realised he would have to work for this success, and he was ostensibly now on his own: the situation with his wife had hardened him. As if to underline this, as the towers of Lincoln Cathedral came into view, Jemima rang to wish him luck. "Great interview on *Newsnight* last night, too," she said, "just caught up with it. The PM was impressed, too, so just be yourself and I'm sure you'll be picked to stand."

Chapter Four

Michael felt relieved: he had given a good account of himself and had also been subjected to an unexpected Q and A with a host of people invited in off the street at short notice, so they could grill him as if he were in the hustings. Some very awkward and hostile questions later, though, he felt he had done well, and was soon on the train back to London with the kind words of the association chairman ringing in his ears: "Well done, Michael. Excellent. Personally, I hope the committee will go for you. You've certainly got *my* vote." The only unpleasant part was the reaction of the waspish Angela Boulbard, the hard-Remainer who had resigned her seat; she had confronted him as he left and said, somewhat viciously, "I hope you don't get it. We need someone to confront the government, not rubber-stamp policy like I know you will. They need to be told the truth."

"I shall tell the truth if I'm nominated," replied Michael disarmingly. "The truth about why you *really* resigned – because you didn't get the job, which miffed you - and also the truth about the corrupt and undemocratic EU, which you should have stayed to fight, if you're really sympathetic to Remaining, as you say you are. And that's the truth I would focus on."

She had sniffed abruptly and turned on her heel to go, then spun around and said, "I hope you have a very difficult time, smart-arse."

On the train, Michael smiled wryly as he recalled the look on her face as she said that. And they were in the same party, too; with friends like that, what would his enemies be like?

In the fullness of time, he would find out.

*

The European Council was meeting: the votes by MEPs in the main chamber had tacitly but effectively given them carte blanche to do what they wanted in order to subvert, thwart and overturn the British referendum result by whatever means necessary. They hated the fact that their power and authority had been challenged by what Nick Lafargue had called "the triumph of the little people" and were heartened that, with him now not leader of UKIP and happily hob-nobbing across the Atlantic with the new American President-Elect, it was a good moment to start the fightback. They had always hated Britain, not just because it had not succumbed to joining the euro, but because it was known as *Great* Britain, always came up with sensible amendments (which they nearly always ensured were rejected out of spite) and had imposed the impertinence of having a referendum in the first place. Democracy had gone too far, in their *communautaire* view; they had tried the subtle digs to make their feelings known, like leaving the word 'England' off the map of the EU, and listening intently to the Germans above everyone else; it was an unwritten law that they were the most powerful country in the bloc and they called the shots. The Germans basically ran the whole caboodle: they were the ones to agree with and listen to. Their manipulation of the euro had been a masterstroke: in one fell swoop they had economically disadvantaged the whole of the rest of Europe as a means to passively subvert the result of the last world wars and it was only the pesky British – as always - who were standing in the way of it. How dare they let their people have a say – *they* were the masters, not a bunch of upstarts, wannabe pop stars and lazybones. Up to that moment, they had been successfully forming the EU in their own image and for their benefit. Now their elitist master-race hegemony was being challenged. They had been outsmarted, and, as they were the elites, it had invited a particular *schadenfreude* amongst some of the smaller and less influential EU nations, which irritated them immensely.

That morning, though, they were heartened by much media attention being given to the movement recently started by ex-Prime Minister Terry Cash, who had openly called for the overturning of the Referendum result. He was consorting with various other 'elites' to try to raise money from 'pro-European' people to whittle away at the general consensus. In time – or as long as it took – the tactic was that eventually the people would give up, give in or be outwitted and – if the predictions of an economic collapse could become a self-fulfilling prophecy – they could get the people to agree to the old EU fallback: another referendum. And another, until the 'right' result suddenly became the democratic mandate. There were precedents. Eventually, they would be cajoled to change their minds and stay. After all, the EU needed their money, and certainly did not want Britannia to rule the waves again, as subsequent global free trade would reduce prices and make their people resentful at the higher taxes and costs which they had up to now managed to convince them were low. Customs unions always raised prices, as they well knew, but the second most powerful EU nation, France, also needed the money for their farmers, who would revolt if their subsidies were stopped and bring their cherished dream of ever-closer union and 'more Europe' to an abrupt halt. And who would benefit? The British! They of the admittedly efficient agricultural practices and instinctively lower taxes: if they were left to influence the world again, not only would the EU's cosy little party be over but they would have no money and no jobs. Yes, it must be overturned. It would cost, but it would be worth it: bribes and support in the right places – which they could blame on the Russians and Isil – would soon make the British regret their choice and succumb again to the 'acquis communautaire'. And Cash was the one to spearhead it, even if he was loathed; he had managed several years in power thus, but had still won huge majorities for his party. Indeed, if it hadn't been for his Chancellor defying him out of pique rather than principle, Britain, too, would be in the euro like almost everyone else in the Union. The fact that most of them were suffering as a result of it was something he and the Germans had always managed to brush under the carpet. So with him back in the driving-seat - and by bribing his own British people with their own taxes as he had done when in power before - even this disparity could be overcome.

He had pampered friends in high places as a matter of course and already many judges in the Supreme Court were on his list – most were already Remainers anyway and had made no secret of it: so they could squash the government's appeal without a shadow of a doubt. Yet the press would not be bought, so more needed to be done to subvert them. It would just take time and a financial disaster – which EU commissioners could engineer. After all, 51% youth unemployment in Spain, Italy and Greece was a crisis they had not bargained for... yet they had got away with it. So they would do so again.

*

It was late on a Thursday evening a few weeks later, and Michael was backstage in a sports hall in his prospective seat of Benwith and Skelling. The count had taken place and the exit polls had apparently given him a larger mandate than his former MP, Angela Boulbard – but, as he was quick to tell himself, polls cannot be trusted. So he waited with the other three candidates in a state of nervous excitement. Then the Returning Officer took them all into a scruffy little room and told them the result: Labour had come last with less than 8% of the vote; the Liberal Democrats had come third with 17% of the vote; UKIP were second on 26%, and Michael had won the seat with 49%. The Labour man was the least complimentary, and not so quietly accused him of being a fascist, wagging his finger in admonishment. Michael just shook his hand and then those of the others and they trooped onstage.

In Brussels, Kate was watching the result in bed in Guifford's flat, which had a feed of the BBC

Parliament channel; Guifford was asleep beside her. When she heard the result, she gasped: her husband was an MP! Stirrings of betrayal, annoyance, pride, excitement and regret were tempered only by the fact that she, Kate, had a bigger prize beside her. It created a kind of uneasy vacuum in her stomach: Michael was much younger, more handsome and certainly more intellectual, but, well, he had voted Leave, and this was the upshot of it: his actions would cut her off from all this wealth and privilege. Guifford could give her everything she wanted. This thought annoyingly triggered a maxim her politically-incorrect father had said to her once when she was young: 'Men like beautiful women because it makes them feel rich and powerful: women like men with power because it gives them riches.' She had berated him for it at the time, but now realised with a hint of shame that it described her perfectly. She looked at Guifford: he was not attractive – but he had enormous power. And riches. And influence. Yet she missed being able to hug her husband. She quietly got out of bed and sobbed for a minute or two in the bathroom, then pulled herself together and texted Michael with her muted congratulations. Then, with a defiant show of resolve, she got back into bed and woke Guifford, demanding that he have sex with her now, hard and violently.

Seeing she was awake, Michael called Kate immediately; but the phone was never answered and reverted to voicemail. He smiled, but he had a tear in his eye, despite his excitement. He knew what that meant: she was with Guifford.

Chapter Five

A febrile atmosphere had gripped the House of Commons. Today was the day that the Supreme Court would deliver the result of the Appeal. To no-one's surprise, it was announced that the right to trigger Article 50 without Parliament's permission had been quashed again. There were whoops of joy in the Commons, and also some stony faces and boos. Yet the Prime Minister got as many cheers and whoops when she said that there would nonetheless be a bill put to Parliament – to be voted on that week – to trigger the Article and anyone who wished to incur the wrath of their constituents should vote for its ratification or there would be a General Election fought on the lines of accepting the will of the people. After all, Parliament had voted for that when ratifying the Referendum, so would they risk again subverting their will? In an instant, the tables were turned, and panic swamped the Opposition benches: the SNP were worried that the Scottish Conservatives – already making headway in the polls since the Labour vote had collapsed in Scotland – would demolish their majority and also wish to stay part of the United Kingdom. Labour had the most contentious and unpopular leader ever and were polling in the low 20s; and the Liberal Democrats – the most fanatical pro-Europeans - had only nine seats and were unlikely to win many more. They were all aware that, should the election go the way of Leave and Remain constituencies, it would result in a 450 to 150 seat majority for the Conservatives, which would mean a mandate to leave the European Union immediately.

The tactic worked. The vote to trigger Article 50 was taken three days later and the Bill was passed with a majority of 498. Yet before Article 50 could be triggered, it had to be scrutinised by the House of Lords, which had an unrepresentative number of Liberal Democrat members who promised to vote against it, whatever – along with many Labour peers and some rebellious Tory ones. Many, too, were willing to vote against the will of the people for different, personal and selfish reasons: they were in receipt of EU pensions and other largesse, which they did not want to lose. It was another example of self before democracy, and it did not go unnoticed. A groundswell of resentment became palpable, and Tessa Lewis was aware of this. So despite much defiance and angry rhetoric from the ennobled house, she decided to call their bluff: if they did not pass the Bill without amendments then she would swamp the Lords with Leave-backing peers to ensure the measures were passed. And if they still tried to thwart it, there would be a General Election, whereupon her expected vast majority would pass new legislation to ensure the Lords were represented by a percentage of the Commons vote.

It had the desired sobering effect. Within a week,

Article 50 was triggered. Britain was on the way out.

In Brussels, patronising anger turned to blind fury, revenge and talk of 'punishment': efforts were stepped up to defy the vote by whatever means possible. The only Tory to vote against the proceedings – a man who had announced his retirement but would now stand on this pro-EU platform – pompously proclaimed the formation of a new party from that day forth, which would openly fight to stay in the EU, whatever, whenever. He would support its new leader, who would not surprisingly be Terry Cash; it would be called the British Democratic Party. The irony of that name was not lost on the press, which had a field day, many arguing it was reminiscent of the old communist German Democratic Republic in East Germany. But nevertheless, ever since Cash's intervention, money had been flowing into its coffers from big businesses and others who had the power, finance and connections to lobby for preferential rates and handouts from the bloc – and wanted to keep them. And, clandestinely – very clandestinely – money was coming from Brussels, too. The gloves were now off: quietly, secretly, the European Union was going to be more direct and intrusive. It would now subvert Britain's will by foul means not fair – even if any semblance of the latter had been forgotten many years ago…

What the EU had not expected, however, was the Italian vote of no confidence in their Prime Minister. He had called a referendum on his leadership, wanting to streamline his parliament, so making it easier for him to impose the will of the EU on his economically-troubled country – and the EU had channelled money to his cause. But the people were having none of it; and it appeared that if the banks collapsed, Italy would have a referendum on whether to stay in the euro. And if that went against the elites, then it was not unlikely the EU would begin to collapse too. Suddenly, the money earmarked for Britain's subversion via the British Democratic Party was better deployed in shoring up the Italian banks and stopping the demise of their treasured euro.

So behind its customary closed doors, the EU decided that it would immediately, via the ECB, channel money to Italy to save the Union - and then throw its weight behind the British Democratic Party a month before any election was called. They reasoned that a short, sharp final push, in concert with the forces for staying in, would work better than a prolonged assault on Britain's democracy. If they openly supported Cash's party too soon, Britain's free popular press would have more time to whip up anti-Brussels hatred and that would, indeed, spell the end of their cosy little arrangement.

As so often, things would not turn out as they expected.

Chapter Six

Michael took his seat in Parliament the next day and was feted by the Prime Minister and many of the Leave-supporting MPs from across the Commons. One Labour MP, Griselda Schwartz, a German who had always shared the opinion of Gorbachev, that, "The EU is like the Soviet Union dressed in Western clothes," was particularly warm, despite their party differences. It made Michael feel good: more so when the Secretary of State for International Trade, Leslie Caxton, asked if he would consider joining his team as an Under-Secretary. He could not have hoped for a better offer. He was on his way, and suddenly Kate seemed much more distant than Belgium - and even less relevant in Britain's impending new global scheme of things.

*

Terry Cash's British Democracy Party was by now ever more in the news: it had secured many prime advertising spots in mostly Leave-supporting newspapers and at prominent advertising hoardings. The launch of their party had been interrupted by a noisy crowd of Leave-supporting people, and there was the inevitable clash outside their headquarters in

Tothill Street to which the police had to be called in to separate the opposing factions. Whilst the Leave protestors had been noisy but well-mannered, it had become ugly when a band of Remainers had taunted them about all being too stupid, too old, too poor or too unwise to realise what they had voted for - and that it was time for another referendum. It was the voices of rich, privileged people with much to lose at the expense of the many who had lost already by gaining little from the status quo. Cash had been interrogated by the BBC but given a fairly easy ride; Sky News, by contrast, gave him a grilling and he subsequently let it be known that, should he be Prime Minister again, he would find ways to close it down. This, of course, played into the hands of the Leave faction: it was all right for him, with so much money and influence, to try to overturn a democratic mandate, the very thing that a majority of people had voted to ensure could not happen again once Britain had left the European Union. Even Andrew Marks on Marks on Sunday was critical, but could not go too far because the BBC was part-funded by the EU and he wanted to keep his job. Yet the polls suddenly wavered in favour of a second referendum for a few days; but events soon advanced with an unexpected alacrity to confound all sense of complacency on either side… And it all started on a Question Time programme when Terry Cash was asked by a member of the audience if he was using his own millions to bankroll this party.

"That's not the point," he retorted. "Whatever my input, the British must rise up and block Brexit. I'm doing this for democracy." Gales of laughter echoed around the studio. Even though many in there would support his quest for a second referendum, most felt that that was the last thing he was doing it for – it was for Terry Cash. Piqued, Cash retorted that he was only doing what people had asked him to do as a well-respected and trusted PM in the past. Yet more gales of incredulous, mocking laughter. To someone who was used to controlled and stage-managed events where no-one with a varying view was permitted, it became very apparent he was on edge and had lost his touch somewhat. In fact, lost it completely: the common view in the studio was that he had finally become 'unhinged'.

Becoming increasingly tetchy, Cash started on another of his pet themes, that it was the rise in populism across the country – and Europe – that had twisted events into what they had become, and it was increasingly fascist in outlook. As he said this, a groan went around the studio: he really had lost it now. Any mention of the 'f' word inevitably signalled a knee-jerk reaction when an argument was running into difficulties – a 'get-out-of-jail-free' card. But the assembly was not having it. A large, vocal man with a booming voice said, "Mr Cash, there has been a rise in populism because the modern elites like you did not look after the people, but only themselves - rather like the old aristocracies did. If you disdain the people, one day they will disdain you." A huge cheer went up and it was clear it had rattled the ex-PM.

Before he could answer, though, another dived in: "Will you be President of Europe if you swing this?" she asked.

It was instantly obvious that this had hit yet another raw nerve, "Of course not. Look, I'm a decent guy and I'm not doing this for Europe per se; I'm doing it because I believe in Britain and love my country."

"So do we," screamed a number of people in unison – and, "That's why we voted to get out," added another, to general agreement.

The programme went on in this vein for some time, until suddenly the BDP Press Officer, realising that Cash was becoming increasingly angry and frustrated because few were agreeing with him, intervened. He stated baldly to the presenter and the cameras that Mr Cash had to get somewhere else fast and his participation on the programme had ended. The mood was ugly. It was obvious the ex-PM did not like it, so he was leaving, and that was that. In fact, he was not so much leaving as retreating, and it was a seminal moment. After all, where did he have to go to so urgently at that time of night?

*

The next morning, Kate was watching the rushes reporting this event in the BBC's Brussels newsroom. She had been asked to do an interview with as high a person as she could get from the EU to comment on the intervention of Terry Cash into British politics again and the questions raised there. It made her uneasy, for she knew something Guifford had told her, and she now wished he had not.

Kate felt it better not to interview her lover as she did not want to antagonise him on camera, but there were questions to answer; instead, she managed to get an interview with one of the EU's five presidents, Manfred Schweiz. His answers were in complete contrast to what Guifford had told her: he proclaimed that Terry Cash and his supporters were working 'for the democratic good and future success of Britain' without any support from the EU hierarchy, other than that they all obviously wished him success. Kate was lauded for the interview by her BBC bosses but even she was becoming concerned at what she had heard from Guifford. That evening, when she went to his flat, she confronted him with it.

"Guifford, you know what you told me about Terry Cash and the promise made by Trausch?"

"Yes," he replied.

"Is it true, or is it just wishful thinking?"

"I don't know what you're talking about," he said with a big grin.

"Yes, you do. So is it true that Cash will get the European Presidency if he manages to get Britain back into the EU?"

"It has been rumoured," he said, quite openly. "But as I said to you before, I never said that, and it would be denied by anyone whom you asked. So please don't." Then he paused and looked at her, with a wry smile on his face: "There's something else, too," he added, "which will ensure it happens – but I cannot tell you what it is."

"What sort of thing?"

"Can't say."

Kate looked at him hawkishly. "You mean, it might be 'helped along', shall we say?"

"I never said that, either." His smile was even bigger. Now Kate felt even more uneasy. Guifford was normally so open with her, and this was unlike him. It must be something big. She was concerned that he had not denied the term 'helped along', either – it smacked of some kind of enforcement. Surely…? – No, it could not be what she thought it might mean – it would be sheer lunacy. Yet she had a strange feeling about it, and she did not like it.

Back in London, Michael suddenly received a text from his wife. Instantly, he felt very close to her again, no matter what. It was potential dynamite.

Chapter Seven

Events moved fast from that moment: in Italy, the run on the banks had continued after Brioschi's resignation, and any money - that only the wealthier people now possessed - had been placed in safe havens such as London and New York. The money injected by the banks into the country had lasted but a few days as Italians withdrew all their cash and increasingly realised they would be better off outside the euro, where they could set their own currency rates and levels without any EU interference. The Florin was mooted as a replacement, and the rate would be allowed to fall as most other global currencies do, so making Italian goods cheaper. With riots looming and the Five Star Alliance in an uneasy coalition with the Lega Nord, the country was on the brink.

The new Prime Minister, Ponti, had only replaced the ousted Brioschi a few days before, and was gingerly feeling his way into the furnace of Italian coalitions with their incessant compromises and horse-trading which had benighted every government since Mussolini's. He was a hard-line federalist, so was completely against quitting the euro and creating a new Italian currency; but with the Germans unwilling to either bankroll a full bailout or sanction a re-structuring via the European Central Bank, there was nothing he felt he could do but wait. Yet things were becoming ugly, and countrywide demonstrations against him, the government and the EU were intensifying. In a last desperate attempt to avoid a revolution, he contacted military chiefs to ask if they would be willing to post troops on the streets if he could get the Senate's permission. But the answer he received from them astonished him. No, the military chiefs were unable to help, for reasons he must know. Ponti was flummoxed: know what? That most of their units were on manoeuvres in Belgium, came the reply. He was stunned; what were Italian troops doing in Belgium without his knowledge? Brioschi had sanctioned it, he was told, and the President had allowed it. But without the Senate's knowledge? Who was running this country? It was requested by the European Union, they had heard. When? Before Brioschi's resignation. But why? His advisors did not know.

Furious, Ponti requested a call with the President of the EU Commission immediately. An hour later, the phone in his office rang and his assistant told him it was Trausch.

He went straight to the point. "I've been told that my troops are on manoeuvres in Belgium. Why did I not know about this?"

"Brioschi knew, did he not tell you?"

"No, he did not."

"I get the impression you're angry with me. Don't blame me, it's your predecessor you should be angry with."

"But I was part of his government, yet I did not know. It smacks of secrecy. Why does no-one else in Italy know of this?"

"Some do."

"This is ridiculous: why? Why are my troops, which I now need here, in Belgium without my knowledge or permission?"

The line went very quiet. Then, "It's very sensitive."

"I am the Prime Minister of Italy. I have a right to know."

"Ask your President."

And the line went dead. In fury, Ponti contacted his President and asked him the same questions.

"A European Army has been created without anyone other than the top military in each state knowing about it," he replied in his even tones. "Things are getting dangerous," he added, "so the Germans and French decided - "

"- Germans and French?"

"Yes – decided that, as things were getting out of hand – like in Britain and, to a lesser extent, here – a European Army was becoming a necessity to put down revolt."

"You mean, because they're training in Belgium, it's handy for invading Britain?"

"I didn't say that. But I think that is its purpose."

"But that's outrageous. Does the British military know about this?"

"Only the top military chiefs, as here. Otherwise,

of course not. The fewer who know about it, the better. As a federalist, you must realise that this is in the best interests of a united Europe."

"I believe in that, of course – but not the attacking of a fellow state."

"Britain is leaving, so it is not any more, as you say, a fellow state."

Ponti was speechless. Then, after a moment, he asked: "So who would be in charge in Britain if this army invades?"

"Terry Cash. And when Trausch retires – which will be quite soon – Cash will be made President of Europe to bind the European Union back together again."

Ponti felt he was in a nightmare he could not escape from. So he asked a more simple question: "Who is going to save *our* country, then?"

"You're the Prime Minister: you decide, tell me, then we see what we can do. We are a sovereign nation."

"Not without our own army, we're not – and especially if it's attacking another sovereign nation. And do you think the Americans will just stand idly by?" There was no answer, so he just snapped, "Look: I need our army back – soon. So please ensure the European Union knows that or I'll tell them myself. And I should still have been informed."

"I didn't tell you because it was safer that way." And the president rang off.

*

Michael studied the brief text, reading it over and

over again to ensure he was not in some hallucination, then anger started to mount as he read it again: 'Just heard Cash being bankrolled by the EU to subvert the Leave vote, will get EU Presidency if it happens. Think something else going on – even bigger - but unsure. Want to be in EU but not like this. It stinks. K xx'

So here was his Remain wife suddenly realising she had to report corruption going on around her; and it was all because of her relationship with Guifford. But he needed more proof – and what was the 'something else going on' she alluded to? Was that of as much importance? Its opaque style hinted at that. He now knew that he needed Kate to continue with Guifford, if only to keep abreast of events and get more information; but she would have to be careful that the man did not realise she had passed on material that was only known by the very top Eurocrats. He would have to 'find' another source - or even create one. He texted her a simple message which just said, 'Great to hear your news – talk soon,' and then set to it immediately.

*

Overnight, the wires had confirmed that Italy was on the cusp of insolvency again and riots in Rome, Turin and Milan – as well as many smaller southern cities where the impact of the euro had been felt more acutely – had prompted the new Prime Minister to 'do' something. Where was the Army when it was needed? Some research by an Italian journalist, Ronaldo Fortini, had established that many Italian barracks were empty bar a few token soldiers at the gates, and locals had been aware of much heavy artillery and troop transport via road and air which all seemed to conclude they were going in a westerly direction. When other journalists picked up the scent, it was in Belgium: many locals there had also noticed large movements of equipment and personnel. And so, a picture began to emerge. And when people in Germany and France began to report the same thing, a pattern began to take shape.

What gave these rumours extra gravitas was that, the morning before, a freelance news photographer had taken pictures of all the EU Presidents and dignitaries leaving the European Union parliament building in Strasbourg. In principle, this was nothing unusual - they convened there once a month; what *was* unusual, though, was that it was not the customary time to be there, and they were not accompanied by the usual hundreds of staff. It smacked of secrecy. More chilling was that they were accompanied by a small host of people who seemed to be dressed in a military fashion. He had recognised them all arriving late the night before and, suspecting something secretive, decided to stay outside overnight to get some pictures when they left. At four in the morning, they did so: not expecting any press, they had become less careful than usual and one minister had some handwritten notes on display, which the photographer duly took several pictures of. On discovering him, their facial expressions told a story of its own, and their anger - plus the fact he was chased by security men – only compounded his view that they had gone there covertly to discuss something they wished to keep from as much of the world as possible. The photographer had managed to escape, then quickly copied the memory cards and e-mailed and posted the pictures to the British,

American and European press. He had good reason to do so: it was a huge revelation. For the notes were proof that Terry Cash's British Democratic Party was being funded by the European Union.

The fallout was intense. It was all over the global news in minutes and the British parliament was in uproar. With extraordinary brazenness, the British Democratic Party denied it totally despite the proof. Inevitably, those who wished to remain in Europe tried to justify it, yet suddenly the boot was on the other foot. Correspondingly, the polls swung heavily against staying in the EU by a margin of 27%. In a state of panic, the assorted Remainers tried to smear the Leave side by claiming it was a set-up and, even, that it was a staged event with actors made up and dressed to look like the top Eurocrats depicted. Yet it was obvious to all that the photographs were genuine: why else were the European presidents and military top brass lurking in Strasbourg if they had nothing to hide? And the fact that Trausch and all the other heads furtively denied it and then disappeared only garlanded the truth.

*

Michael had racked his brains for what Kate's text had alluded to, but with the rumours about possible troop movements circulating, by the middle of the next morning, he had a good idea and requested an urgent meeting with the Prime Minister, who called in the Minister of Defence and the Foreign Secretary. On hearing Michael's prognosis, they summoned the Joint Chiefs of Staff in the British military down to London to meet them all immediately, charging them, in the meantime, to gather any reconnaissance of troop movements in Belgium. Within a few hours, the word came back that there were, indeed, troop movements there which no-one in Europe had told the British government about. More sinister still was that GCHQ had suffered a cyber-attack from that very area and had no intelligence at all. It was becoming obvious that France and Germany had secretly colluded to form the European Army, and roped in the Italians for added support. Britain was about to be delivered a 'helping hand' to sort out its troubles as a supposedly 'warm-hearted gesture from its European friends'. Worse, there was evidence of troops and equipment coming in from the north through the EU's Baltic states: it could only be the Russians – all three Baltic state armies added together would have registered less than the movements detected. But were they exploiting the weakness of the EU at this dangerous time with a soft invasion of states they wanted back under Russian control, or was it an unholy alliance with the EU to subvert Britain's will?

*

In Italy, the issue of a European Army training in Belgium only fed the flames. Ponti went public with his knowledge of Italian participation in the forces and openly castigated his former prime minister for neither informing him nor involving the Italian parliament. The president was accused of a massive cover-up, and as Italians spontaneously convened in massive demonstrations once more, demanding the return of their army, he suddenly found himself being impeached. It was not long before the Italian forces were quickly recalled to help quash the growing demonstrations, much to the embarrassment and continuing denials of any invading army from the EU hierarchy. Across Italy, people started burning EU flags and even flying the Union Jack as a token of solidarity with the British.

*

Michael had heard nothing more from Kate, and he supposed she was wrestling with her conscience – not regarding him and her, of course, but whether her loyalties rested with her sovereign country or the EU. And she would be an easy target for EU wrath if it came out that she had betrayed a confidence from her very influential lover. In one sense, Michael wanted to do that: but as his loyalties had shifted more in favour of his country than his perfidious wife, he decided that restraint had become the better part of valour. It would also help him. At Prime Minister's questions that day, Tessa Lewis had been asked a planted question about any intelligence of an army amassing in Europe and her answer that troop movements had been noticed there which the government was 'keeping an eye on' had inevitably seen the newswires run hot with speculation, denial - and confected outrage from Germany and France. The British forces were immediately granted a huge rise in funding and put on full alert, with all manner of strategic positioning being implemented, particularly in the south-east and on the eastern seaboards. Yet, not unsurprisingly, the European Union issued a statement denying it had any intention of invading Britain, and most who had voted Remain now unequivocally supported this as the truth, angrily postulating that the government was creating its own version of Project Fear to whip up support for Brexit.

As with so many objectives, however, the intent was soon obliterated by unintended consequences.

*

It was not long before the press and politicians started to put two and two together: if the EU was bankrolling Terry Cash's party and had possibly created a European Army, then surely the purpose was to invade Britain and install him as a puppet Prime Minister. Needless to say, Terry Cash and his party denied it all. Of the many denials he had made years before when PM, this one would turn out to be the most contentious of all. And it would have devastating consequences.

Chapter Eight

These events gave those in Britain wishing to leave more confidence and determination; demonstrations were hastily arranged outside Parliament, where, for once, those who wished to stay were the ones being intimidated. They had provoked an anger that motivated people across the country. Even many Remainers felt that what they had heard was probably true and they despised it. To disagree was one thing: to have one's country threatened like this, with the intention of overturning the democratic will of the people, was turning many more into Leavers in an instant.

A spontaneous uprising began: great swathes of the population – mainly from the North-East, the South-West, the Midlands, the East and Wales – impulsively left their jobs and travelled to London by train, bus, car, bike or on foot. Likewise, hardline Remainers came from Scotland and the South-East to swell the ranks of those Londoners who had voted to stay. It was an explosive cocktail.

Six million supporting Leave and two million supporting Remain converged on Parliament Square, with the whole of London brought to a standstill. The capital was packed with people from Croydon to

Enfield, Hounslow to Ilford. Fights and skirmishes were commonplace and gangs of either faction had pitched battles wherever they found themselves in confrontation. But where was the army? Surely they should be deployed to keep the factions apart?

The Prime Minister's appeals for calm and for people to disperse fell on ears which were either deafened by, or oblivious to, the arguments. As the obvious threat to order with so many of conflicting views became increasingly critical, she contacted the Joint Chiefs of Staff to intervene; but they said they could not contain or disperse such a large crowd now that it had gathered and so could not help. With the police already overwhelmed, the anarchy continued unabated. At the headquarters of the BDP, six high-ranking members found themselves discussing strategy when the doors were burst open and an angry mob of people from the political left and right bludgeoned two of them to death with whatever came to hand. Con Smithers, the one Tory who had voted against the passing of the act to allow Parliament to trigger Article 50, had to hide in a cupboard as the crowd invaded. Where an MP well-known for his or her standpoints was recognised in the street or in a building, a crowd of loyalists to their particular cause would protect them against the baying of those who felt betrayed the other way.

The riots ran unchallenged for the rest of the day and through the night: London was in the grip of anarchy – for such it was, whichever side people were partisan to. Yet neither side would relent; each had acquired a perpetual motion of its own. Realising that she had to do something dramatic to regain some order, the Prime Minister did the only thing she felt she could do – call a General Election, set for six weeks hence. Although it would mean more division and the possibility of defeat, she felt that the ensuing debate, not physical confrontation, would stop the riots and the Brexit she had nailed her colours to would succeed if she got a full mandate from the people. Article 50 had been triggered, so it was only a question of how the process panned out, rather than whether Britain would leave – it was the terms, not the facts that would be the issues dividing or uniting the electorate. Instantly, she dissolved Parliament. But the genie was out of the bottle and the unrest would only worsen: it had the potential to become a second Civil War.

But the proposed General Election would never take place, and what happened next would be seminal and completely unexpected…

*

Early the next morning, in Parliament Square, a flotilla of helicopters suddenly appeared and dozens of troops were landed on the roofs of Westminster Abbey and the two Houses, as well as government buildings around the area. Armed personnel carriers, too, were suddenly passing through the throng down Whitehall and Millbank, converging on Parliament Square. Soon, shots were being fired and panic set in as the crowd started to flee – especially when the troops disembarked from their vehicles and advanced on foot, pointing their guns at anyone who appeared intent on resisting their progress. Down Whitehall, from across Westminster Bridge, Tothill Street and Broad Sanctuary and Millbank they came… Yet some retired soldiers protesting in the crowd were uneasy: why were the helicopters not the Army's customary Chinooks? They were twin-rotored, but they were not Chinooks. And the APCs were unusual, too, despite their British markings. There were other dissimilarities to the trained eye and - to add to the confusion - the public had learned that Tessa Lewis's request that the army should intervene had been denied for fear of fanning the flames. So where had these troops come from? Rumours started to spread that there was something not quite right. Yet around Downing Street, the armed police who had been deployed there for many days were now pleased to see the Army starting to take back control. Destruction was all around them, placards and blood everywhere; smashed windows, graffiti, rubble and litter defaced the previously proud area. In Trafalgar Square, Nelson's Column was climbed and a man and a woman placed a 'Vote Leave' placard around the famous admiral's statue, only for them to be thrown off the column to their deaths by four opposing people who then replaced it with an 'I'm In' sign. A man and woman scaled Big Ben and hung a placard from one of the famous hands, which soon dropped off as the clock's time advanced towards the half-hour. A couple with a small child were crushed by an APC which did not stop as people tried to arrest its advance, and the crowd attacked it – only stopping when the doors opened and the troops started firing into the crowd, killing several protestors of both hues. Again, doubts started circulating: surely the British Army would not fire on its own people?

Then, there was a moment which changed everything: one of the helicopters, depositing soldiers onto the roof of the National Liberal Club in Northumberland Avenue, had its blades hit by a missile – later found to have been a cricket ball – and was in difficulty. The pilot tried to make it to the Thames so no demonstrators would be hurt but the aircraft did not make it and careered grotesquely into the crowd on Victoria Embankment. Screams and terror rent the air as people tried to escape the swirling blades slicing them to pieces as it crashed in a ball of flame, many jumping across the historic barrier and into the river to escape. Just before it spun into the crowd, a soldier was heard from inside shouting, "Sautez, sautez," to his comrades. And suddenly, like a searchlight penetrating a darkened sky, the crowd realised that the soldiers were not British, but French. Was this the rumoured European Army, here, in London, trying to intimidate and silence their right to demonstrate against an institution which they felt was stealing their democracy? The discovery swept like wildfire through the crowd, and even many supporting Remain found themselves sickened by this act of treachery and felt equally as angry as Leavers; but worse was to come... As the helicopter burned, the paint bubbled and peeled off to reveal a Russian flag underneath. Russian! No wonder the hardware was unfamiliar – but French soldiers in Russian hardware? Now even the soldiers were targets of the crowd's wrath – and more so when another incident proved that some others – again in Russian hardware – were German. Chaos and conspiracy theory had never had it so good...

Whatever the politics, the result of the Army's intrusion – from wherever it came – imposed an uneasy order on events and soon the capital was calm again... only for fury to rise once more as it was rumoured that the Remain-supporting Joint Chiefs of Staff for the military had apparently turned a blind eye to the invasion to ensure that the Referendum result could, they hope, be overturned. Such treachery would not remain forgotten...

Once the area around Parliament was cleared and made secure again, questions flew as to how this invading army had been funded when the Eurozone was in such a parlous state. Yet the answer was not difficult to see: the Russians had augmented the EU's hastily-convened Euro Army less to help its invasion than to destabilise the bloc in the long term. The trade-off would be that the Russians would then stay in the Baltic states, citing it as a return of a favour, so enlarging their empire and reducing the European Union's. The Russians were well aware, too, that the EU would miss these states far less than the obstreperous cash cow that was Britain. The relatively small cost of the invasion and possibly losing the Baltics would be small beer compared to the restoration of Britain's huge budget contributions and a sated Russia - for a while, at least. It escaped no-one, though, that Britain's continuing membership of the European Union had been achieved by force – and it instantly made people rebellious, angry and desperate to redress the insult.

However, a further treachery soon also emerged which would underline the duplicity and harden attitudes even further; the British Joint Chiefs of Staff had not just turned a blind eye - they had actively colluded with the EU and given orders for the British forces to be involved, without the knowledge of

Parliament or the Prime Minister. These orders were then passed on by the generals in English to their British and European Army counterparts, the British regiments initially unaware they were betraying their own people and country. Indeed, it had been a fully British decision to deploy only European Army units in London, rather than British ones, as the commanders believed there would be less hostility in such a cosmopolitan city. European soldiers would also be more intent on crushing the people's will and less concerned about casualties - British troops would not have wished to fire on their own people. Yet once British personnel realised they had been duped, their anger intensified and many started to rebel and desert.

The final insult of the invasion was to immediately close the House of Commons and the Lords. But this affront, the stilling of British democracy for the first time in over three hundred and fifty years, was surpassed by a clandestine visit from the top European Commissioners and Presidents, who flew unannounced to London and discreetly entered the empty House of Commons. In a symbolic but mock and jocular debate, they then 'passed' an act in the empty chamber to dissolve Parliament and close it down. They laughed and gloated as they did so: it was a huge joke and a historic put-down of the country which had created the Mother of Parliaments but always 'got in the way' of what the rest of Europe wanted. Guifford Neveu sat with his feet up on the green benches, lolling around as the others laughed at how they had finally suppressed the British. And to think this had all started as a catfight between different factions of a democratic party in this very building, they chortled. Then they left and went back to Brussels, only the Serjeant-at-Arms being privy to the event as he watched – unseen – from the Strangers' Gallery.

He secretly filmed the offence on his phone, and sent it to the BBC. But it was never shown. Yet he kept it to ensure that it soon would be, on social media. It went viral in minutes.

The Prime Minister, Tessa Lewis, had disappeared, as had all Britain's MP's: all were under house arrest or in hiding, frightened of being found. By anyone.

When the EU hierarchy openly dared to show their faces again in Brussels, it was predictably less than enough, and they garlanded the insult by proclaiming that Terry Cash had been proclaimed Prime Minister by the European Union President. A visibly cocky and smiling Trausch announced this at the same time as he proclaimed they had invaded Britain, "to help a member state in difficulties, not to betray or compromise its sovereignty." Yet everyone knew this to be a fiction: the Serjeant-at-Arms had ensured that - and it was seen for what it truly was, a naked colonisation of the UK to overturn the Referendum vote by force. There would be no more debates or votes in Parliament for the foreseeable future, the voice of the British people had been silenced. The 'Democratic Proclamation for the Protection of Britain', as they had called the act they passed in the Chamber, was sent to Cash and his supporters, who were expected to rubber-stamp it – and did, without discussion. Ministers and MPs were not only proscribed from entering Parliament but told to stay at home, and those who were sympathetic to Leave or in the Cabinet were put under even closer watch than the others. Tessa Lewis was interrogated by judges from the European Court of Justice, flown in from Luxembourg to underline the subsumation of the country: she would later describe it as the most terrifying episode in her life. Because two of the six judges were from Spain, it soon became nicknamed 'The Spanish Inquisition'.

*

The Queen was constitutionally not allowed to make any comment on these events, but with her Prime Minister having been compromised, she made it clear she was unimpressed – which was a majestic way of saying 'furious'. As someone who had previously made no secret of getting along well with Cash, she summoned him to the Palace for an explanation. He told her he had always been determined to keep Britain in the European Union, whatever it took – a stance which ensured his swift departure from her company.

After Cash had been dismissed, the Queen's advisers recommended she leave the country; with most European states being republics, no-one could be sure of the outcome of this insurrection - or her safety. Her response to this was resolute and typical: she would stay – just as her mother and father had done during the Blitz. She was still head of state – albeit one without a functioning Parliament - and she was going nowhere.

Britain had become a Dictatorship: democracy had been crushed, assisted by powerful people in its own country who once championed it when in their interests to do so. But now that these people had the power and influence they wanted, it was suddenly unimportant. 'Ever more Europe' now assumed an even more sinister tone: Britain had effectively become a totalitarian state.

But from now on, events would take a very different course.

Chapter Nine

Due to the defence cuts made by previous governments, it had become painfully apparent that the British Armed Forces would have been pushed to match even the hastily-convened Euro Army, especially buttressed by the unwelcome hardware from Russia. As expected, the Russian trade-off for keeping Britain in the EU was the unannounced but obvious annexation of Latvia, Estonia and Lithuania, this treacherous act motivated by pique and revenge by the European Union for Britain having had the temerity to vote to leave it. But things were as they were, and the Euro Army troops – now in enforced collusion with their British counterparts - were stationed at strategic points around the country. Parliament Square and the area around it from Trafalgar Square to Vauxhall Bridge and up to and around Buckingham Palace had been proclaimed a virtual no-go area accessible only to people who lived and worked there. EU Army soldiers patrolled the streets of major cities. Germany and France had at last succeeded in doing what they had been trying to do for centuries – conquer and subjugate Britain. Yet, loyal British servicemen and women were deserting and rebelling in their thousands, often taking their weapons with them, privately beginning what would become a resistance movement in concert with civilians who would not be subdued. But it would be a long, protracted uprising, for with hardline Remainers now assuming power, it looked bleak for any future democracy in Britain. Those in government who had supported Remain were cock-a-hoop, and the entire government machinery for exiting the EU was abolished. Those who had vocally supported Leave were stripped of all duties, dismissed and effectively retired. As if to cock the final snook, the 'Spanish Inquisition' impeached the former Prime Minister, Tessa Lewis, on a trumped-up charge of 'anti-EU activities' and Terry Cash moved into Downing Street with the slogan previously used by the Vote Leave campaign - 'take back control'. He went at it with gusto, unhindered by his chancellor or concerned about elections, in the manner of EU precedents and in the full knowledge the EU would always support him on any issue.

*

In Italy, however, its returning army had gone beyond its remit and shot and killed many protesters there. What with events in Britain, it was not long before the EU hierarchy had to answer some searching questions across the rest of Europe: after all, if they had done this to Britain, who was next if they did not comply with the EU's new hegemony? For days afterwards, they kept a low profile. It was rumoured that they knew they had overplayed their hand; worse for them, hatred for the EU around Europe was at its most extreme yet, with sympathy for Britain and demonstrations in support of democracy and the overthrow of the EU reaching fever pitch. Even Greece became deeply Eurosceptic overnight and voices started to demand a referendum on leaving the euro, which independent economists had been advising them as their best course for many years to save the country. At the same time, the Front National in France went far ahead in the polls; and in Germany, the AfD were level-pegging with Anna Seidel's Christian Democratic party. Revolts in Estonia, Latvia and Lithuania were commonplace as people were shocked and repelled at the EU's duplicity in allowing Russian troops not only to occupy their soil but to help attack an EU member state. And would the Russians stay, now that the EU had achieved its goal? It was no secret that this was what its president, Rastov, wanted...

Yet things were about to change. In America, the outgoing President, being no friend of Britain - and who had even removed the gift of a bust of Winston Churchill from his White House office – did nothing. If his friend Seidel had sanctioned the invasion, then that was fine: the Special Relationship meant nothing to him and he had even proclaimed that the European Union was one of the greatest achievements in world history. Other more democratically-leaning observers took a different view – especially when they contemplated the actions the bloc had just taken to suppress and invade a sovereign state. Yet the germ of populism had been born with Brexit, and this President had just been defeated by a populist Republican insurgent: America was about to be transformed. The President-Elect was pro-British, and the main movers in the Leave campaign were managing to keep in constant touch with him, despite EU crackdowns on communications, which had echoes of Germany in the 1930s. The EU was treating Britain more harshly than any of its other states, wishing to keep, contain and re-educate its prize: its prime annoyance in its panoply of states was vanquished and it was not going to give it up.

But there was one thing they would never control: the British spirit and its thirst for true democracy.

PART TWO

REVENGE

Chapter Ten

The truth about all empires is that they eventually collapse under the weight of their own assumed importance – it is a recurring theme of history. If a will is imposed on a people, or even an enforced collection of peoples, as in the European Union, it will eventually fall. The cracks started to appear very quickly after Britain's subjugation: the Americans, under its new President, had stood by his belief in a free Britain and was covertly supporting any resistance to the occupying powers by supplying intel, small-scale weapons and money for the rebuttal of state propaganda. Social media threats, abuse and hit-and-run attacks against prominent Remainers, judges and military top brass became daily occurrences, rather in the mode of the French Resistance in Nazi Germany – which was frequently cited as a comparison by both sides. Inevitably, the Remainers were patronising and indignant about these events, proclaiming that it was proof the people were not intelligent enough to realise what they had voted for when Leaving – yet conveniently ignored that fact that their supporters had done precisely the same thing.

In the UN, although motions were passed to enforce the EU to leave Britain and dissolve its army, it had a veto and it would not comply: this battle had taken centuries to win and they would not give it up easily. Also, the British government, of course, would not support it either. However, five eastern states – Poland, Slovakia, the Czech Republic, Romania and Bulgaria – joined forces to form their own bloc opposing the invasion. In Italy, the anger at the EU action had escalated, becoming a catalyst provoking further national riots and then elections, which ushered in a new government pledged to fight the EU and give Britain back its democracy – and retrieve its own. The European Union hierarchy was aghast, but dared not try another insurrection for fear of more widespread uprisings. The relatively few troops they had were stationed in Britain and they quite simply could not afford another invasion – nor believe it would succeed.

Left on its own, the new Italian government passed many so-called populist acts which the EU would normally have resisted but were now in no position to thwart. Despite being nominally against the Italian Constitution, its brazen first act was to banish the euro and start its own, new currency, the Florin, which had caught the popular imagination when mooted before. People were tired of the straitjacket of EU rules and wanted action, so any domestic Italian legislation which got in the way could now easily be disregarded for the common good.

Instantly, the Florin's value fell against a large number of currencies and subsequently, within weeks, the economy improved. Investment from tiger economies and the United States flooded in, industry started to grow and joblessness began to fall: what had been the British miracle was becoming the Italian one, too. Italy had achieved truly sovereign nationhood again, becoming once more the single realm that it had always wished to be since the Risorgimento movement of the 19th century. North and south became colleagues rather than enemies to promote the cause of a united, proud Italy, unbossed by external forces, just as the British had voted to do. They instantly refused economic migrants from other EU countries for a ten-year period, in a bid to cut the youth unemployment rate of 46%: it soon started to work. In a fit of futile pique, the European Union expelled the country, which attracted a lot of mirth and the observation that it had locked the stable door after the horse had bolted.

In the Baltic states, elections were called for, but Russia resisted a plebiscite and they were quietly repressed with as little disturbance as possible. Despite protests, the EU said and did nothing: indeed, it was secretly pleased that the Russian iron fist was still in force as it kept things there in a state of osmosis. For its part, Russia did not wish things to move too fast either, for fear of giving away its true intentions: it would have to wait until either the EU collapsed completely or Britain became a sovereign power again. If or when that happened, these states could become a bargaining chip between Rastov, the Americans and probably a new alliance of European nation states, where the fractured new geopolitical situation could be used to broker a greater Russian hegemony. It would be Yalta all over again. For now, though, it was just a holding operation.

In Holland, the populist Freedom Party forced elections on a vote of no confidence in the EU, using its invasion of Britain as its main reason: after all, was not one of the founding principles of the EU to prevent wars in Europe, not start them? This opinion was augmented by anti-Muslim rhetoric - and it won by a landslide. Appalled, Brussels had intervened in the poll but overplayed its hand, helping to gift the result to its nemesis; the EU now had so many battles on so many fronts that it had lost its focus and did not know where to turn or whom to support or subvert next. Holland's new leader, Gerritt Hendriks, instantly did what Italy had done and banished the euro, reverting immediately to the Dutch Guilder.

There were other problems for the EU, too: due to complacency and under-funding by some member states, the American-led NATO had been allowed to wither – some said with the tacit encouragement from an ungrateful France and Germany who had, for some time, wanted it replaced by a European Army. Yet now that they technically had the beginnings of one, it was going spectacularly wrong; not only was it already fractured, under-funded and in the wrong place, but their rhetoric had also managed to annoy the Russians, who suddenly and cunningly changed tack to argue that they saw an EU army as a replacement for NATO and, being closer to their existing and former countries, was therefore an even greater threat. It was one reason that they had played the EU against itself, offering support for it versus

Britain and NATO but managing to annexe the Baltic states at the same time if they could get away with it: they were playing a very clever game.

The new US President had been vocally critical of this lack of NATO funding and support. Now that the EU had played its hand so badly, he knew that, in concert with the nations which were leaving the EU, NATO could be prominent again if a free and liberated Britain could show western Europe once again how very important it had once been – and could be again. Even if, for the moment, it was subjugated by a fledgling and fractured European Union army.

Stalemate prevailed, while a cocky but nervous Russia, a furious and frustrated population in Britain, a fractious assembly of current and ex-EU states and a newly-motivated America waited to see what might happen next. Yet during all this uncertainty, the very existence of the European Union was in the balance, facing existential threats from inside and outside - and maintained only by arrogance and righteous indignation.

The BBC had been glad to help the new British government, and made no secret of its support for the newly-appointed Prime Minister, Terry Cash, and the status quo. It was also tasked to re-align a large part of its programming to reflect the new 'reality' – what would normally have been called propaganda. In Brussels, Kate had been swept up in its over-arching ambitions and was now happily espousing – and living - the new dream. Neither she nor Guifford could understand how the EU had allowed both Italy and Holland to leave the Union and both felt that more could have been done to prevent it. Yet, with the situation as it was, their ideology was clouding what was actually possible. She was aware that the EU Army in Britain was acting not unlike the Germans had acted under Hitler, in that any attacks on EU officials or installations were harshly dealt with. Not with executions, but certainly beatings, mild torture, deprivation and extreme prison sentences. She also knew that this would provoke the British spirit further, which was a point she expressed to Guifford on several occasions. But he would not listen: he confided he had not been so happy for a long time, despite the other crises in the EU. History ran deep with Guifford. As it did with the British, in much the same way. On one occasion, though, she asked him: "Guifford, how long can you keep up this repression in Britain?"

"My dear," he said patronisingly, "you British must realise that it is not repression, it is liberation. A new history. You have been under America's influence for so long you have forgotten the benign European characteristics of altruism, charity and humility - the will to act responsibly and socially towards other people. You will change. And thanks to you, my darling, I know that this voice will be heard in Britain via the BBC. It is a new dawn for your country."

"So why have Italy and Holland left, then?" she enquired.

His face turned to thunder. "They will come back," he exclaimed. "We have the moral upper hand, like your Terry Cash. He will help ensure that they return to the fold you wait and see."

"Look, I'm with you in principle, but others are going – or want to – as well: look at Greece, the Visegrad states - the Baltic states if they can get rid of the Russians... They all have resentments. What you did in Britain – whether I approve of it or not – has motivated other countries to revolt against you. And what with the new President Gold in America, they now see Britain as a suppressed state and will probably do something about it, too."

"My little flower," he said, stroking her chin. "You mustn't let your British sensibilities and sense of fair play distort the bigger picture. We will win over the rest of Europe again because everyone knows our brand of benevolent but liberal socialism is what people really want – they just don't know it yet."

"But Cash tried that twenty years ago, and look what happened."

"Yes, indeed – look what happened! He's back in power again, and Britain will soon be turned into a springboard for the resurgence of the European Union across Europe. It will happen." And with that, he gave her a peck on the cheek and left for his office. Whatever his exhortations, though, Kate felt differently. She thought that the invasion of Britain - by what even she privately regarded as an illegal invasion - would prick the British into a quiet revolution, supported by America, and the rest of Europe would follow – as it was already doing. Resistance was already happening in Britain, even if not yet particularly apparent, as the BBC, media and the press had been clamped down on and instructed forcefully that there were to be no reports of any anti-EU incidents. But she knew they were taking place.

She had been in touch with Michael and her suppositions were correct: rather like a gliding swan serenely appearing to paddle across a placid lake, under the waterline its feet were paddling frantically. Michael and the rest of the proscribed government, and all those who voted Leave and were patriotically attached to the democratic processes now so abruptly torn from them, were doing all they could to reverse the situation and overturn the result. The irony of this situation was not lost on either of them – it was just what the Remainers had fought for the other way around. Yet the resistance was starting to succeed – more than mild stirrings were afoot.

For the moment, though, a very uneasy calm had apparently descended on Britain and Europe. Due to losing two member states in quick succession, though, there was less money coming into the EU coffers. Britain was still being forced to contribute its £367 million per week, the true figure, rather than the £350 million, bandied about and damned as lies during the Referendum campaign. It was no secret that the EU was running out of money and, to make matters worse for them, the new American President – guided by hawkish generals and a determined new secretary of state - applied sanctions to the EU until it withdrew its army from Britain and allowed new, free elections.

This act was bitterly condemned by Britain's new Prime Minister, Terry Cash. Despite his history of bellicose interventions in North Africa and the Middle East with previous Republican US Presidents, now that his dream of a Britain subjugated by the European Union had been unexpectedly realised, he had a Messiah-like belief in trying to prove that the rest of the world was out of step with him and that Europe could be globally predominant. Indeed, he had grandly seen himself to be the embodiment of the Second Coming. He had already done his best to ignore the events going on in other parts of the European Union. Like Guifford, he was confident that his brand of a resurrected third-way socialism would eventually be a beacon for the rest of the bloc and he would lead a grateful Britain back into the fold of European hegemony, thus attracting back the deviant states who were now mistakenly starting to believe that true sovereignty and democracy was benefiting them. In this, he was supported by many who had once been enemies from opposing political parties; indeed, it was part of his plan to create a 'grand coalition', the only mandate being that Britain was led by him and back in a glorious and improved European Union. To further cement his ambition, he formed an alliance with the Scottish National Party, giving them a more powerful parliament and nominal independence, which of course it could never have had as a standalone part of the European Union, where policies tailored to ethnic groupings and areas were always sacrificed on the altar of 'ever more Europe'. Scotland was euphoric: no more rule from Westminster, yet still part of Britain, the EU and its single market. They could have their cake and eat it, too. As a further act of defiance, and moving fast so that popular resistance could not gather momentum, Cash made it clear that he had also started preparations to join the euro, despite his previous chancellor having managed to prevent him from doing so. Yet that decision – made out of resistance to him rather than rational judgement – was the reason why Britain had succeeded economically where Europe had failed.

Yet his almost religious vision of a celestial EU would not come to pass in the way he intended.

The feeling of anger at having the result of a vote on their country thwarted, taken away and ridiculed was being augmented strongly as British Leave supporters were increasingly aware that businesses were stagnating further in the Eurozone while Italy and Holland were becoming economically stronger. Indeed, the British economy had taken a hit of Project Fear proportions. This news was being suppressed by the BBC and ignored by Cash's EU elites, yet, it sparked an unexpected revolt amongst the young. Instead of making them feel better about the country's new situation, the collapsing economy had jolted them into a hostile mood. Although most had voted to Remain, social media and modern communications had ensured that nothing was hidden for long. Indeed, even though the BBC had been instructed to broadcast only good news stories regarding Cash's policies to stay in the bloc, the young were beginning to realise that their freedom to converse and make money was being compromised. Indeed, it was the younger journos who were starting to question the status quo, in defiance of those who were supportive of Cash; the resentment might be coming from a different base, but the stirrings of resistance were beginning. Middle-aged people would do as they were told without demur, but older people who had lived in a Britain free from EU interference before were now bookending the age gap. Younger people could see, and had access to, both sides of the truth and realised their basic instincts of a balanced press and free speech were being compromised. Thus dissent began to accumulate from a previously very unexpected quarter...

Kate had watched and reported all the news restrictions and state propaganda with a growing sense of scarcely-concealed horror, despite the prevailing mood of joy at the BBC. Despite being a solid Remainer, she had never envisaged a situation like this, where a sovereign state was invaded by its own master, and it was reminiscent of what her father had told her about the Prague Spring in 1968, or the erection of the Berlin Wall. Against her will, she found herself likening the European Union to the old Soviet one. And she could not help thinking how strange it was that Seidel, who had come from East Germany and been raised under its repressive regime, was now seemingly part of a similar conspiracy. Kate's partner, Guifford, was still making no secret of his delight that Britain had been humiliated; but now even he was becoming concerned that the perception of overkill to sustain the achievement of one of the bloc's most treasured goals could now overturn it.

Chapter Eleven

Michael, like a growing majority of British people, had been shocked into numbness and disbelief at what was happening in Britain. It was becoming obvious by the day that revolt was brewing, and although demonstrations and gatherings had been banned as 'not in the national interest', everyone knew that polls would have shown a huge majority for an uprising to overthrow the imposed government, the invading army - and to leave the EU without any deal or compromise whatsoever. And it would not necessarily be of the quiet kind. Everywhere there was discussion, people spoke of their hatred for the EU and Cash, and especially the clinging elites in the judiciary, the top of the armed forces and global businesses who were bankrolling their capitulation. Especial hatred was aimed at the cabal of ex-prime ministers and those MPs of all parties who had taken their democracy away from them and yet had all the plum posts and influence.

But democracy would not be stilled in Britain. For however the 'elites' – many of whom were not so but had manoeuvred themselves into positions of power and liked the soubriquet – tried to distort its true meaning for their own gain, there were a growing number who understood and revered Britain's innate feeling of fair play and truth, burnished by the spirit and grit of two world wars and countless battles throughout the country's noble history.

And so it was that Nick Lafargue, now spending most of his time in America as the unofficial British Ambassador to the new President, found himself yet again trying to get Britain out of the European Union, but this time from afar. His party, UKIP, had been banned from the European Parliament, and MEPs of parties from other sympathetic countries which had not by now left were intimidated, silenced, and often expelled. In one case, an MEP for Poland had just disappeared, and few thought he had just gone away. Across what was left of the European Union, police and armies were being used increasingly in the manner of the Stasi in the former East Germany; control of television news and suppressing the press were the main tactics. More sinister and personal was the knocking on doors in the middle of the night, the infiltration and breaking up of even the smallest of demonstrations and the denouncing of anyone who was critical of the European 'project'. Any so doing found themselves in deep trouble and under close surveillance from then on.

From his office in Washington DC, Lafargue had found himself a magnet for those who loved Britain and were appalled and astonished at its demise, and he was having no problem recruiting staff who would work for him without question. Many were not even British – indeed, most of his core staff were American Anglophiles – but the majority of his adherents were

British people who had found themselves in America on holiday but had subsequently not wanted to return to their once great, democratic country. Funding came from all over the world, but primarily from Americans who had been particularly appalled at the previous President's disdain for Britain, which they felt had encouraged the take-over: he had even haughtily proclaimed that any trade deal agreements post-Brexit would have seen Britain 'at the back of the queue'. By contrast, President Gold would put Britain right at the front of the queue but only when the country wrested itself away from the EU: at the moment, he could not encourage trade – even if it was beneficial to America - whilst Britain was subjugated.

Suddenly, due to the muzzling of Tessa Lewis by the Cash administration, Michael found himself at the forefront of his party, despite being compromised by the draconian new rules emanating from Brussels, where free speech was a part-time bystander and a chill of fear and distrust was prevalent. This was no more so than in the now re-opened but half-empty House of Commons, where the hand-picked Cash-supporting MPs were enjoying their new-found one-party power and treating those whose constituents and consciences had supported Leave with exclusion, ridicule and hatred. For there was no Opposition – the House was appointed and unelected. Just like the House of Lords, which was effectively in mothballs – a situation many thought it had been in for hundreds of years.

When he had become a new MP, Michael had not made alliances or particularly caused dislike, and had mostly managed to keep a low profile. This would now help him, for whilst he had to be careful, he had by chance managed to establish a clandestine conduit between himself and Lafargue. But total secrecy was the only way to survive – possibly literally. He had by chance found himself in a good position, but total secrecy was the only way to survive – possibly literally. For these reasons, the deposed Prime Minister had secretly – and at great risk - managed to come to him early on in the annexation; she had slipped out the back gate when her 'minders' were changing shifts at the front, and as far as they knew, she was still inside. Her husband would 'put out the rubbish' when it was time for her to return, so she could slip back in again. She resented being a pariah in her own country, but it gave her an extra resolve to restore democracy as soon as possible. For even as someone who had previously reluctantly supported Remain, out of respect for democracy and the will of the people, she would do all she could – again - to achieve Brexit. It was no surprise that she was now treated with even more contempt by Remainers, ironically being dubbed a 'turncoat'. Yet she would not be turned: she had the closest experience of the new administration, and what it represented was against every bone and belief in her democratic British body. Yet here she was, furtively meeting someone she trusted in the back room of a pub: had they been seen or followed, they would have been photographed and arrested. In addition, the new government-controlled press and BBC would accuse them of collusion against the state, which would carry harsh penalties.

"I should have acted faster," she had said to him

after she arrived, her head covered in a scarf reminiscent of the 1950s. They found a table under a particularly loud speaker so their conversation could not easily be heard by others, then she quietly but forcefully opened up to Michael.

"I should have triggered Article 50 the second I won the leadership, then none of this would have happened: the revolts, the challenges…"

"… and the invasion," Michael added helpfully.

"Indeed."

Cognisant of the fact that they had to proceed quickly lest they attracted any attention from forces loyal to the EU, she continued, "I understand you have attracted some sympathy from other 'people'."

"Yes."

"I will do anything I can to help."

"We have financial backing, and the goodwill of almost every country outside the EU."

"Rather like my plans to create a global economy based on WTO rules," she quipped. In true British spirit, it was good to see that her sense of humour had not suffered.

"Exactly," Michael concurred. "Just what the EU had always been afraid of. The good thing is, there are far more of them in the world than are in the EU."

"Just not in this new unelected government." Michael nodded. She sighed. "And so you're in touch with 'him'?" She referred of course, to Lafargue. Michael nodded again. "Should have made him British ambassador," she confided. "Not that it would make any difference now," she then added ruefully.

"Although, if you had, he'd be stuck here and unable to help us," Michael noted. This time, she nodded. He continued: "He can now help us more from there than he could here, actually. And I understand," and he leant close to her to say this, "there is the probability of military help if we need it."

She sighed. "It really has come to this?" she breathed. "Oh, God, what have I allowed to happen?"

"It'll turn out OK eventually," Michael consoled her, although privately he was concerned at what might have to be gone through before it did.

"Do you still hear from your wife?" she asked.

"Hardly. And communications between the EU and the BBC are compromised as they're sympathetic to one another, of course. So that makes it even more difficult."

"What does she think of all this?" she asked with a vague wave of her hand.

"I can't be sure. But she's 'with' Guifford Neveu and so I have to treat her as an enemy."

"Guifford Neveu?" Michael nodded. "The German commissioner?" Michael raised an eyebrow. "My goodness, I had no idea. I'm so sorry. She has no idea we're meeting, does she?"

"No, of course not. But in fact, I think she's as horrified deep down as I am, but she'd never admit it. And especially while she's still with *him,* of course. She's gone native; but I suspect that's for power and influence reasons rather than anything else."

"She was a journalist I had trusted," she said with a sense of sadness. Then: "How could such a supposed bastion of Britishness be so complicit in all this?"

"Are you talking about the BBC or my wife?" Michael asked with a wry look on his face.

"Both, I suppose." After a long pause, she continued: "And you're so much nicer-looking, too."

"Thanks – small solace though it is." She smiled. Michael went on: "I have my own theories about that, too, though."

"Yes, I'm sure you do."

There was a silence as they both delved into their inner thoughts. Then Michael said simply, "I think we ought to have a name for our new movement for if – when – we start the real drive to take back power."

"And control." It was Michael's turn to smile. "Hm. Good thought: any ideas?"

"Restoration," he said instantly. "It has historic, positive English – and British - overtones, and is reminiscent of when England was liberated from the rule of Cromwell in 1660. It fits, and resonates, perfectly."

"I like it," she concurred. "From now forward, that is what we'll call it." She looked at the floor and then up at Michael, and rolled the word across her tongue. "Restoration… It has a good resonance. And it should catch the imagination," she said.

Their meeting concluded after they had discussed when and how they could further the cause of what they had to admit was an uprising: 'revolution' was too strong a word and had connotations of what the very socialist leader of the Labour party not so secretly wanted and Cash had installed. It was thus more reminiscent of the very forces they were now committed to defeating. They were both sure an uprising would happen, but neither were in any doubt as to how dangerous or difficult it would be.

Immediately afterwards, Michael went to his 'safe house' as he called it; from there, he could relatively securely get in touch with Lafargue. The news was good: the new President was still fully behind them and already channelling money and weapons to sympathetic areas of the UK, where they all hoped an uprising would start. The further good news was that their intelligence showed the EU was in paralysis as, with Russia occupying the Baltic states, Italy and Holland out of the Union and the Euro Army trapped in Britain, there was little they could do without everyone knowing about it. In addition, most countries outside the European Union – the rest of the world – had stopped any trading with them and refused to export any goods or raw materials to them. This was having a dual effect: what was left of the bloc as such became far more integrated than ever before, with the will of Germany and France being imposed more politically than they had managed to get away with previously. Essentially, it was a question of survival – they had to stick together and trade only between themselves. Secondly, the economies of Germany and France, particularly, were suddenly unable to manufacture many goods as their previously-imported supplies dried up. They had placed themselves in a vice-like grip and were turning the screw on their own people. Their mantra of 'ever more Europe' was suddenly becoming a reality, but only in the sense that there was less of everywhere else.

There were some brighter spots for them early on, however, but these would not last long. As an example, Greece found itself being visited by millions more Germans and French than before because Europeans were not now permitted to travel to Italy; and, with the austerity of the European will imposed more rigorously - and their people now forced to pay their taxes - its economy started to recover. But with this came a resentment of being controlled by what was essentially a foreign power, without the checks and balances occasionally afforded by a greater diversity of opinion in either a national parliament or other EU states. So despite limitless recent bailouts to buy their souls and keep them in the European Union, the Greeks' hatred of their masters started to manifest itself into the first meaningful stirrings of revolt. Reluctantly compliant for many months, the iron German hand, arrests, interrogations and control of the media were starting to turn the Greeks against the euro again and, hence, the European Union itself.

This knowledge was known to Michael as he had established good connections there, like he had done in other states; this he passed on to Lafargue and his implicitly trusted supporters of Leave in England and Wales. Scotland, for the time being, was not included, as most of its MPs had willingly joined with Cash in subjugating 'the auld enemy'. Grassroots organisations – known as 'Posh de Resistance' in the more educated avenues of the supportive underground pro-Leave press - were gaining courage, momentum and finance. And, like the French Resistance, growing arsenals of firearms, which were being hoarded for what was already being planned for Britain's 'Independence Day' – June 23rd. Yet there was also a more modern twist: young hackers and social media fanatics were now mostly keen to be rid of this hated new administration, essentially a puppet government run by unelected and unaccountable people from afar, and they were busy disrupting any TV and radio stations that were willingly disseminating government propaganda. (Those independent stations which had dared to criticise the government or spread anti-EU views had been quickly 'advised' to toe the line – or else). These people were also planning a huge wave of cyber-attacks on government and EU institutions and installations. They had hacked into Europol, too, which had records of many British people now considered dissidents: these were targeted for support – some did not even realise they were on the database, having perhaps only once made what had previously been innocent opinions in more open and democratic times.

Thousands of British soldiers were still deserting, too: many, though, had decided to stay in their regiments so they would have access to weaponry when the time came. They would be only too happy to undermine and contradict any orders from their now-despised and compromised Generals and Commanders. British expatriates from European states still in the bloc – especially those old enough to have had experience in sabotage and parents who had seen action in the last war - had managed to return. They remembered what Britain had been like before and, although it was far from perfect, the country was significantly better than what it had become now.

The main areas of support were a swathe through

the middle of England, starting in the North-East and passing down through East Anglia and the Midlands towards the South-West and Wales – in short, a majority of the constituencies which had voted to Leave. As such, it was creating a band of resistance that would cut off London and the South-East from Scotland.

This would prove to be a crucial factor.

Chapter Twelve

As June 23rd approached, Cash's government was doing all it could to suppress the swell of support they knew would be apparent. Regiments of mainly Scottish battalions and civilian volunteers sympathetic to him – including many settlers from the EU who had electronic or 'persuasive' skills and had suspected they might lose out from any Brexit deal – were stationed in places of high Leave support. And this despite Tessa Lewis having previously tried to ensure that EU people could stay, provided it was reciprocated across the EU: yet that humanitarian request had not been forthcoming from Seidel. In addition, the stationing of Scottish battalions on English and Welsh soil only inflamed tensions further: it seemed proof that England and Wales were being bossed by vengeful Scots and Europeans from a foreign institution they despised; so Cash quietly returned the Scots to their barracks.

Yet with open borders still EU policy, many British had started returning to Britain; several had reported being harassed by EU citizens who had family and friends in Britain and were keen to make the same point in their own countries. It was instructive that the phrase 'freedom of movement' still held good for people wishing to travel back to their own countries – as well as invading armies.

*

Nick Lafargue had managed to contact Michael from his office in Washington: they had to be brief and also hope that their young techies had managed to use a line that was unhackable, but when nations are at stake, risks have to be taken. Lafargue went straight to the point.

"Michael, I have some very interesting news, which I think will help us for our big day."

"Excellent."

"President Gold has been very helpful. You may not know that he had his first meeting with Rastov last week in Alaska – very hush-hush. It went very well. In a nutshell, this is what's happened. He put it to Rastov that although the EU is trying to replace NATO with its pathetic Euro-army, the way it's going, the whole thing is going to crumble soon anyway – and I probably get more inside news on this than you do, by the way: I still have sympathetic MEP contacts."

"Indeed."

"Well, Gold put it to Rastov that NATO will survive, despite – or perhaps *because* of – the EU collapsing. He and his Pentagon blokes – top brass and all that – managed to make Rastov aware that NATO was the devil Rastov knew, rather than the other way round. So – and this is where it gets interesting – Gold got him to discuss what he thought on Earth he was doing invading the Baltic states and supplying Russian hardware to the EU to invade

Britain. Rastov tried to deny it, of course, but Gold wasn't having any of that and his military chiefs soon showed him they had the proof. However, he said they'd keep that quiet if Rastov would help him to get rid of Cash's government and re-instate Britain's sovereignty. At first, Rastov wouldn't budge, but he started to see the attraction when Gold offered some sweeteners. For example, he said he would drop sanctions on Russia, which means they could start selling Siberian oil and gas on the open markets again – which would do their economy no end of good."

"Won't that make them more aggressive and powerful, then?" Michael asked, perturbed.

"I'm coming to that – but not necessarily. So, added to that, he'd announce a new trade deal with the Russkies *as well* if they left the Baltic states due to a new US-Russian accord. Mind you, that bit – leaving the Baltic states – would be kept quiet, because the Russians could never admit to having invaded them in the first place."

"They slipped in easily enough," said Michael, "so hopefully it'll be just as easy for them to slip out again."

"You're right. And, of course, it's never been announced, confirmed or denied that the Russians are in the Baltic states anyway. *We* know they are, as you do – but it's never been admitted. They've taken over all the state and private communications, media, etc., but made it look as though normal daily life is continuing. Obviously, many Latvians, Estonians *do* know, but fear - and the ostrich principle – are keeping them quiet. They still have fresh memories of what it was like under the Russians before, of course, so don't want to rock the boat. But for now, Gold wants to keep it like that because he doesn't want to look as if he's got Rastov in a pincer movement. And it'd be easier for them to leave if it had never been over-obvious they were there in the first place. Between you and me, though, Gold actually needs to reduce military spending and Rastov knows he can't keep up with American might anyway. So it's win-win for both of them – and so Rastov agreed to the deal."

"That's great – but what about the Baltic states? Are they going to be given back to the EU?"

"That's up to them. But, candidly, the answer is 'No'. Gold and Rastov have agreed that the Russians can stay in the Baltic states for the foreseeable future because having them there will help both keep the EU on its toes and also be useful to Britain. The Baltics are still hopping mad that they were, one, invaded, and two, used as a low-key launch-pad to help invade Britain. There are so many of their people working in Britain now that they were livid. But they'll be made to realise that it's in their best interests to suffer the Russians for a bit longer and get rid of them after they've helped Britain become a sovereign nation again – which they'll be again, too, of course, after the Russians have left."

"Do you really think it'll work?" asked Michael, incredulous.

"Yes, I do. As long as Rastov really does leave – and Gold will ensure the world knows he must or all the deals they've discussed will be null and void - I think they'll see the bigger picture. Frankly, though, with what's happened recently, I'd wager that they'd be happier to have the Russians back than return to being under the EU."

Michael pondered what he had said for a moment, then asked, "I suppose there's a tacit understanding that they're *both* invading armies so Rastov would rather withdraw so he's not tarred with the same brush."

"Exactly. And the Crimea and east Ukraine are more important to Rastov politically than the Baltic states, so they'll probably be tacitly allowed to keep them – for now, anyway. And, of course, could the EU go to the support of the Baltic states anyway? No. It hasn't got the money or the hardware."

"So that means that Gold will lay off the rhetoric regarding getting the Crimea and Ukraine back from Russian control," Michael re-iterated thoughtfully.

"Probably. After all, Rastov's less worried about a Euro-army now or states joining the EU, so it's another win-win for him."

"And what do we Brits get out of it?"

"Erm… probably quite a lot – although I think just having Rastov on our side again with the Americans is a coup enough. I'm sure he'll help if he knows Gold will stick to his part of the deal – which I know he will."

The conversation soon ended, with both feeling more optimistic than they had done for some time. They had concluded that it was a brilliant ploy, and should have the desired effect: the EU did not want any further Russian incursions and was powerless to stop them anyway, especially with the bloc in crisis and its fragmented army now stationed in Britain and trying to hold down potential rebellions elsewhere that could cripple it further.

In fact, the deal would work better than any of them hoped – but not in the way they expected…

Chapter Thirteen

In Brussels, Guifford Neveu and Kate had been discussing the latest developments: she was still making her reports for the BBC but had unofficially become his most trusted assistant, a conflict of interest which would never have been allowed before the current situation. As such, though, she had unfettered access to the vast majority of European edicts and regulations, of which there were a frightening number. Even she felt that its insidious penetration of all aspects of life had gone too far, but she was still broadly wedded to the project. When she became unsure, she just thought of how life had dealt her a wonderful hand and that when all this was over she would be wealthy, powerful and influential. And all thanks to Guifford. It was her own little justifying panacea, and it never failed to work.

"We have an idea that there's revolution brewing in Britain and we have to be wary of it," he had told her. "Now that those Dutch and Italians have left, though, we don't have enough resource to fight it – either militarily or economically. And the Irish won't pay the fines we imposed on them for having their own business models unless we leave Britain which, of course, is the last thing we want – or will do. But the fact remains – and keep this outside your BBC broadcasts - we're in trouble."

Yet Kate knew that the European Union always thrived on adversity: one of its founding fathers, Jacques Delors, had even proclaimed that, "it should never allow a good crisis go to waste." In other words, if there was a stand-off between the EU and the people, use the uncertainty and the excuse for subterfuge to create the result the EU had wanted in the first place. It had always worked, especially with the creation of the euro and treaties such as Maastricht and Lisbon, all overcome by re-aligning the facts to triumph over adversity and so create ever-closer union.

*

Michael was in a state of nervous panic: he had been summoned by Cash, whom he had not met before, but was aware of his charm and ruthlessness. He knew he had to be careful not to betray anything by default, knowing as he did all the details of the impending uprising. He was concerned that he had been betrayed or found out, and he was racking his brains to try to remember any indiscretion he may have made, but he could not. Then the knock on the door meant that his car had arrived, and he was on his way to Downing Street.

"Good morning," said the Prime Minister coldly as Michael was ushered in by a member of his Cabinet, passing two armed soldiers on his way in. He also instantly noticed the presence of the previous Lib Dem Deputy Prime Minister in the previous Coalition. He did not like it. Or him.

"We've been hearing some rumours," began Studd, as the door was firmly closed behind him. Michael said nothing.

"Rumours that you're involved in organising an uprising," added the Prime Minister. Michael's blood ran cold. He, too, had heard rumours: that people suspected of treachery to the new government had been thrown into prison on spurious grounds, with water-boarding a possibility. And some people had apparently disappeared completely.

"I don't know what you're talking about."

"I think you do," said Studd, with his usual air of miffed indignation.

"You tell me, then."

"Are you in touch with Lafargue?" Cash enquired.

"Not in any sense more than the usual international dialogue one has with people of other countries."

"He is not of 'other countries'," snapped Studd. "He's British but a proscribed person. We do not have dealings with him. So nor will you."

"Oh. Well, I'll remember that from now on."

"You certainly will," said the Prime Minister. "Or there'll be consequences."

"Like the restoration of Parliament and a democratically-elected government by the British people without any foreign interference?" said Michael. He knew he had gone too far but his blood was up.

There was a pause as they stared at him coldly. Then Studd said: "There is no foreign interference, except from the United States. Britain is part of a union of states - "

"Sovereign nations," Michael interrupted.

"A union of states agreed by the people in 1973. We are only sustaining their will." Michael could feel himself about to boil. Calm, stay calm – this was what they wanted.

"I beg to differ. We had a binding Referendum a year ago which expressly stated that the people wished to leave the European Union."

"It wasn't binding," Cash said tersely. "It was advisory."

"An opinion poll," added Studd, "fuelled by lies on the Leave side."

"Lies? And what about Project Fear, then? Until your insurrection - "

"This is not an insurrection, but a taking back of control."

Michael had expected them to throw that at him, because they knew it would cause anger: the irony of hijacking the winning slogan of the Leave campaign was daily being used blatantly and frequently by these unelected people to try to confuse the populace into thinking that this insurrection, invasion, was actually what they had voted for. It was being done to sow confusion, distrust, imbalance – just like the EU would do in the same situation. Well, this was the same situation, of course. Yet however they tried to spin it, Michael knew that their acts were the total antithesis of the direct democracy the Referendum had presented - the ultimate tyranny of denial.

Michael took a deep breath and calmed himself with difficulty, desperately trying to suppress the fury in his voice so he still sounded rational. "The Referendum result was constitutional, well understood and reflected the voice of the people. And we were in the process of delivering on it until... all this. Everyone knew the facts."

After a moment, Cash looked up and said: "People had an imperfect knowledge. As we have been in politics for many years, we see all sides of every debate, and we therefore know the people made a terrible mistake which we are now rectifying. They *didn't* have the facts, so they need to be re-educated." All through this, Studd was nodding dementedly like one of those dogs that used to sit on the parcel-shelves of cars, unable to stop until the journey finished.

"Well, I believe the people showed more understanding of 'the facts' as you call them, than you ever have," exploded Michael. He now knew he was in trouble but as a British person his innate sense of having to speak the truth got the better of him. "The true facts – and all the evidence - exists to the contrary. Forty-three years of being under the yoke – in my and seventeen million people's view - of an undemocratic, corrupt, bullying, interfering, unaccountable, expensive, anti-sovereign and unnecessary imposition is enough to make anyone realise the folly of the vote in 1973. And it was sold as only for a trading bloc, not a political union. The Prime Minister at the time, Ted Heath, even told us that, "there would be no 'essential' loss of sovereignty." That was not true either and the Referendum was a reaction to that – as you, Mr

Studd, voted for when Parliament gave you the opportunity to decide whether to have one or not over a year ago. Yet you're not honourable enough to accept the result, just because it didn't go your way. That might be the EU way, but it's not democracy; in my view it's the beginnings of fascism."

The look on their faces showed he had scored a point – one which these two normally directed at others as a final insult. "Anyway," Michael continued, "I doubt I was summoned to debate the finer points of true democracy with you: what is it you wish to discuss with me?"

"The fact that you're in league with people planning an insurrection." The sudden quiet in the room highlighted the buzz of the office he could hear through the closed door.

"And where did you get that – incorrect – information?"

"Your wife." Michael then realised they knew nothing – it was all bluster, and designed to throw him off guard and admit everything. He had not spoken to his wife for two weeks, and her views – although diametrically opposed to his – would not have been discussed by either of them. There was no point any more. She did not know of his nascent involvement with the counter-revolution, and certainly of no collusion with Lafargue – he just had not told her. No, it had obviously come from someone else - someone who was trying to compromise him, expose his sympathies to the unelected British government and cement his relationship with his wife. Neveu.

A sudden determination – not anger – borne of indignation and being insulted welled up in him. "I haven't spoken to her for two weeks. We have nothing to talk about any more. She has become a stooge of the BBC and, ergo, yours. And she's having a relationship with Guifford Neveu, who must have put you up to this for his own purposes. So, if you'll forgive me, gentlemen, I have work to do. Good morning." And he turned on his heel and left.

They were so astonished, they just let him go. After Michael had closed the door firmly behind him, Cash turned to Studd and said, "I didn't know Guifford was having a relationship with his wife."

"Neither did I," admitted Studd. "Lucky sod. She's gorgeous."

"And one of us," added the Prime Minister, diplomatically.

*

Outside in the fresh air, Michael breathed deeply. He had come through OK, he thought, although the accusation that he was implicit in an uprising was too close to the truth for comfort. Yet they had let him leave without hindrance, so they obviously weren't sure, which is what had given him the confidence to stand up to the claim that Guifford had found out through his wife that he was implicitly in collusion with Lafargue. He did not actually think that she would have told Guifford, though, even if she had known. Or would she? It was, indeed, true that they had not spoken in two weeks: was this her indignant way of finally telling him it was over and that she would soon be filing for divorce? He doubted it, Kate was always careful to ensure the grass was, indeed, greener on the other side and she still didn't know he knew about Guifford. Perhaps she would do soon, though, now he had told Cash and Studd, but it was his only defence. Either way, she would probably wait until this whole debacle was over and she could see clearly that the EU would survive, that Britain was irrevocably subjugated again and her rich future as an EU Commissioner's wife - with all its perks and handouts - was assured. He sighed. It was a beautiful summer's day, the birds sang and all seemed well… until one noticed the surveillance cameras, military posts, army vehicles – whether they were British, Russian or European he did not know as they had all assumed British colours. Huh! To make people feel less intimidated! Yet the palpable sense of pervasive fear expressed on people's faces told a different story. There was no laughter, no sarcastic British humour, no levity. It was like life without soul. To cap it, there were EU flags everywhere. And not one Union Jack to be seen.

Chapter Fourteen

There was no reaction in the Baltic states to what the Americans and Russians had agreed because they were not told. Resistance movements had been thin on the ground anyway due to the reasons Lafargue had articulated to Michael, but the right channels were discreetly ordered to keep things quiet for the time being as it would ensure a better future in the long term. And so the Russians maintained their discreet, if vice-like, grip. The military and trade deals between Russia and America were kept quiet, too: it was better to continue things as they were than give hope or propaganda to any faction. One story did get out that the Russians were intensifying their hold and had shot a resistance fighter, and the European Union put out a terse statement decrying the 'invasion of a sovereign European Union state', without accepting the irony; yet their indignation was dismissed as everyone knew the truth - that they had used Russian hardware and the Baltic occupation to crush Britain and further their aims.

But this story had been released by both parties: it was all part of the plan. The Russians accused the Americans of interfering in their affairs, the

Americans that they had invaded a sovereign country. With the world looking the other way and the spotlight off Britain, the Americans had amassed two aircraft carriers and a fleet of submerged submarines off the Irish coast under the guise of Atlantic manoeuvres. This had been arranged with the complicity of the Irish government which, although still a part of the EU, was increasingly angry at the EU's imposition of extortionate taxes and fines to compensate for Ireland's low business rates, which had resulted in the American government moving huge software and electronics companies there. To compound this, the EU had manipulated reason to fine the Americans as well, which only added another insult to injury. The standoff had continued when the Dail had also sent a proclamation to Brussels denouncing the EU invasion of Britain and had consequently secretly allowed America to station troops on their soil. The Irish might not have liked Britain once, but their kindred sense of being part of the British Isles – if not of Britain itself - had touched their sense of fair play. Democracy had been outraged and they wanted to help liberate their closest country, for their good if not Britain's and America's too. Quietly, it had also been agreed with the Americans and the British Restoration government-in-waiting that – if any counter-invasion was successful - they would refuse to pay any fines or taxes back to a humbled EU. Whether they then stayed in the bloc or not was an issue for another day: for now, the important issue was the restoration of democracy to the country closest to it - both as a trading necessity and a statement of honour.

Although most in the Irish Republic had been

minded to stay in the EU, (despite having had two referenda foisted upon them when the first had not gone the 'right' way) Dublin was nervous of any Brussels retaliation: the referenda had caused major rifts in Ireland, as the Referendum had in mainland Britain – but they needed to keep their bread buttered on both sides. If the public mood changed again – as the many financial impositions by Brussels had caused it to do – the Taoiseach wanted the ability to bend either way. For the moment, he was mindful that Ireland did more trade with Great Britain than it did with the EU – an identical embarrassing fact for Scottish Remainers too. He also did more trade with America than Europe and wanted to keep it that way – so to support Britain and, thus, America, was key.

*

The night before the Independence Day uprising, a power failure had been orchestrated right across the southern part of Eire; there was not a light to be seen. It was blamed on a linked malfunction of power stations across the republic and was calmly passed off as a local difficulty with no sinister undertones. But under the cover of this darkness, US Marines and paratroopers moved to the East of the country to prepare for an invasion. They would start by retaking the US air bases scattered around Britain which had been neutered by the compliance of the British Army and RAF when Cash's putsch started, which was another annoyance to the new American administration: the previous President may have temporarily accepted it due to his respect for Seidel, but the new one would not.

When the power failure started, things had moved

rapidly in their pre-planned way: 'sleeper' soldiers and RAF staff at all the British and American bases in England and Wales had surprised both the British and European occupiers in a co-ordinated and synchronous attack, taking back control of communications and authorities so that the Americans could land their troops and equipment unimpeded. As this happened, any British and European soldiers, airmen and auxiliary personnel suspected of sympathy to Cash and the European Union were rounded up and kept under lock and key. Their PCs, mobile phones and codes were confiscated and only comms needed to give the semblance of being on alert were left open under the command of counter-invasion, Restoration forces. Then they sent messages to government installations to say that they needed anti-insurgency training flights and troop movements to put down disturbances: this would explain the extra noise and activity resulting from the dissemination of forces across the land. To keep the nation unsuspecting, the American planes had been re-painted with Army and RAF markings, and their troops had been issued with British clothing. At the same time, all the military British top brass not in their bases were arrested in their beds or wherever they were at that moment, having been tracked ruthlessly but unseen by army volunteers who wanted their country back.

It was a supremely well-organised event and, within a few hours, all the airfields and barracks around the country were filled with personnel who earnestly wished to take Britain back to its democratically-elected future outside the European Union.

*

Although elected MPs were not allowed to engage in debates or voting under the new regime, they had been allowed back into their Commons offices. Yet they suspected that all the lines and communications were being tapped and no-one risked any correspondence unless it was to do with everyday constituency issues.

Michael was in his office there when Jemima Grice knocked on the door, furtively entered and whispered the news to him: "It's started – bang on cue. June 23rd – Independence Day! And it seems to be going so well that no-one seems to have realised yet."

"They will by tomorrow," Michael whispered back, "and with a vengeance. Is it all happening in the right places – from the North-East down to Wales and the West country?"

"It would seem so. Fingers crossed. I don't know yet whether Lafargue and the main Brexiteers have met up yet, but I should imagine so. When are you joining them?"

"When I get the call."

"Good luck." And she left. Michael had not felt such a thrill of excitement and optimism for a long time and he felt invigorated by the news. If Lafargue and the Brexit cabinet – including the previous Prime Minister but not the Chancellor – had met up and could integrate the fightback for a free Britain, it would be an amazing coup. In every sense of the word.

Michael pondered the plan again: it was that the swathe of Leave-supporting constituencies would be taken over and secured, but not London, the South-

East and Scotland. Even though support for the EU invasion had shrunk significantly in those areas, it was felt that they were – for the moment – a bridge too far. And the masterstroke was that this cross-country swathe would effectively cut Scotland off from London, where the bulk of Remain-voting support still lay. The whole of the centre of England and Wales would effectively become a no-go area for the EU army: industry and commerce, farming and pro-Remain areas within this area – such as the University towns of Oxford and Cambridge – would be especially well monitored to win hearts and minds - but also to ensure that the new trade deal freedoms to be announced were seen to benefit them as well as the rest of the land. It would mean an uneasy stand-off between military sites and barracks which the EU army invasion units had managed to conquer and hold on to, and loyalist British ones where they had been resisted or thrown out. But there was an uneasy recognition between each faction that the other was there - and a tacit understanding not to provoke a shooting-match. That would have been in no-one's best interests, and each side knew it.

Chapter Fifteen

Nick Lafargue stepped out of a Chinook helicopter and sniffed the East Anglian air being excited by its whirling blades. There was a stiff breeze blowing in from the east coast, too, and it smelled of the Fens and fish, which made him feel good. He smiled at the assembled press, soldiers and previous government officials. They and he had all mutually agreed to work together to help restore Britain's sovereignty – there was no place for any infighting: this was Britain's most important day since the Second World War. He was quickly escorted to a car with a military escort which would take him to Peterborough, where cabinet members of the previous government and the former Prime Minister were waiting for him. As he sped through the thickening light which revealed sleepy English villages, he mused how the majority of people in this area were supportive of him and how proud he was to be representing them, trying to get back this wonderful country from the clutches of an oppressive minority. Again, a previous Prime Minister's words, "the tyranny of the majority," passed through his mind. Well, he was going to try to impose the will of the true majority, and there was not a tyrant in their whole set-up. He chuckled: it was good to be home.

An hour later, the outline of Peterborough Cathedral could be seen and, as the cavalcade reached it, the military outriders peeled off and his car pulled up near the West Door. As they did so, it opened and some familiar faces from the previous government approached him, smiling, their hands held out in welcome. Petty party differences were irrelevant now; they had all pledged to bury the hatchet and do all they could to end the occupation.

In Downing Street, Terry Cash entered his office. It was early, and there were only a few people in the entire building. The phone rang: it was his Cabinet Secretary, who had been re-appointed by him when he acceded after the invasion.

"Morning, Prime Minister."

"Morning, Jim. You're a bit previous today, aren't you?"

"Yes – bit of bad news, I'm afraid."

"Oh. What's that?"

"'Fraid the wife's ill – soaring temperature and excruciating stomach cramps, so I'll need to look after her today. Sorry. I'll have to leave you in the capable hands of Julia Reeve. You know her well enough."

"Yes, indeed. Sorry to hear about the wife: just hope nothing dramatic happens today."

"Don't worry, Julia's one of us. She'll be in soon. She was on leave but has stepped into the breach."

"Well, thank her and say I look forward to seeing her later. Hope your wife gets better soon. See you tomorrow?"

"I'd hope so. I'll keep you in touch with developments."

"Excellent. Speak soon."

They rang off. At his home, the Cabinet Secretary looked up at the man with the gun to his head as if to ask if he had passed. The man nodded. Behind him, Julia Reeve, a closet sympathiser of the counter-invasion, stood ready to go in to Downing Street and keep the Prime Minister as uninformed as possible.

*

Peterborough Cathedral had been chosen for this first meeting of the putative Restoration government for many reasons. First, it sat in a generally benign part of the country where Leave was prevalent; second, it had limited communications so no-one there could leak anything; third, its open spaces all around would make it very difficult to storm – and the cost to Britain's heritage would be significant if it had been; finally, there were several exits and hiding places if the need arose. It would also never have been expected. The ex-Prime Minister and Lafargue had had their differences and, in principle, loathed each other: yet the prospect of a shared goal and the replacement of this hated undemocratic government made their policies converge both simply and constructively across most of their agendas.

Tessa Lewis had never met Lafargue but they had been in touch via Michael. Lafargue's easy charm and intimate knowledge of Brussels had soon had the ex-PM wishing she had, indeed, made him her Ambassador to the United States, as suggested by the then President-

Elect; but it was obviously meant to be, because – having been a high-profile anti-EU MEP for so many years - he told her of the many intimate details and institutionalised corruptions of the EU as he perceived them. She soon realised he was better off with her than stuck in America and they realised their shared aims were more important than their differences. Deep down, she was almost pleased it had turned out this way because, if and when the Restoration happened, she suddenly realised she would enjoy working with him. He was not the fascist and racist ogre as implied by the BBC and the left-wing press; rather an old-fashioned and principled reactionary from much the same background as she had come from. Yet she was not going to be with him in Peterborough – she had decided on another plan which would make the Restoration announcement look more national and more representative. And it would be safer, too. Many of the leading Brexiteers in her previous government were there, though, as well as a handful of the Leave side from the Labour party - and several prominent UKIP people, too. Needless to say, there was no Liberal Democrat in sight as, to a man and a woman, they had all thrown their support behind the insurrection and were now back in government under Cash.

Having decided unanimously to call it The Restoration, they quickly moved to consolidate their position. It seemed that no-one had realised the counter-invasion had happened yet, such was the thoroughness of the organisation and the loyalty of those involved. BBC East in Norwich had reported complaints from people around the Lakenheath area of unusually extra flights, but they did not yet seem to have made any connection. In the spirit of Dunkirk, flotillas of cars and vans were, at this very moment, ferrying American and loyal British troops to all parts of The Swathe – as it would now be called – so that any resistance or retaliation could be dampened as soon as possible. Where there was not enough barrack space for the liberating army, people willingly put them up in their spare rooms, inns, hotels, B&Bs and more: but this was only in places where the prevailing majority had voted overwhelmingly to leave – now swelled further by the EU's invasion. Sunderland had become a command centre for that reason, as well as Stoke-on-Trent in the Midlands, with the highest concentration of Leave voters in the country: conversely, Cambridge and Oxford would not be attempted for a while yet. It was better to leave them surrounded without their knowledge than provoke any possibility of a Remain backlash. And once all the hardware and personnel had finished accumulating, the Swathe would expand from the area northwards and southwards, with the main prizes being Manchester and, of course, London. From there, they could rule the country again once the other areas were secured.

A vast number of people had been clandestinely recruited across the Swathe area in particular from the ranks of vocal Leave-voting people: economists, doctors, ex-services personnel, trades, retail, delivery, carers, designers, writers, actors and many more had been carefully signed up for this moment without any resort to computers or online communication, which was too easily compromised. Mostly, it was organised by word of mouth, discreet landline phone calls, coded leaflets and notes and so on – rather like during the war. Many gave ill-affordable money to the campaign: industry leaders in particular who had been vocal in their support of Britain going it alone before the Referendum had stumped up the most to provide and pay for support, propaganda, office space, secure locations and more. Most were in the industrial areas around the Midlands, yet there were also many in the north-east, south-west and East Anglia: the old wartime adage that 'walls have ears' became a guideline for those planning the uprising wherever they were involved or knew about it, so that the counter-invasion could proceed as unhindered, fast and relentlessly as possible. Keep Calm and Carry On became the catchphrase once again.

Yet, inevitably, there were people asking probing questions, and many were hostile. In cases like these, they would be assured that all was normal and that they were acting on the orders of the Cash government; if they persisted or looked as if they were about to blow the whistle, they were taken to hastily-arranged detention centres with supposedly pro-Cash propaganda to quell their suspicions. British personnel were used to bark orders – or even in French or German if they could get away with it: but no American accents were to be heard, even if they were actually giving many of the orders behind the scenes.

*

It had always been hoped that there would be no loss of life and that it would be another "quiet revolution" as Tessa Lewis had said; yet, inevitably, there were initial skirmishes where an iron fist had to be imposed on people who were resistant to what was being planned. And there were casualties. These were sent to hospitals in areas sympathetic to the counter-invasion and the carefully-chosen staff were under strict instructions to keep difficult and vocal patients drugged until after the putsch had been announced – or discovered.

*

Rumours were starting to come into the European Union concourse in Brussels that something was wrong. But they had not yet twigged that it was in Britain. With the calm, calculating charm that was Cash now in charge, the general consensus was that Britain would be quiet, safe, suppressed and compliant - at least for a while. After Cash had used his influential global supporters for the money – supplemented by £10 million of his own from his various foundations - to bend people's views towards another Referendum, he would then win it. And he would, too: for his brand of persuasion would brook no discussion or dissent and would make Project Fear look like a children's tea party. After that, the European Army could return to their states and all would be well. And he and his chums could start influencing the world again in their own image and for their own gain.

*

During the tumultuous recent events, even the European Union had been complacently disregarding France, despite the fact that presidential elections were due. Despite the tumult of Brexit and Britain's subsequent invasion, Brussels was singularly unprepared for what might happen there, believing that France's involvement in Britain's invasion had enraptured the country: yet the event had polarised it. A majority were delighted in principle but horrified in practice – it was what could happen to them if things went wrong; and although many were happy to see Britain humbled, they knew there would be repercussions. And that would reflect badly on France. Political leaders outside Europe had already condemned the EU for its act, and were obviously pointing the finger at Germany and France as the main perpetrators. Many countries had pledged not to invest in France or buy French products, and the boycott was worsening its already dire employment statistics, augmented by the high taxes and economic policies of its current president.

The ongoing austerity – aggravated by France financially supporting the invasion of Britain, which it could certainly not afford – had also exacerbated the situation. This had driven many into the fold of the Front Nationale, whose leader, Laporte, was leading the polls. She was expected to win the first round but lose the second to Ernest Faucheux - an untested banker who was popular mainly for not being any of the other candidates and had just founded a new movement called En Marche! Yet many French bankers and industrialists had started to laud the British pre-invasion way for, even after the Brexit Referendum had been overturned, their economy was still growing – although it had slowed considerably since the ensuing invasion. To these perceptive French, it was proof that the EU was going the wrong way, and a takeover of its own country by their own army – and no interference from any other - to subdue the unions was the only way to get France working again as a representative sovereign democracy. Laporte had, of course, made much of this: her ratings soared when she proposed this as a possibility. In addition, she had always maintained that the euro was destroying businesses and jobs as much as the dangerous situation that the nation found itself in immigration-wise; to boot, Seidel's 'open door' policy had only made it worse. A number of terrorist atrocities in France had helped her cause, too: the French suddenly began to believe too late that they were losing their identity, and this swelled her populist ranks even more.

At this point, too, external events intervened. In the Elysee Palace, the outgoing President Hugande was informed that the President of Algeria had suddenly died. This was a huge further blow to him, as the man had left no obvious successor. As with so many North African states, the country was instantly falling into factional, lawless anarchy now this strongman was no more; to add to the crisis, suddenly even more refugees were arriving in Marseilles and along the Cote d'Azur, so testing France's tolerance further. And when a new wave of bombings and suicide attacks began and Hugande hesitated, the polls started moving even further in Laporte's favour. Allied with the febrile state of Europe generally and the aftermath of invasion in Britain - which Laporte had roundly condemned - she was now trying to trigger a motion of no confidence in the outgoing president's government. It started to look possible that the prevailing winds might propel her to success in the first round – an unprecedented situation, where the second round had been created solely to stop anyone not from the elite classes ever winning a presidency. She was also sure that events in Britain would help her. In that, she was about to become a much happier woman indeed.

Chapter Sixteen

Julia Reeve had been a career civil servant for many years, and its complacency, snobbery and sense of entitlement had often disgusted her: but she had kept her nose clean and done well. Unlike most of her peers, she had voted Leave and was a fervent supporter of the Referendum result, but had always played along with the majority view so as not to risk suspicion, isolation, and therefore her job. The fact that Cash was back in power – and especially how it had come about – disgusted her even more, so she had decided early on to be a 'sleeper' for Leave and, if at any time her services were needed, then she would be ready. This was that time.

When she entered the PM's office, she was relieved to find that there was no sense of panic or horror, so she knew that, for now, the Restoration counter-invasion was still a secret. And she intended keeping it that way. After notifying Cash that she was there, she set about ensuring that the newswire had been compromised. This had been achieved several weeks ago by another fervent Leaver who was in charge of IT at Downing Street. He had constructed a programme to hack into Whitehall's entire broadband network when the time came, which would then be programmed into providing a steady stream of humdrum news and replies to intercepted e-mails and communications for as long as necessary. He had already procured a list of all the e-mail addresses of staff across Whitehall and Downing Street, which was being monitored 24/7 to ensure that any communications from anyone who might suddenly reveal that the counter-invasion had begun would not get through. It had taken him months to create the programme, but he was confident he had succeeded. More difficult was compromising the entire TV monitor newsfeed operation, but her driver, whom she had asked to wait downstairs for an hour in case Cash needed her to go somewhere in a hurry – was in reality an electronics engineer who knew exactly what to do. He had been tasked to compromise the whole of Downing Street and Whitehall with the same news – also shutting out any that might be counter-productive. Having done this, Julia called him whilst in front of Cash to say that she would not need him until much later, which was his cue to leave. For the moment, it all seemed as if the hard work had been worth it.

Meanwhile, in Peterborough, a plan was emerging. Although she was not with them there, Tessa Lewis had – with Michael's help - discussed the strategies they wanted to see done immediately, which would be disseminated and discussed under Michael's guidance with the other fellow Brexiteers. Now the Reformation was starting, they were all of one concerted mind - to ensure Brexit was delivered fast.

Each one of them would be in charge of a region,

and covertly pursue their original briefs as if they were continuing without the current hiatus. In effect, they were going to act like a government in exile, even if they were currently still operating secretly.

Chapter Seventeen

The first thing the Cash government would know of anything unusual happening was when the jocular and very popular former Foreign Secretary was spotted in Sunderland, apparently just walking around. But this was actually a ruse to begin gaining attention for an innocuous-seeming start to the events which would soon escalate to grip the country.

"Oi, Borya – when we goin' t'get rid of these bastards fom Lunnen, then?" The first shout of support attracted attention and, within minutes, a huge throng of people were around him, all asking the same type of question.

To say they were angry was an understatement: "My brother was about to buy a fishin'-boat so we could start catchin' our own British fish until these arseholes came back."

"I had a job manufacturin' clothin'," another said, "but the bloody EU bribed the bosses to relocate our factory to Turkey."

"I'm a midwife, and when my sister was about to have a baby she couldn't get a place 'cos they were all taken by incomers – ridiculous," said a robust lady. As the tenor rose and the crowd enlarged itself, Borya knew they were going to be all right. The will of the people, expressed in a controlled, indignant anger, would win, he believed. And here, in Sunderland, he was the bait, and the plan was seen to be working: for suddenly, the expected happened. From nowhere, an EU Army personnel vehicle swung around the corner and four heavily-armed combat troops jumped out. In an instant, they dived into the crowd to try to arrest the man, his mop of blonde hair being jostled about as the soldiers tried to reach him and the crowd tried to stop them; a couple of burly Northumbrian men grasped one of them and brought him to the ground, pinning him there as members of the crowd – including a number of female shoppers – jumped on the others. Then the cameraman who was filming this – so that the first incident in the fightback for a liberated Britain could not be suppressed - saw another EU soldier getting onto the top of their vehicle and aiming at Borya.

He screamed, "Get down, Borya, get down." Having expected the possibility of a scene like this, Borya dropped instantly to the ground as a bullet whistled past his ear and hit a mother carrying her child behind him, who slumped to the ground. Screams and shouts rent the air as people started running in all directions and the soldier aimed at the cameraman: the soldiers on the ground were all still being held down by the crowd, and one young man in jeans and a hoodie grasped one of their guns and pointed it at the soldier. "Attention, Maurice!" cried the floored soldier in a thick French accent to his comrade on the vehicle, "Attention!" This had a dramatic effect: the crowd stopped running, and many returned to ensure that these occupying troops from another land were well and truly incapacitated, as the young man fired at the soldier on the vehicle, hitting him in the arm, and his gun fell from his grasp. Suddenly, a British Army vehicle swung around another corner and a dozen British soldiers, their uniforms emblazoned with Union Jacks, jumped out. Four picked Borya up from the ground and bundled him into the back as the crowd, confused, looked on: were they impostors or truly loyal British soldiers who had revolted against the occupation of this undemocratic government?

"They're our boys," roared the cameraman, "they're loyal to us, the people of Britain – the restoration of democracy starts here!" With that, a huge cheer went up as the British soldiers disarmed their European counterparts and bundled them into another van – festooned with Union Jacks - which had arrived almost unnoticed in the clamour. The wounded French soldier was taken down from the roof of the vehicle and given immediate attention by the crowd and then a British Army paramedic. In true British fashion, there was just a disdain for him: no vitriol, no violence. That was reserved for the man now sitting in Downing Street.

*

A couple of hours earlier, the ousted Prime Minister, Tessa Lewis, had brazenly walked out of her house and defied the minders outside to allow the democratically-elected Prime Minister to leave so she could go shopping. The minders had followed her car but sympathetic loyalists had devised a plan: a stage-managed car-crash took it out at a busy junction, causing chaos. She had travelled serenely on, then switched to another far less conspicuous vehicle, the first being quickly hidden in a garage down a suburban back street in Watford.

She was heading for Sheffield, and arrived outside the City Hall in its main square with some of her Cabinet, who had joined her on the way. It was a bold choice for her, as Sheffield had always returned a majority of Labour MPs, and it also included the Liberal Democrat Studd's seat; yet it had also voted overwhelmingly for Leave, so the magnificence of the Hall and its relative security and wide space in front was the perfect place to make an announcement – provided all went well.

Unlike in Sunderland, she arrived in the middle of a convoy of military vehicles comprised of loyal British units. More discreetly, two armed American vehicles had joined them, their white stars covered with Union Jacks. If there were any incidents, it could then be argued that a friendly force had been attacked, which would cause a diplomatic incident, and the wrath of the whole world outside the EU.

Two cameramen set up on the steps, as supporters around the square – ready and aware of this historic occasion – began distributing leaflets to bemused onlookers. On the leaflets, and echoing aspects of the Leave campaign, were the words: 'British people: it's time to take your country back and fight for sovereignty.' Soon there was a large crowd, and the ex-PM began her speech.

"My friends–" she began.

"You're no friend of mine," shouted a strong

Yorkshire voice. "Get back to London."

Calmly, she looked at him directly and said: "I have been deposed from London by the forces of the European Union, from which I was trying to get an amicable divorce before our country was invaded under the auspices of the man now sitting – unelected – in my chair in Downing Street."

"You weren't elected, either," the man shouted back.

Some in the crowd bristled at the man, as she calmly replied, "No, but I was part of the democratically-elected government which the country voted for: I was your Home Secretary. I think that gives me some right to lead the country – and certainly more so than the millions of pounds given by anti-democratic forces to and by an ex-Prime Minister to subvert the democracy he pretends to uphold as long as it's right for him and his cronies."

A big cheer went up and someone next to the man pointed out that she was for Britain, not the EU and, like him, she wanted her country back, too. The man nodded. "Sorry," he shouted – "I thought you was one of them invading buggers. I'm with you all the way."

Another cheer – louder this time – went up as the ex-PM thanked him and then continued: "I am here to start a counter-revolution. We are calling it The Restoration." With that, the crowd erupted into a frenzy of support, cheering, whistling and shouting. When it subsided, she continued, "All across the country, people like you who are just managing, deserve a better outcome – not a continuation of jobs for the elites and the influential, who snobbily deride your hard work and are happy to export your jobs to other countries or have your trades supplanted by unregulated numbers of people who have access to our land." Another cheer, which drew in more people from around the square. "You have been conned, you have been misrepresented, and you have been invaded for the first time since 1066. It is time to break free from this imposition of an alien will that has no respect for the democracy established by the mother of all Parliaments. It is time to fight back and take our country back. Join me – join *us*. From today – this moment – thousands of people are starting to take back control by harrying, questioning, overcoming and repelling these people who were once our friends abroad and representatives at home but who have now turned our great British democracy against us. We *will* be friends again with Europe – if not the EU; but they need us more than we need them.

'Not for the first time in our history, it will be us – you – who will teach other lands the true meaning of democracy and the rights it espouses. They must be taught that the government they have imposed upon us is not the British Way, nor ever shall be." Another huge cheer went up, which covered the sound of four EU army vehicles driving into the square. She saw them, but continued: "With our democratic friends from across the Atlantic - who treasure true democracy as much as we do – we shall overcome this interruption to our thousand-year history and be free again. I may not be the Iron Lady, but I am like the Women of Steel represented over there," and she gestured towards the statue at the base of the steps commemorating the women of Sheffield who worked in the steel mills during the Second World War. "And

I will set you free." The reference to the Americans was a sign that an unwelcome presence had arrived and, instantly, several British and American soldiers rushed to intercept the European Army vehicles, which stopped instantly. As the ex-PM continued, the EU vehicles were surrounded – first by the troops, then a ring of British and American personnel carriers. They were going nowhere. Again, there was the usual British restraint, and they were not booed or cursed, nor attacked, just disdained. With that, she finished by saying, "We have work to do. The Restoration starts here," turned, and went into the building as the sound of riotous cheering and clapping escorted her inside.

The counter-invasion had truly begun.

*

In France, a terrorist outrage had been perpetrated in Montpellier: an Algerian suicide bomber from Daesh had exploded himself in a shopping mall and an accomplice had driven a hijacked cargo lorry through the Place de la Comédie in the centre of the city, killing forty-four people, many of them children and university students. The president had reacted quickly and sent what was left of his army not stationed in Britain to the centre of the city and some others to imply a national presence. But it had had little effect, and the French penchant for rioting had become widespread, with Left, Right, black and white fighting on the streets across France without restraint. Not one to miss an opportunity, Laporte loudly asked why a neighbouring, democratic nation state had been invaded by a part-French army yet the French Army itself was now too ineffectual as a result to control its own cities. Once again, she claimed it should be repatriated immediately and Britain should also be freed: what would the French think if that had happened to them? Well! It already had – they were now being invaded by people hostile to their very way of life! The army's re-patriation was, of course, resisted in the Assemblée Nationale; France was a stalwart part of the EU and had agreed to the provision of troops in Britain, so they must stay. But Laporte's polling numbers swelled inexorably once more. As the president's hands were tied, the riots persisted; after fractious further Assemblée debates and more disturbances, Laporte actually proposed her motion that the French troops stationed in Britain should be returned to France to face down the existential threat to the country. She also knew this would help Britain and weaken Cash, and she mercilessly pushed the point that a democracy should deliver the will of the people rather than that of the ruling elite as constituted by the EU. When the Assemblée rejected her proposal, she changed tack and managed to table a vote of no confidence in the president himself; she was ecstatic when she won - and the Presidential election already scheduled for less than a month's time looked as if it might be won by her on a single ballot. *'La France En Premier,'* she said and, as in America, the intent of the phrase started to stick.

Chapter Eighteen

In Britain, these events would soon play a part in Restoration's plans: but the news of a resurgent Laporte had not yet got through the official barriers. If it had done, it would only have emboldened their campaign. Julia was still in the dark, too, which only underlined that her careful planning to keep news out of Whitehall and Downing Street was still working. By now, all she knew was that Borya in Sunderland and the ex-Prime Minister in Sheffield should have started proceedings and that Nick Lafargue was soon scheduled to start a similar proclamation in Colchester. But whether or not these British events were being transmitted nationally, she did not know. Her techy friend had also managed to beam a force of electronic 'chaff' into the Whitehall and Downing Street areas which disabled mobile and data signals, and would hopefully give them more vital minutes before the counter-invasion and its breadth was noticed. This would inevitably happen, of course: one could not keep the nerve centre of government shut out for long. But with the House of Commons chamber now shut down, this unwittingly helped Julia's plans: there was less chance of anyone knowing anything about them. The downside was that because she had to be under the same electronic shutdown as everyone in Downing Street, she was none the wiser about external events either.

In Colchester, Nick Lafargue adopted a mix of the tactics used by both Borya and the ex-PM, in that he was dropped off in the middle of the city with a number of his advisers and four loyal British soldiers, and toured the Lion Walk shopping mall until he was noticed. This, of course, only took seconds, such was his support in the area. But he aroused strong passions both ways so had to be careful, especially if the radically-inclined and free-speech-resisting students at the local university got wind of his visit: people like them were often more dangerous to deal with than the invading army. So there were also several exits for escape. A throng soon gathered, and he was fielding the usual questions while slowly winding up the idea that he was at the beginning of a fightback for democracy, joining with the leading Leave-supporting members of the deposed government. "I told you I feared treachery," he began, "and I was right to say that. The forces of darkness have turned our country into a puppet state. But we're British, and we will fight back for our democracy."

"How did you get here?" asked a man belligerently. "I thought you weren't allowed to be here. The government has told you to fuck off."

"Charmingly put, if I may say so." The crowd laughed and made it clear the man was in a minority, and he shifted uneasily from one foot to the other. "No, it is our undemocratically-unelected invading government supported by the European Union which has told me not to come here or I'll be arrested. Yet that is what I have done because today we are starting a nation-wide fightback to give you all your country back. It's called The Restoration." Huge applause and cheers rang through the mall, but the man was unperturbed. "You're just sucking up to that new bastard President in America."

"Quite apart from the fact that is an intended insult to his parents and not to him," Lafargue smiled back, "frankly, it's thanks to him and the forces of global democracy – which elected him, remember, unlike the situation we now have in our country - that I am indeed, here; for – with the Americans' help, and not for the first time, I might add – they have managed to get me here to help restore our democracy. And, d'you know? With their help, we might truly do it and get our country back." There was a huge cheer, clapping and whistling, and the crowd grew bigger. The man slunk off as the crowd of supporters grew: they had a strange idea they were witnessing something special – and they were.

Events like these were happening at the same time all over England and Wales, with the swelling ranks of Leave-leaning voters being bolstered by huge numbers of many who had voted Remain in the Referendum but were furious at their country having been invaded; many on the Left and Right of politics had had enough of Cash the first time around, too, and his brazen support for unelected elites and the snuffing of the flame of a sovereign freedom by an essentially occupying army was becoming the counter-invasion's biggest recruiting-sergeant. Everywhere, the spirit of revolt was palpable, with ever-swelling ranks of Remainers rueing the European Union bludgeon that had so tried to extinguish the will of the nation - whether they had originally wished for it or not. Perhaps, they were beginning to believe, the Leavers were right after all: either way, there was now a focus for people to support, and they were about to start pushing for Restoration in ever-greater numbers.

*

With this onslaught of pop-up assemblies happening across the Swathe, it was not long before the media got hold of these rumours and actively started to seek out the possibility of their truth and a local scoop. News crews were despatched to as many major towns and cities as they could and any possible sighting was fervently chased: but one of the policies of the counter-invasion was to cause a stir and then evaporate back into the countryside as soon as possible. Yet, inevitably, it was suddenly headline news - but thanks to Julia Reeve's subterfuge, it was still another three or four hours before the information got to Terry Cash in Downing Street.

*

The rumours had, though, started to reach Europe, as tourists and local newsrooms sent pictures and reports across the wires around the world. When it hit the European Union headquarters in Brussels there was, as would be expected, apoplectic fury. Yet it was difficult – and dangerous – to accuse the Americans of aiding an insurrection, as that was what they had done - and at least until they had further proof; yet the probability of the Anglosphere ganging up on the EU was not unexpected. As Britain had started preparing to leave before the invasion, the noises of support, not just from the USA, but Canada, Australia and New Zealand – as well as other former Commonwealth and global countries – had been of growing volume, especially when the superb trade deals that could be attained after Britain's exit were taken into account. Just the fact that food and clothing in general would have been around a third cheaper in Britain due to no EU tariffs was enough to cause indignant concern at Berlaymont, yet their stubborn refusal to listen to the mood of the people across their EU empire had caused their peoples to react in the hostile and crushing way they had – and would increasingly continue to do.

*

As soon as Julia realised Terry Cash had indeed finally got the news, her electronic engineer was notified by the simple expedient of her putting a page of white A4 paper in a pane of glass at the rear of Downing Street. The window overlooked Horse Guards Parade, which was where her engineer was stationed in a bogus telecommunications provider van. He had been expecting it and instantly sent another engineer – for safety, in a differently-marked van - to Downing Street to fix 'the problem'. Julia had posted the page and then run into Cash's office with the news that it appeared his comms had been compromised but she was sorting it immediately. Cash was livid: he had spent a lot of his own money on this project and he was not going to let it become derailed. As soon as the real comms were back and the engineer had left, all the people in the PM's office crowded around the televisions to hear what had been happening under their noses but behind their backs.

Fury and indignation were some of the reactions: yet there were also many in that room who felt pleased. Deep down, they knew that they had been part of the betrayal and that what had happened was not 'the British way'. And they were secretly hopeful that the Restoration would be successful.

Not so in the Treasury, of course: there was instant panic as there would now be a run on the pound. If only they had joined the euro immediately, they lamented, the event would have made little difference – the euro was plummeting anyway. Now there would be friction once more between supporters of Remain and those of the newly-announced Restoration – and Cash was furious that this emotive word had been appropriated. He immediately called a Cabinet meeting to work out how to combat 'the insurgency', as he called it, and discussed the use of British troops – not European ones – on the streets. Yet it soon became apparent that the Army and the RAF had been supportive of Restoration by more than 90% of their personnel and that their superiors had been incarcerated so they were helpless to give orders or form any kind of cohesive strategy. Most of the new commanders were from the lower ranks – just like the people who had voted Leave, he furied – and he felt indignation at the stupidity of this island race being supported by people who were not as intelligent as those they had replaced. And being against *him*! Yet if the military *had* been appropriated, he was powerless, and could rely only on the EU. The Defence Minister was, indeed, a German, drafted in to ensure that the 'purity' of the military side of the invasion was upheld; he had been in the building when the news hit, yet even he suggested that deploying obviously foreign troops in large numbers would only make things worse – Lafargue and Borya would see to that. The EU could neither afford any more money nor supply any more troops, anyway. And what was Russia's game? Were they really occupying the Baltic states or was it make-believe? Was their President in league with them or with the Americans, or was it all a huge bluff? Would they indeed, devour these states as part of a deal with America, using it as a trade-off so Britain could become a sovereign nation again and so diminish the size of the EU further, to the Russians' joy? How dare the Americans support the occupying of other states – they would not allow it to happen to them!

But Cash now knew he was in trouble, and he rapidly had visions of the fate of Mussolini, strung up on a lamp-post in Rome by the crowd. Perhaps he should get out while he could: even his huge wealth could not save him if the mob got into Downing Street. Then his Cabinet members started to arrive and all seemed normal again. Except that they would soon be summoned by Trausch and his entourage to Brussels: all five Presidents and as many Commissioners as could make it would be there, too, including Guifford Neveu. Cash's government was fortunate in that all the main air routes in and out of London were well outside the Swathe, as the Restoration people had so nauseatingly called it: Heathrow, Gatwick, London City and RAF Northolt were all available. A flight from Northolt with an EU military escort was soon arranged for them all by Julia, and the outriders soon arrived in Downing Street.

For the first time since the insurrection, Cash felt

trapped and not in control: it was even worse than having his erstwhile Chancellor telling him what to do, and he did not like it at all.

*

Meanwhile, in Bristol, Michael had orchestrated the visit of Martin Glover to the city, and as one of the most prominent figures of the Leave campaign, was attracting a hugely supportive crowd in the Cabot Circus shopping mall; it had been noticed early on that excited younger people were increasingly engaged at these impromptu walkabouts, too. This was explained by their realisation that, being outside a customs union applying tariffs and barriers, trade could now help third-world countries to thrive as their products could be imported, so helping their development without the need for costly foreign aid. This would also economically help the countries involved and help bring them out of poverty. With Africa and India becoming technology centres, too, with whom Britain could trade freely if out of the EU, electronic devices and phone costs would start to plummet as the expenses of manufacturing also dropped. And this suited not only their pockets but, more importantly, their consciences as well. Having explained all this as part of his pitch, it was no surprise that, within minutes, Glover had a huge audience in the palm of his hand and, at the mention of the new prime minister, boos and shouts of derision were heard. Even the local BBC news programme, Points West, appeared at least not hostile, unlike its sneering and apparently contemptuous reporting from BBC Centre in London. The Restoration was becoming more likely by the moment.

*

Cash and his Cabinet were now airborne and on their way to Brussels on a hastily-convened cargo plane adapted for comfortable and secure government use. They watched Northolt disappear as, on board, cabinet members, press secretaries and researchers, advisers and mandarins were in panic, not least when they were joined by a protective squadron of Typhoon fighters from the same airfield. Were these jets hostile or benign? In this atmosphere of suspicion and uncertainty, fear was the predominant emotion – not something many of them had experienced before in their cocooned and reality-impervious lives. After they reached the Channel it was, however, obvious that they were heading for Brussels and their concerns subsided. Over France, four French F1 Mirage fighters joined them, the RAF fighters peeled off to return to England, and Cash then really knew he was safe and in friendly company. For the moment, at least.

Chapter Nineteen

In the press hostile to the Leave vote and supportive of Cash's takeover, it started to refer to the Restoration administration as a 'Vichy' government, in the hope of associating it with fascism and the Nazis; but the ploy fell flat as more and more people were realising that Restoration was closer to the true representation of support for the peoples' will, which cut right across the political spectrum – as it had during the Referendum. It was nothing to do with fascism or racism but patriotism, sovereignty and common sense.

On the plane to Brussels, Cash and his Cabinet were drawing up plans to consolidate their grip on power with the help of what was left of the European Union. And it was, indeed, becoming more fragmented: the Baltic states had just announced that, despite being unofficially occupied by Russia, they would not support the EU's takeover of Britain in any talks with Cash, a decision that had already been taken by the Visegrad countries a few hours earlier.

Kate had heard that Cash and his cabinet were on the way to Brussels and had been instructed to doorstep them outside the Berlaymont building. She had been pushed to get full interviews with as many of them as possible before and after their meeting. Her news editors at the BBC were keen for her to get any demonstrably pro-EU comments from them to head off the growing support around Britain for what they would insist on calling the 'so-called Restoration government'. Her partner, Guifford, was as keen as her superiors to do this, too. Indeed, he had smoothed any access issues so she could help the Commission to pour scorn on this nasty little insurrection. Yet Kate was uneasy: she felt that her instinctive British regard for fair play and free speech was being compromised and she wanted to ask questions that might sound probing of the EU and Cash side but which could help them demolish the Restoration arguments: yet she did not want to appear a patsy, as it would just look like what it was, bias. No, she wanted full and fair interviews with the protagonists from both sides. Of course, she would not get Restoration views in Brussels as none of them were there and all UKIP MEPs had been banned long ago. A free press and media was a basic British right and she felt better arguments could be made by challenging Restoration rather than just treating them with disdain or ignoring them. Yet, when she had mentioned this to Guifford, he had slapped this notion down immediately: "It is an EU edict that no-one is allowed to criticise it," he stated bluntly.

"But I don't officially work for the EU," she had protested.

"If you're with me, you do."

"But the BBC is supposed to be impartial," she tried again.

"Why do you think we contribute funding to the BBC?" he had riposted tetchily. "It's so our views are represented. You should know that. It is our funding that essentially ensures your job, too. Don't forget that." And he had walked out. She had never seen him angry with her before and she did not like it. Worse, she did not want to jeopardise her future with him, the BBC or the EU. She suddenly remembered a situation which had made an impact on her when she was young: in the 1970s, an early British member of the European commission had suddenly had a 'lightbulb moment' and realised that, in his view, the EU he was part of was a sham - overpowering, corrupt and unrepresentative. Consequently, he had written a book called 'The Rotten Heart of Europe', which had heralded the birth of Euro-scepticism. He had subsequently been vilified, abused, ostracised and eventually banished from Brussels for his views, losing his job: even then, it had disturbed her deeply. Economists and other whistle-blowers had, over the years, received the same treatment: so Kate, at that moment, decided to do as she was told and toe the line. But it sorely troubled her, and she wondered what Michael would have said. Actually, she knew.

*

Michael was leaving Bristol with Martin Glover at that moment, and was surprised to get a text from his wife. He had not heard from her for a long while and he suspected that she had sussed he knew of her situation with Guifford, which made things even more difficult. But Michael was not going to admit to knowing, ever: he wanted her to suffer the pain and embarrassment of telling him to his face - if he ever saw her again. He looked at the words on his phone: 'Don't like being told to push the party line here. Would love a discussion with you. Miss you. xxx' Well, that was a change. But he would not reply – not yet, anyway. Let her stew. She had compromised her principles to pursue power, influence and wealth and he had, he realised, rather gone off her. The girl he had fallen in love with those few years ago for her principles, intellect, trenchant wit and sense of balance had now become a stranger to him. Her beauty, too, suddenly seemed less obvious, which only underlined how much love is associated with attitudes and beliefs, and not physical attraction alone.

And then there was Jemima. Jemima Grice, his mentor who had got him into the Commons before he – and she – had been banned by Cash's government, along with any other Leave-supporting MPs. He was still technically an MP, could attend the House to do his constituency duties and was still paid, but was not allowed to vote. No-one was. So much for democracy. Yet he had found himself attracted to her only after it became apparent that Kate was having her affair. He had not told Jemima this, either, so was quite surprised – and delighted – when she had invited him back to her room after a long organisational session just a few days before – in fact, the evening before the Restoration campaign and counter-invasion had started. They had been in a Peterborough hotel and he had agreed to a nightcap. They had gone into her room exhausted and she had kicked off her shoes and flopped onto the bed. He had offered to pour her a drink and he joined her; they were both excited about what was going to be happening the next day and he suddenly noticed what beautiful legs she had – and pretty feet. Kate did not – her only unattractive physical attribute. Unlike her lover, though, who was completely unattractive from top to toe. But Guifford had influence. So would he, soon, though.

Jemima had dozed for a second and nearly spilled her drink, and Michael had caught it and found himself holding her hand. She looked at him, squeezing his hand in thanks. Then it had happened, and she and he were rolling around the bed, fondling, kissing, discovering… She was beautiful, yet they were also two souls instantly lost in a timeless and infinite union, instinctively and profoundly believing not only in each other but a shared vision of the country they loved and soon hoped to return to sovereign democracy. And when they had somehow become naked, their clothes strewn around the bed and the floor, they just knew. Her breasts were as beautiful as the other parts of her anatomy, and her olive-coloured skin was soft and scented, her tousled hair like a garden of flowers as her natural perfume mingled with the fragrance of her shampoo and a hint of *Chanel*. Her lips had the shape of butterfly wings and were sweet and soft: and when he penetrated her, he suddenly realised what true love was. He thought he had had this with Kate but now he almost felt deceived because he realised he had not – this was the real thing and it would last forever, he just knew. They had eventually fallen into a dreamlike sleep, soon after Jemima had whispered in his ear, "Oh, Michael, I've wanted to do this since I first saw you. I knew it would be wonderful." He had concurred: it truly was.

Chapter Twenty

Kate was standing outside the EU building. It was wet and windy, and the cavalcade was late. She occasionally glanced at her phone to see if Michael had returned her text message, but he had not. She became grumpy as she had wanted to discuss the paradoxes which had arisen from her spat with Guifford, although she could not be specific: Michael still did not know. She felt guilty: for although she had made the decision to do what she had done, she still wanted him to reply to her when she expected it. They were married, after all. Then she wondered if he was having an affair, and she became angrier still, just in case he was. Then the cavalcade swung into the space at the front of the building and her private thoughts were banished, to be replaced by all opinions EU. But she could still not stop thinking about Michael.

The EU Commission council had met with Cash *in camera*, which they always did when passing final resolutions. Parliament would then be asked to vote on the decision which, like the Politburo in Soviet times, had always rubber-stamped the outcome. It was becoming obvious that popular resistance to the imposed Cash-led EU government was growing exponentially and the consensus in Britain and many other EU states was that they had exceeded their remit and had shot themselves in the foot. Getting Britain back into the EU by force had a dwindling number of adherents - only in Germany, Belgium, Luxembourg and France were there still defiant calls for an even stronger invasion, which would destroy the Restoration and get the country subdued again – and for good, this time. Then the predominantly German and French exports could flow there again and the British people would eventually see how lucky they had been to have averted a financial and structural disaster, and would be led again by those who knew what they were doing for the good of the European dream.

Cash, of course, was supportive of this view, but he still knew it would be ever more difficult to sustain: there was no point in him appealing to the masses for they not only hated him but the Referendum had proved beyond doubt that the people wanted out. And that sentiment was even stronger, now; and another Project Fear would be ridiculed as – prior to the invasion – Britain's economy and inward investment from outside Europe had soared, with employment growing rapidly. All this had only come crashing to a halt after his invasion, with non-European democracies refusing to invest or have anything to do with him until the EU withdrew from Britain and fresh elections took place. Before, the EU had depended heavily on Britain sucking in their exports; but now Britain was dependent on the EU to keep it subdued. And America had become involved, too, the country he had always loved and waged war with in the Middle East; but they were supporting the wrong side, distorting the true meaning of his type of democracy. And what were the Russians really up to? No-one knew – least of all, him.

What Cash and the European Commission had begun to realise, though, was that even if he did want further EU support for a bigger invasion, its Parliament might not sanction it – there were now as many states against it as for it. They would not let Cash circumnavigate the democratic process as he had done in Britain by shutting down Parliament, either. Cash became tetchy again: to him, this was not the meaning of 'ever-closer union'.

Chapter Twenty-One

Kate had done her interviews and been applauded for them by her BBC bosses. Cash and Studd had showed resolve and resolution in the face of a very close vote in the EU Parliament, which had been passed only by seven. Yet extra troops had not been sanctioned; instead, the creation of a secret service with extra powers to infiltrate, arrest and try people had been. With Trausch and his cohorts proclaiming this as a great victory for common sense, for Europe and a cheaper way of suppression than an army, it would become a further chilling motivation for people to rise up when the news got around in Britain. The country had spent two world wars fighting this sort of thing and now this Stasi, this SS, would be administered on their soil by a remote, brutal and unsympathetic external force. Yet if it had been created to quell the flames of revolt, it would have the opposite effect, for although the BBC and media were ordered not to report this development, when the news filtered through onto social media channels, it spread in minutes. There were immediate reports that huge numbers of people in England and Wales were rising up in even greater numbers to demonstrate against EU rule, the silencing of their historic Parliament and the takeover of their country. The new American President pledged to become more overt in giving the British people back their control and, whilst Cash and his supporters felt generally lauded and feted in Brussels, the truth was that they were now terrified of returning home. They had favoured a more diplomatic solution, where the sovereignty of Parliament appeared to be respected, and free elections would be tolerated as long as only pro-Remain MPs were allowed. Yet this was anathema to the EU mandarins: they wanted virtual blood, if not the real variety. Britain must be punished, and Cash was the best person to do it – with their guidance and support.

*

At that moment – keeping a careful and close electronic eye on the events in the European Parliament for optimum effect - Russia privately declared to the EU that they were formalising their takeover of the Baltic states and would only consider leaving when the European Union returned its army – and their hardware - from Britain to French and German soil. In an apparent change of usual tactics, when this happened, they said, there would be free elections in those states and candidates would be allowed to stand from all parties and persuasions. Their most pertinent point, though, was that the result would be binding, as the British Referendum had supposed to be. The hand of the new friendlier relationship between America and Russia was suddenly obvious. And it was designed to weaken the EU further.

And soon there would be another challenge to European Union hegemony – the French elections were soon due. Just one week later, in fact.

*

As the meeting in Brussels was breaking up, Nick Lafargue was in a central Cardiff shopping mall, with the usual – yet growing – riotous support. But suddenly a shot rang out from one of the floors above, and Lafargue fell. Panic began as people tried to get out or hide. Instantly, the assailant was seen and two salvos of bullets ripped into him, fired by the soldiers protecting Lafargue, and he fell across the parapet, then – lubricated by his own blood - slid over the handrail and crashed to the ground floor. The soldiers were American, and they had killed a man on British soil. In theory, that meant the country – as it was constituted under an EU government – was now at war with America. Events would now move faster still.

*

Cash and his entourage were being driven back to the airport. He was aware that there were more military and police outriders than when they arrived which underlined how events had rapidly changed even since his arrival from London: FN signs were everywhere, and also signs and graffiti supporting 'Grande-Bretagne Libre'. This was a new development for France, and it made him shudder. The French had almost always tended to be against the British as a matter of principle, supporting their own government's line: even during the war, they had supported Britain through its Resistance more due to hatred of Germany than any love for the British. Yet here was proof that everything was changing. If

France voted FN on the following Sunday – which was looking quite likely - then the EU was finished anyway as France would leave the euro – and even he could not quite work out how he might spin that fact to his advantage. Indeed, there wasn't one: he had always wanted the single currency in Britain. Perhaps he would soon be finished after all.

In the event, what happened over the next few days would not be controlled by him anyway, nor by the French elections, for circumstances would soon confound expectations in a very different way.

*

The reaction to Lafargue being shot by a French soldier and then himself killed by an American one threw Brussels into even more chaos. Indignation and anger were not enough as they knew they were in a failing organisation now caught in a clever pincer movement by two superpowers, both of which had out-manoeuvred them with guile and speed. Yet such was the resentful righteousness of their organisation that, rather than construct a carefully-worded response, they hurried out a tirade of denials, threats and bluster. When this was laughed off by both Russia and America, the European Commission found itself at odds with its own parliament as to what to do. It was not an edifying spectacle.

*

Kate was studiously trying to make sense of all this: secretly, she was of the opinion that Brussels was making a complete mess of the situation, but she could not imply this in her interviews. Although she still believed in the concept of the European Union, she craved that Britain could somehow overthrow Cash's government and return Britain to a sovereign democracy under the auspices of the EU, albeit with more control and self-determination than before. The Brussels hierarchy, though, were in meltdown: yet she wondered if she preferred being under American influence rather than a European one. She had to admit to herself that she did not really wish either, and this flash of insight was a revelation to her. Not for the first time, she began to wonder whether she would have a future with Guifford after all: if the EU collapsed, then she would be out in the cold with no prospects. She would probably be sacked by a BBC compelled to be a less partisan employer, even if she had been forced by them to be such, so she had cooked her own goose there. Yet she was well known in Europe now, so could try her hand there, with or without Guifford, if his prospects and influence really were on the wane. She suddenly felt isolated and realised she wanted to go home. But Michael had still not returned her text.

Nor was he going to: Michael was on a roll. His relationship with Jemima had blossomed in concert with the rapidly-expanding support for Restoration and the ex-Prime Minister. The shooting of Lafargue had had a cathartic effect, too: polls – proscribed but abundant - wanting an end to EU domination went skywards and he, Jemima and many others in the movement were gaining influence and popularity: so much so that in many BBC newsrooms in the Swathe, the news editors with autonomous local regions decided to defy the London line and report events with a slant that would match their local viewers' opinions. This was unprecedented: London had always had the whip hand – but no more. In Bristol, Cardiff, Norwich, Birmingham and other cities, subtle changes in attitude were perceived. The reaction from London was savage: toe the line or else. Yet, as these executives were reluctant to leave the safe haven of London and travel into alien territory to impose their will, the instructions were ignored. The British Army and RAF had hidden those Chiefs of Staff who would try to overturn their loyalties and had been given a simple choice: be flown to America under close house arrest and keep quiet, or just keep quiet in Britain and let the counter-invasion run its course. It was the same for the judges of the Supreme Court: they had been placed under an informal house arrest and had had the same impositions placed upon them. Four of them had admitted to being wrong, too, and had openly suggested that they had been too keen on wilful misinterpretation of precedent, their own privileges, and the status quo. Yet it was pointed out to them that if they had followed the democratic mandate of the people, differently interpreted that precedent and then judged accordingly, the challenge to Parliament would have been crushed. And Article 50 would have been triggered immediately.

Rather like Sarajevo and the cause of the First World War, if the Kaiser had been wearing his silken bullet-proof vest none of the ensuing events leading to conflict would have happened.

*

There was also some prescience creeping into other areas of Britain's fabric as support for the Restoration intensified. Those who had wished to thwart Brexit by any means, fair or foul, (and increasingly desperately, the latter) had started to see the writing on the wall and their challenges were becoming more muted and less frequent. The hairdresser and ex-model had decided to return to their countries of origin rather than risk the possible consequences of an uprising: for this, the people who treasured our island story rejoiced. The ugliness predicted by Remainers – just as their bankers, elites, 'experts' and economists had mis-predicted the catastrophe of a Leave vote – was palpably becoming silenced as they realised the situation they were in was far worse than any Leave vote could have delivered. Yet it was only when Cash and his EU invasion crippled Britain's economy once more – and EU moves were made to hasten the movement of jobs from Britain to other EU states – that even these people had slowly and reluctantly begun to realise that the whole thrust of EU policy was fundamentally and severely wrong – and especially for a liberal and tolerant country like Britain. Project Fear was now eating itself.

Chapter Twenty-Two

Lafargue had been hit in the shoulder, and was not in danger; as he was hurried out by sympathetic paramedics, he laughed as he proclaimed that the assailant must have come from the EU army. The gun recovered from the potential assassin was standard French kit, and he joked that this was the third time he had cheated death and he would soon be back. A huge cheer went up as he said this. And he was right: the dead soldier was from a French under-cover regiment, and part of the elite and feared crack unit, the GIGN. As Lafargue was stretchered out, he proclaimed a Restoration government would soon be with them. The cheers and applause grew only louder as he disappeared down a passageway into the waiting ambulance.

In the background, the sniper's 'spotter' – a soldier accompanying the potential assassin - realised he would be next if he showed himself or tried another attempt. He was reluctant to do so, anyway: he did not like shooting in civilian areas but that was usually where Lafargue was most seen and they had been ordered to neutralise the man whenever they could. But now the plan had gone wrong anyway, and it was not secret any more. So he would try another time: and with his colleague dead and he himself undiscovered, he wanted things to stay that way. Wisely, he slipped away and hid, so neither faction would discover him.

*

Cash and his Cabinet arrived at Brussels airport and entered the plane to take them back to London. There was a sombre mood: the news of Lafargue's attempted assassination by a French soldier had provoked a couple of smiles but even these were beginning to fade as they realised it would be a difficult event to gloss over. The underground Restoration press and the media outside London's control would have a field day, and they knew it.

After the plane took off, Cash convened a meeting. The instructions from Brussels were not helpful – they wanted him to crack down and arrest the perpetrators of the Restoration, use their army and the soon-to-be-created Strategic Security Force - or SSF - to release the Chiefs of Staff and judges, 'liberate' the British Army and RAF so they would be forced to help the invasion, suppress the media hostile to it and be ruthless in doing so. If he did that, Europe would be saved and he would even sooner be appointed President of Europe: yet now there was menace in the instructions. Previously, it had been a prize: it had now become a condition. To the European Parliament, they hoped this would be the end game, but even Cash realised that this would only make matters worse. Spain might be pushed, perhaps, but Portugal was Britain's oldest ally and he could not see them agreeing to a policy that was effectively a takeover. History ran deep, and Portugal only had a small army anyway. On top of that, he confided to himself, did he really want to be President of such a dysfunctional and collapsing union? One of the great myths of European integration was that it would bind these countries together and prevent war. Yet it was currently having precisely the opposite effect – as many of his opponents had predicted.

They were now over the Channel and as the French Mirage jets peeled off he noticed the RAF aircraft swiftly and silkily substituting them. He had to admit that he felt safer now and wished he had fought his previous Chancellor more robustly in giving the armed forces the funding they needed. If he had, then perhaps fewer personnel would have mutinied and supported the counter-invasion. He was furious that this had happened and he reflected on how even his later successor as Prime Minister had used smoke and mirrors to cover a serious shortfall in budgets for defence of the realm and NATO. With a happier army, perhaps, a European army might not have been necessary at all and he could have appropriated them at will for his ends.

As he pondered, he noticed that the jets were now guiding the aircraft into a very slow, wide arc that seemed to be taking it further north than he had expected. Perhaps the weather had changed. Then he saw the worried looks on the faces of many of his staff as the arc suddenly became more pronounced and steeper. They were climbing – why? One of the crew ran down to him. "Prime Minister," she said: "I think we're being hijacked."

*

At that moment, in France, Marie Laporte was holding her final Presidential rally in Toulouse. The response of her supporters was ecstatic. At the same time, Faucheux was having a harder time at his final rally in Nantes: his attempts at a proposed centrist revolution in France had been derailed by a vicious campaign spearheaded as ever by the unions. He also seemed to have no answer to the ease with which 'Seidel's jihadis' – as elements of the press had branded them - and now the Algerian situation was reducing the centres of many French cities to disaster zones. Consequently, the polls were still on a knife-edge between him and Laporte. In essence, the contest was solely between these two. It was a frightening time in France - and it would become even more so over the next few weeks…

*

Cash and his entourage did not know where they were. Somewhere over Scandinavia, they presumed. The British fighter planes had directed them north up the English Channel and had then turned a sharp right across what they suspected was Danish airspace. It was surmised at that point that the planes were heading for one of the Baltic states, as Denmark was the smallest land mass to be crossed if the RAF pilots sympathetic to the Restoration had wanted to reach there. In fact, Cash and his advisers also wondered whether Denmark had allowed free passage over their land, being more Euro-sceptic than their mid-European counterparts; they might have instinctively turned a blind eye if they thought it could cock a snook at the EU – or even hasten its break-up. This supposition was soon confirmed when the four

British fighters suddenly disappeared – only to be instantly replaced by eight Russian MiGs. The world was being turned on its head – and Cash was at the centre of this outrage. This was the first time in several years that events were now controlling him, but his sense of righteous indignation from him and his team – particularly Studd – was not enough to make the plane change course. He was trapped – not just in a plane but in a diplomatic global nightmare.

Chapter Twenty-Three

The fallout from Lafargue's attempted assassination was profound. Despite the government following the edict from the EU that UKIP was a proscribed organisation, the polls rocketed towards it as the full realisation of what had happened sank in. In London, even the BBC was forced to admit that it was a grave event, perpetrated by what amounted to a foreign power trying to engineer a political coup. Yet it could not quite suppress a feeling of glee in its journalists, only let down by the fact that it had not been successful. Yet to be, as the letter 'B' represented 'British', it had to try to be seen as balanced, taking in the opinions of its country-people whom they instinctively mostly disdained, being outside its gilded coterie in opinion and intention. After all, if the invasion ultimately failed there would be blood on the carpet if there had not been even some apparent facade of balance. The worm was, indeed, turning: the corporation would have to get used to following the news, not shaping it.

Yet there were still forces in Britain that wanted the EU to subordinate the country at any cost, and a group of militant Remainers who had benefited hugely from EU largesse and influence suddenly announced that it was they who had attempted Lafargue's assassination. Calling themselves 'The 48%', they were unequivocal in their intent to enforce the Cash government's pro-EU agenda and remove as many obstacles as possible to him not regaining full power – even if this involved the use of undemocratic means. The fact that '48%', by definition, expressed themselves as less than a majority was overlooked: as always, they felt they possessed the moral upper hand. Again, the underground polls rose in support of the proscribed UKIP and Restoration, but the 48% were defiant. Yet what they, nor anyone else, knew at this time was that Cash was now just landing in Riga with his entire Cabinet, all prisoners of the Russian occupying army.

The Russians, of course, said nothing. As far as the world was concerned, they had simply disappeared.

*

In Downing Street, Julia Reeve was giving a class performance in calm efficiency. She was giving the impression of business as usual and suppressing the more hysterical reactions around her to the non-return of the entire Cash administration: after all, it was she who had planned it. She had always wanted to do something for her country and now she was doing it: she had not let the Restoration movement know that she was the perpetrator for they could not be seen as being complicit. Yet as the media news reached fever-pitch, she knew they probably suspected it but were wise enough to say nothing: they would just be grateful for what she was doing and could thank her later. Politics was, indeed, a dirty game: but how she was now enjoying it. Any who were suspicious of her in the complex were disabused of her intentions when she announced that the ex-Prime Minister and arch-Remainer James Gatting was to be the new leader until Cash returned. Her plan was to ensure that by quickly inviting another man sympathetic to Brussels to take charge she could keep the momentum against them alive, whatever had happened to Cash; this would ensure that the polls continued to go against the new but very un-British status quo. She had worked with Gatting in the past, too, and knew his weak points well. By cleverly inviting him to the post and out-manoeuvring any opposition in this helpfully febrile atmosphere, she expected that Restoration would be able to press a decisive coup very soon.

*

By contrast to Julia's optimism, in Brussels they were in a state of blind panic, not helped by the fact that Laporte's Front National had now gone seven per cent ahead in the French opinion polls, which were about to close according to French law: the euro was looking doomed. As Cash had observed a few hours before when he had seen the graffiti imploring a 'Grande Bretagne Libre', the impulse for the European Union to 'punish' Britain was now bringing a continent-wide opprobrium down on its head. This was helped by Italy publishing its first economic results since leaving both the EU and the euro, and the investment which had poured in from around the non-EU world had ensured superb trade deals agreed in days, which were now showing in their first-quarter results since leaving and showed its economy had grown by almost 2%. Millions of jobs were already being created: it was a further spur to the probability of a Laporte win in a week's time.

*

In Latvia, Cash and his Cabinet were stepping off the plane into the chill air. There was an easterly wind from Siberia and it matched the situation. There was no hint of any excessive military presence, despite being a small military airport, situated in what appeared to be a remote part of the country: the MiGs had disappeared after their aircraft had landed. In front of them were several black ZIL limousines and a few dignitaries who looked officious but not quite hostile. Cash and Studd aggressively walked up to them with an indignant sneer and unpleasantly asked where the hell they were and why. They received no answer and were politely but firmly directed into the cars, which then sped off to an unknown destination. No-one said a word – either the Russians or Cash and his staff. They noted that the outriders were Latvian police, not Russian soldiers, and wondered when anyone would explain to them what was going on. For the moment, though, all they could do was wait and hope that they would be well treated.

An hour later, after passing through forests on mostly empty back roads, they arrived at a huge palatial building, well outside the city. It was quite new, but built mainly in the Czarist style with white stucco and ornate window lintels adorned with painted fruits around them: and all complemented everywhere by a large amount of filigree ironwork. The grounds were open and largely treeless, but in the distance some low mountains could be seen. A wide river curved gently around the front and sides of the house, as if it had been built in the centre of a meander. A good prison, and difficult to escape from. And miles from anywhere. The palatial central doors opened as they were shown out of the cars. Cash indignantly barked at the besuited man in dark glasses who was approaching them but still some way away: "Why are we here? I am the British Prime Minister and I demand to see someone in authority immediately. We must be returned to Britain *now* or there will be diplomatic repercussions." The man just looked at him and pointed his arm to the front entrance of the building. Instantly, Cash recognised him as Russia's Foreign Secretary, but he could not remember his name.

"Good day," the man said, "and welcome to the returned Russian state of Latvia."

Cash disregarded the pleasantries and shouted: "You have no right to hold us here – this is a kidnap and I demand you return us to Britain immediately." The man just gave him a wry smile and again intimated towards the door. "You cannot do this," Cash announced again, "I am the British Prime Minister."

The man continued grinning and then waved his finger in a negative sideways manner. "No," he said, "you *were*. But you're not now."

Chapter Twenty-Four

It soon became the accepted belief around Britain that the plane had been hijacked either by the Russians or by British soldiers and airmen sympathetic to Restoration; but whether either had acted alone or colluded with the Americans – or not - was a fervent point of debate. Inevitably, this is what the European Union proclaimed, and also many outside the Swathe. The BBC and other news media were sure this was the case as it fitted the perfect scenario: to kidnap the unelected PM and keep him hidden until events would restore the deposed Prime Minister who had been in charge before the invasion. Yet with claim and counter-claim so rife, and rumour the first call for truth, no-one knew anything positive at all. Any involvement was denied by the Americans and contemptuously dismissed by the Russians. Much of the maelstrom of speculation was, of course, correct and many had actually got the analysis right. It was just that no-one was admitting or denying anything - no-one *knew*.

*

Julia Reeve, meanwhile, did her best to create a replacement Cabinet which was still ostensibly represented by Remainers – appointing any overtly Leave MPs was both impossible and a bridge too far for the moment. However, she had, as part of her subterfuge, managed to find and appoint a number of closet Leavers, whom she knew to be sympathetic ever since the economy had grown dramatically in the brief pre-invasion period. Whatever their previous beliefs, too, they were indignant that British democracy had been abolished: to them, their country was now a dictatorship.

It was a hard task for Julia to balance this new Cabinet without giving the game away, but she was in constant touch with Michael and Jemima who had guided her brilliantly and availed her of those whom Gatting would think were still Remainers but in fact now supported Leave and the Restoration. It helped, too, that Gatting had started to show some very strange views when speaking up for the EU status quo, and she felt that despite all his experience his judgement had been compromised; this could be useful to her – she would be more easily able to control him.

In all this, the Queen had constitutionally been forced to be silent. In fact, since the invasion she had been treated graciously but firmly by the occupying government and was still afforded a weekly meeting with her Prime Minister, which was still awkward. She had also been visited early on by Trausch, who had told her he was sorry all this had happened but that it was for the best for Britain and would create a more stable and prosperous Europe. Yet it had gone on record that the Queen had asked him to remove his troops and allow another election, which he had flatly refused. They had not met again. But the lady had sowed one tiny seed: she had made it subtly obvious that she liked the association with the monarchy to the word 'Restoration'. Even the BBC had been carefully keen to report that.

*

Immediately after France's Presidential elections, Marie Laporte had been presented with some evidence that Faucheux's campaign had been bankrolled by money appropriated from secret EU funds. The EU indignantly denied any such impropriety, but such was the history of denials which had been proved true, that suddenly no-one believed them. Once again, riots were rife throughout France, with factions angry at the EU's interference in national elections directly battling those who wanted the election of Faucheux to stand. After several days of paralysis – the confusion augmented by hackers from countries which had hostile interests on both sides – Faucheux was driven to announce a new Presidential election between just him and Laporte, which he believed he would win easily – especially if none of the other candidates could stand. He hoped a swift mandate would quell the violence and give those antagonistic to his presidency less chance to find – or concoct – any more rumours against him, and called for a re-run of the election for two weeks' time. The EU was in a state of shell-shocked inertia: it was known within the organisation that they had, indeed, given money to Faucheux's campaign, but could never admit it – so they just had to keep on denying it. Yet whether it was a true genie out of a real bottle, no-one could easily tell; and so it was that, two weeks later, Laporte won the re-run French Presidential election with 51.9% of the vote. This inevitably threw both France and the EU into chaos: the euro, already in crisis, collapsed further, and a run on French banks and cash machines was only arrested when the new President decreed that, if she won a referendum to do so, she would re-create the French Franc, which would initially have parity with the euro until the currencies diverged in value and found their true levels. This was what many economists had been agitating for – if it found its own rate against global currencies it would help the French economy, just as not joining the euro had helped Britain. The markets calmed, but inevitably the invective emanating from the Berlaymont building did not... The inevitable disbelief in France was accompanied by further rioting against the democratic result, only confirming attitudes to similar events which were now becoming eerily mainstream. As in Britain and America, the supposedly impossible had happened and the polls had been confounded. The people had had enough and voted accordingly – much to the distaste of the liberal elites and their cronies in power across the continent and the rest of the world.

And still no-one had any idea of the fate of Cash and his Cabinet.

Chapter Twenty-Five

In Downing Street, Gatting had made some fresh Cabinet additions to tide the government over until such time as Cash returned. Julia had ensured that all those secretly sympathetic to Leave and Restoration were well briefed on any external events, and in contrast to the chaos of France and the recriminations in Brussels, Britain seemed relatively calm. With the removal of Cash, the country entered a lull – or so it seemed on the surface. Michael, Jemima and many others, though, were in constant touch with Tessa Lewis, Borya and Lafargue, and all the other supporters: yet she also encouraged them to be less visible and more careful whenever possible as 'The 48%' had started to recruit more sympathisers. It might have started as a 'quiet revolution' but these people had every intention of stopping it by any means possible – whether violent or not.

*

As Lafargue left the hospital, he stopped outside to pay tribute to the courage of those who had looked after him and the soldiers and volunteers who had protected him. He had been recovering in a sealed and guarded ward as 'The 48%' had brazenly declared again their intention to assassinate him. Although surrounded by soldiers and armed police, suddenly a shot rang out. Everybody dived to the ground, screaming in panic. Lafargue was on the floor again but had not been hit. A moment later, a police marksman spotted the gunman in a window and fired back. For three minutes a gun battle ensued as Lafargue was shielded by police with riot shields and bullet-proof jackets and taken back inside the hospital. Two soldiers managed to get into the back of the building where the sniper was believed to be and soon came up behind him: he was losing blood from a hit in the neck but still tried to resist arrest. He was not in any type of protective clothing and sounded British when they challenged him: yet his rifle was state-of-the-art and very accurate in the right hands. Once overpowered, the police took him into the hospital: they wanted him alive so he could be interrogated, but it would be touch and go. Lafargue had been lucky once more.

The police went through the man's scant possessions but did find some ID – a driving licence. And a fistful of euros and a Eurostar ticket in the name of Angus McClellan. He was Scottish. Yet that was not all: when they searched his address in Falkirk – which was initially resisted by the SNP leader, only relenting when it was pointed out she would appear complicit and do her own referendum plans no favours at all – they found protestations of loyalty to the EU, lists of Restoration and Leave assassination targets, maps, explosives other types of assorted weaponry and ammunition. At first, it had seemed as if he was acting alone - until the spooks found a squeaky floorboard, under which was damning proof of his funders: 'The 48%'. The cache also included details of all those belonging to the organisation. Most were high-ranking executives and managers in international financial companies and global food businesses. But this was just the tip of the iceberg.

*

In France, as Gold had done in America, Laporte instantly did what she had promised to do if she won: she ensured that multinational companies either signed a decree to bring as much production, design and intellectual property back to France as soon as possible, or they would be heavily taxed. She restored union demands of a 36-hour week and gave more money to security forces and intelligence agencies to crack down on terrorist organisations. She also proclaimed that no more French money would be used by the European Union to relocate jobs from France to other parts of the bloc – and especially potential members like Turkey - as Britain and other EU countries had been forced to do. Most importantly, she quickly organised the referendum on whether France should leave the euro. The polls were close but there had been a consistent majority for doing so over several months: despite historic enmities, the French had noted the economic mini-boom that had happened in Britain after the Leave vote. Due to this, despite warnings of economic and social doom being predicted if they left – just as had happened in Britain – the public had reasoned that they had been conned into being part of a failing currency which only benefited Germany. Surprisingly, perhaps, it was the younger generation who were suddenly more in favour: they had become desperate as it was their age group who were suffering disproportionately: with youth unemployment sticking at nearly 40% for several years, it was not surprising they felt that way. And as in Britain, it was the elites who were blamed for their smug insistence that all would be better if they stuck with the EU. The common response was that it was certainly better for them, yes: but not everyone else. And when a vocally pro-EU judge was murdered, Laporte decided – for their own safety as well as of benefit to France – that they should all be dismissed and new judges appointed who would better reflect the mood of the French people. It had the potential to be a French Revolution all over again.

*

In Angus McClellan's flat, a further, more extensive search into a cupboard over the bathroom tank revealed documents bearing European Parliament crests and information. Also, his bank documents, which were found to have links to a covert EU slush fund containing proof of large payments to him; and most importantly, the name of his main contact – who was traced to the offices of a leading German industrialist with links to British entrepreneurs, judges and tycoons - all known to be sympathetic to 'The 48%'. And there was more: chillingly, they in turn were linked to another slush fund which led straight to the office of a very high-ranking European Commissioner indeed. Guifford Neveu. 'The 48%', too, was being funded by the European Union.

This discovery would be a devastating blow to 'The 48%' in particular and the whole militant Remain movement in general.

*

When Julia got hold of this information incriminating the EU, she knew it was time to trigger the full insurrection. She ensured that every newspaper and television station had the news as soon as possible – without telling Gatting. The calls and protests for Parliament to be re-opened again had already been reaching fever-pitch, with even once-hostile opposition forces demanding the same thing. It was only hard-line Remainers, as exemplified by 'The 48%', who were resistant, and ironically tried to make a diplomatic incident of the US invading British soil against the will of the people. Yet it was increasingly a cry in the wilderness and Julia knew it: now that Cash and his Cabinet were appropriated, the Army and RAF were being run by sympathetic personnel and backed up by US forces, and the realisation that EU connivance and money was subverting the elites and chaos was rife in France, Julia felt it was the perfect moment to unleash the popular will. As if to underline this, it became apparent that The Swathe was getting bigger and gaining massively in support, with pockets of vocal resistance becoming widespread in even the hardest of previously Remain areas – including London, the south-east and Scotland. The conviction of Angus McClellan helped in this, much to the anger of Scotland's First Minister. But the portents might never be so good again to create a major flashpoint: now true democracy could be restored. Yes, the timing was perfect.

Yet this was almost instantly supplemented by an event which had been predicted but now manifested itself at precisely the right moment.

When the Algerian president had died and his country had erupted into violence, causing waves of immigrants to try crossing the Mediterranean to get to France, the ensuing maelstrom of humanity had, indeed, contributed to the terrorist attacks and then the Front National Presidential election victory. Yet events court strange results: due to this victory, a bigger number of immigrants tried to get into France before the intensified crackdowns and inevitable restrictions could be implemented; this caused flotillas of boats, dinghies, inflatables and yachts being stolen by traffickers, terrorists and innocent refugees all at once – wherever they could find them. Rich people's yachts were targets, too, and many installed armed guards on their vessels to protect them. Laporte's reaction was to get the entire French navy – which had not been involved in the invasion of Britain – to blockade the coast and forcibly repel or sink the armada. This had huge popular support in France and also countries inundated by immigrants who had been encouraged by Seidel's refugee policies without their approval. As if in support of Laporte's positive actions, AfD ratings in Germany passed those of Seidel's for the first time: the EU-supporting elites across what was left of the EU were in tumult, and becoming not a little terrified. Was their diminishing and cosy little world of wealth and plenty about to disappear completely? Perhaps: but the French people were jubilant. As in Britain, it was time to take back control of their country.

It was in this increasingly florid situation that Julia organised a clandestine meeting with Tessa Lewis,

Jemima, Michael and Lafargue, her full Cabinet-in-waiting and the entire contingent of Leave-supporting MPs across the political spectrum. As a way of showing their increasing spread of support across the country, they decided on a bold move: to meet in a large conurbation – Manchester - where their support was moving decisively towards them from a lower base. But they would have to rely on supporters and the loyalist British Army and RAF to ensure their venue was very carefully secured against any subversive action. The police were ambivalent – many still supported Remain due to their indoctrination of EU rules and nostrums and currently were more involved in social and 'hate' crimes than protecting the public. Yet, although there were also many who saw the invasion of their country as the ultimate betrayal and were fiercely for the uprising, the danger for Restoration was that the police network would announce any rally to forces nationwide, which were all still part of Europol. In short, the knowledge could be leaked to people hostile to the counter-invasion and Restoration, as well as to the EU command itself. It was decided a better plan, then, was to bypass the police and trust the loyal Army regiments who were already alert and committed. It was the safer option. The rally would be announced only the day before, with loyalists contacted via social media, phone and hearsay to ensure that minimum disruption was encountered.

In Brussels, Guifford, with Kate in attendance, was denying categorically any complicity in funding 'The 48%' to neutralise any British nationals the EU decreed to be irritants, or that he had any slush fund or other financial arrangements to assist it. Yet, as millions of euros went missing every year and the EU's accounts had not been ratified or signed off for more than fifteen years, few believed him. In fact, he started to notice that many interviewers and journalists from around the Union were distinctly less warm, sympathetic and overtly supportive of him than they had been before: he had even noticed it in his partner. He insisted that the EU was based on democratic principles and would never do such things as he was being accused of – and it was fascists that were sowing these rumours. Yet as soon as he used that word in his defence, Kate knew he had lost his case: the two words, 'fascist' and 'racist' were predominantly only used by people with no distinctive argument. And she now knew that this was true of the man she had grown to love.

Chapter Twenty-Six

In Riga, Cash and his deposed Cabinet were being treated royally, yet were still under what amounted to house arrest. All mobile phones, computers, laptops, tablets – anything electronic that could betray their location or be used to communicate with the outside world - had been confiscated. They also felt that these had been searched for contacts, opinions, links, hidden peccadilloes and secret documents: many were deeply concerned as to what the Russians would find and how it could be used against them for years to come. The only thing they had been told was that this was a Russian involvement and nothing to do with Latvia. And, of course, Latvia would be set free again if or when the European Union left the UK for good and its army was back in France and Germany. It was a clever ruse, as it was a cheap way of showing Russia apparently respected boundaries and sovereignties – but it would also hasten the break-up of the EU.

The mansion they were in had everything a person could want – except freedom. There were sumptuous bedrooms with astonishing bathrooms, a gym, swimming-pool and superb food and wines. Sports were available, too; in short, they wanted for nothing.

One extra request had been fulfilled, however: a newsfeed of the BBC, so they could keep up with events – which they then frequently found they did not want to see. They perceived, too, that the BBC was becoming less objective. To them, so steeped in the habits and prejudices of the EU for over forty-three years, the BBC was becoming more attuned to the sensitivities of the Restoration movement, and they found themselves in a state of anger on many occasions, with no recourse to do anything about it. For the first time in their professional lives, nobody would hear them: they were impotent. This powerlessness was exemplified on one occasion when one of their younger researchers – as a way of creating discussion - had suggested that perhaps the elites' influence and sense of entitlement over that period had become so entrenched that anything not full-on pro-EU was seen as a retreat from the truth and a shared destiny. He was regaled with a furious denial and a torrent of abuse by the angry Cabinet and was not spoken to politely for several days.

In fact, the dominant London BBC had not shifted its opinions one iota: it was only in the regions where some minor news stories got through that there was occasionally an inkling of benevolent balance. But this episode, allied to Cash's incarceration and lack of any power or contact with the outside world, rendered him into a continual state of apoplexy and fury. Short, brusque, indignant and impolite, some wondered if the strains of seeing his beloved EU imploding daily on a screen, which he could do nothing about, was beginning to impinge on his mind.

*

Yet the collapse of the EU was happening without their resistance anyway: only a few days later the euro referendum in France took place. The result was definitive: 68% voted to leave it. In an instant, the riots of the few weeks before were replaced by street parties, bunting, a proliferation of the Tricolour on official buildings and the mass burning of the European Union flag. Free spontaneous concerts were given, with little-known French rock bands and solo performers suddenly so keen to get onto the bandwagon of a new French identity that they became household names overnight. Any people who railed against them – especially in politics or the media - were roundly ostracised and labelled as apologists for repression. A new spirit of freedom of opinion, so hated by the liberal groupthink which had descended like night upon a people once known for their philosophy and art was suddenly ubiquitous.

Protests against 'Enarqués' and their patronising beliefs were frequent: in television studios, those still wedded to the nostrums of the EU were vilified and often sacked, to be replaced by journalists and reporters more sympathetic to the current mood. Even the French Left became supportive and the unions – *'les Syndicats'* - saw within the emerging and supposedly Right-wing freedoms the chance to grasp the moment and help create a more egalitarian country. The fact that a clampdown on Muslims taking over whole Parisian streets to pray - and financial incentives offered for those of a militant nature to return to their own basic countries of origin - was hailed by the Left as well as the Right as an intelligent move and a re-affirmation of the Nation State, gaining far-reaching support. It was France that had pioneered and developed that idea through monarchies and revolutions – and the French people suddenly felt free and inspired to lead that enlightenment once more. Laporte had managed to re-unite France in the most unexpected of ways: and those who persisted in crying out for the saving of the EU in France to counteract these 'acts of racism' were themselves branded as 'inverted racists' – those who would rather see foreign workers and creeds overcome the new liberality of diverse French opinion. Although many academics, elites, judiciary, media personnel, bankers, government lackeys and a few industrialists were vocal in their opposition, for the majority it was a sudden release: it seemed as if a huge collective weight had been lifted from the massed people's backs and their joy was palpable, if somewhat unexpected in its magnitude. The Nation State was back.

For the European Union, it was a disaster: and with a surge in support for populist parties starting in other states – notably in Scandinavia, Spain and Portugal - the only countries left to fully believe in the European project were those whose intended hegemony had once propelled and most benefited from it: Germany, Belgium and Luxembourg.

*

In Latvia, the Cash coterie was in despair. All their cherished liberal nostrums and influences designed to keep people in their place – a patronising, gilded patriarchy where the elites would guide people's thoughts and needs in a condition of overtaxed benevolence – were disappearing before their eyes. By comparison, in Britain, the prevailing view became one of joyful indignation. The majority of people were happy that one of the founding countries of the European Union – France! – had managed what Britain had started, if tinged with annoyance that their own liberation had been thwarted. But France, of all countries! Yet the irony that Britain had been primarily invaded by troops from Germany, supported by France's army, ensured that people's anger was sustained.

Whatever the intricacies, it now became apparent that at last the invading army would soon have to go. Yet despite Seidel's diminishing influence, she made it clear that, whatever the French decided, hers would stay: France was France, but Britain must remain subdued. Germany would be resolute and immutable to the end; after all, she had the most to lose – from an economic and a historical point of view.

It was this one defiant statement that was the tipping-point: it made thousands more British support the Restoration. They wanted the recall of Parliament, and they wanted it now. Everywhere, those still supporting the EU's dictums were in retreat. 'The 48%', from a position of growing strength only a few days before, had now become isolated and ridiculed.

*

Julia had spun some excuses to the acting PM, James Gatting, that she needed to be in Manchester to discuss how to handle some anti-government events. In a sense, she was right, yet it was she who was planning them – against Gatting's government. The Restoration event had been organised specifically to catch the moment, capitalising on events in France and to proclaim that Britain would soon be a sovereign country once again, too.

When she arrived, Michael and Jemima greeted her with some more good news which had just come in: President Gold had told Seidel in no uncertain terms that if she did not start withdrawing her troops at the same time as France's – that was, now – he would cease all trade with Germany from midnight. In addition, she would have to pay for any reparations of damage on British soil if there were any repercussions. He and Tessa Lewis had agreed in secret before the ultimatum that he would not betray her major announcement – that elections would be held in six weeks to install a new government that would respect Britain's will to leave the European Union. In this, she was confident: not only was the EU in a state of near-total collapse but if it still existed soon in any shape at all it would be but a quarter of its previous size.

The overall reason for optimism that Tessa Lewis would champion was that if an overthrow could happen in France then it could certainly do so in Britain. The growing wish for the country to take back the control wrested from it had been mirrored by a continental precedent. And – palpably – that the mood for a sovereign government which rewarded aspiration for all the people rather than the privileged few was mounting across Europe. Around Britain, this was seen as a re-affirmation of British principles and was becoming increasingly, hugely resonant.

And whether the media liked it or not, it was a story that they would have to broadcast.

Chapter Twenty-Seven

Michael stood up, the bright pool of light on the podium a contrast to the dimly-lit but packed hall in Manchester. Many were standing in the aisles and the balcony was full, too. A thread of nervousness tinged with excitement was running through the others next to him - the ex-PM, Jemima, Borya, Leslie Caxton and the rest of the Restoration hierarchy. Cameras clicked and flashed as he made his way to the lectern and started to speak. "Ladies and gentlemen. Welcome to the first public meeting of Restoration, which is now on the cusp of taking our country back to being a sovereign state, so cruelly and undemocratically wrested from us just a short time ago." Some polite but loud applause and a few cheers greeted his opening comments. "Our country has suffered some historic setbacks in its time, but we prevailed; until a few months ago, we had only been invaded twice, by Rome and the Normans. We were nearly dominated in 1940 but our belief in ourselves and decency, bulked up by lashings of British spirit, saved the day. At that time, we were eventually saved from an invasion by Germany with the help of the Americans, and I am pleased and proud to say that they have again come to the cause of honour, decency and democracy in order to help restore our sovereign land to those to whom it belongs: us." Some sporadic cheering ensued with shouts of approval mingling in with the applause. "And yet, our country has been taken from us by people who posed as our friends, even though they were constantly working to beat us down. I make no apology for saying that – I was duped, too. In fact, you could say that it took me all my life since birth to realise the terrible thing we had done to our country: we had allowed it to be taken over piecemeal by laws and strictures that emanated from people with whom we had alternately fought and allied with over centuries but whom had always resented our success. Yet the one country that tried – twice - to take over Europe and, ultimately, us, failed. Both times. Yet over the past 44 years we have been invaded again – insidiously - by ideas and interpretations of democracy that were not our own: their idea was to ensure that if they could not conquer us militarily, they would do it economically. They were right, and they almost did.

"Now, I am no fan of the years of government presided over by the man who has now apparently disappeared - " he paused as a cheer went up from many members of the audience, "but his chancellor did one of the best things he could do to start saving our country: he kept us out of the euro - although it was only done to pique that current PM rather than because it was the right thing to do." A gale of laughter and applause swept the hall. "And if we *had* actually joined the euro... we would now, indeed, be conquered. You might say that we currently are – for the first time since 1066 an alien army invaded our land, in direct defiance of a referendum to leave the European Union, the outcome of which was not advisory as our Faustian friends would attest, but binding – just poorly phrased because they thought we had no chance of winning, so it wouldn't matter anyway!" Many stood and applauded at this, mirth all over people's faces. He waved a hand to stop them and continued, "Yet thanks to anti-democratic forces from those within our own land - " taunts of 'Shame' echoed round the hall, "we are going to prove that democracy *does* still exist here and we are some of the best exponents of it. Yes, our country has been compromised and our supposed friends have betrayed us, delivering us into a subservience which we did not vote for. Yes, we are still technically invaded - true. And that was bad enough: but what was worse is that it was done under the pretence of their being our colleagues and stopping war in Europe. Yet is it right that they waged war on us in order to stop it closer to them? NO! It is NOT!" With that, the hall erupted. "So, over the past few weeks, we have been working tirelessly with our true friends - the Americans, and not for the first time – to gain the support of our people to topple those from abroad and their traitorous supporters in our country who can only see their dominance in terms of power, control and the subjugation of the British spirit. Well, as from this moment on, we are fighting back! Thanks to our wonderfully loyal armed forces who put principle before the orders of our compromised generals, judges, bankers and more – they know who they are: people like 'The 48%' - " a huge boo reverberated around the hall, "these benign and wonderful forces have started the liberation of our country that was under the hegemony of the EU. I say 'was', because even their most fervent poodles – and I use the word advisedly," – another big laugh – "have now realised the folly of their ways and have decided to follow us out of the EU, in defiance of their economic masters – as have Italy. Yet we are still trying to leave it ourselves, I hear you say, because we were *literally* invaded. Well, as from today, we are going to make good that Referendum result and WE ARE STARTING THE FIGHTBACK NOW."

The hall went mad: those on the podium smiled, none so more than the ex-PM. Michael turned and waved a hand, whereupon a huge blue cloth with 'Restoration' on it unfurled behind him, to the sound of massed trumpets. Cheers, whoops, whistles and hurrahs accompanied the revelation. He implied quiet, and continued, "'Restoration' is a word with serious meaning here in Britain: it was used after the Civil War ended in 1659 and meant that the freedom of expression we are so famous for now was born after a period of gloom, persecution, religious intolerance and lack of freedom of speech against an invading army – albeit a British one. Indeed, the similarities are numerous as to where we are now: a foreign army has invaded us to sap the will that propelled us to greatness and was woven into our souls. Well, after the events of the past few weeks – last week – and now here in Britain as from now, the European peoples are one step closer – as we are – to the Restoration of the Nation State, with all its idiosyncrasies, different languages, freedoms, laws, customs, foods, beers, wines, spirits, senses of humour and – yes – currencies, that make people proud to live where they do. So I – we – look forward to the resurgence of the Nation State and the end of a homogenised, pan-European pooling of ideas and freedoms. The only union we need is the British one – not the European one. Yes, our Scottish friends might feel closer to the European model," some friendly 'boos' were heard – "but I still think that their innate sense of fair play will keep them with us – I hope so. And I mentioned drinks a moment ago – well, they should stay with us, because the Scots sell more whisky to us than they do to the whole of the rest of Europe!"

Laughter and agreement pervaded the hall again. Then, with a stretch of the arms as if he had scored the winning goal, he proclaimed: "The Restoration starts here! And now I pass you to the lady soon to be our rightful Prime Minister again - who will announce what and how we are going to take back our country and deliver the Brexit a democratic majority voted for. Here she is!" With that, Tessa Lewis stood up amongst tumultuous cheers, applause, whistles and whoops. When it subsided, she gave her outline of what would happen next. With a build-up like Michael's, she did not have to work hard. She finished with the words, "Michael is right: the Restoration starts here – and from now on this milestone in our island story will be known as the Manchester Convention, when the first steps were taken to return our democracy – and the Mother of all Parliaments – back to its people."

*

"Sir James – I think you should come and watch this," a fretful-looking secretary had said to the stand-in PM as the Restoration event started, the excitement of which had interrupted the banality of daytime TV. "I think a revolution has started in Manchester. 'Restoration'. The BBC is showing it live now."

"The BBC? How did they know about this if we didn't?" Sir James hurried in to watch. He glowered. "What tosh," he muttered as it progressed, instinctively realising his days as Prime Minister were again numbered. "Why did Julia not tell me about this?"

"Well, that's another thing," the secretary confided: "I think we've just spotted her on the Restoration podium in Manchester."

*

In Brussels, Guifford was in the awkward position of being interviewed by his lover. Although this had happened a few times before, today it was different. Overnight, the BBC's Head of News had resigned in protest at the corporation's reporting of events. He had willingly gone along with the status quo until recently, but had realised that the growing feeling of the majority for the re-imposition of Parliament, the ousting of EU influence - and now events in France - should be better reflected in bulletins. This had made him a pariah in his own department. He found himself savagely accused of being a stooge for the Restoration government, which he vehemently denied: all he wanted, he said, was the balance expected by the British population. He added that news not necessarily in tune with the corporation and its EU masters was being reported in the regions and so the London operation should catch up with them. Yet this did not go down well with his sub-editors, who – preferring to toe the party line they had joined the organisation for - refused to agree to what they ironically called 'partisan' reporting. Faced with this revolt, he accepted a job from a rival organisation which would be more sympathetic to diverse views that were not necessarily their own. His parting shot was a very public filmed resignation speech accusing the London newsroom of 'muddled thinking' and that they should 'stand up to the excesses of power' that emanated from too cosy a relationship with influential elites. Especially those from the EU. It went viral in minutes.

Guifford had seen this and quickly realised that things were not as they used to be: he was also about to be interviewed by Kate again and was very concerned that she might have subscribed to the new reality – which would do him no favours at all. She might even feel bold enough to ask him about the so-called slush funds to his face, a topic he was desperate to keep away from. But, as it happened, her first question was not quite what he was expecting at all.

"Commissioner," she began, "you are aware, I take it, that the Restoration movement in Britain has just announced a counter-government to the one installed by the European Union by force a few weeks ago. What's your reaction to this development?"

Expecting a question about France and its aftermath having left the euro and – by definition – the EU, he was caught out. His face betrayed that he had no knowledge of this development and, therefore, no answer. Tetchily expecting imminent further intrusions regarding his complicity in the alleged bankrolling of 'The 48%', he just gave her a filthy look before lashing back at her: "Oh for goodness' sake – I have no wish to talk about that stupid little country when so many other things are happening. Why do you keep asking me about things which are nothing to do with me?" She had replied correctly that as she worked for the BBC, it was therefore of interest to the British, and that before the invasion and their subsequent subjugation he had been a Commissioner with influence over Britain's terms for leaving the European Union - so it was everything to do with him. He stared at her for an instant with ice in his eyes, then stood up, threw off his microphone and stormed out.

Later, he admonished Kate for not warning him of this explosive question, especially as he had not known about the development. "But you should have done," she chided him.

"Perhaps," he admitted, "but you didn't have to leak my reaction to YouTube."

"YouTube? Has it? Well, it wasn't me. I wouldn't do a thing like that to you."

"Well, one of your lot has. Probably from the BBC newsroom. I tell you, they're starting to not be supportive of Brussels. We'll have to... fight back, let them know who's boss - or cut their subsidies if they go on like this." And he walked out. It was true: the clip had already been seen by hundreds of thousands of people in Britain and America – and many parts of Europe, too. Yet events were happening at such a pace in Britain that any threats to the BBC would soon be irrelevant anyway.

Chapter Twenty-Eight

The Restoration meeting in Manchester was disassembling: it had been a spectacular success, and was now openly being referred to as 'The Restoration Proclamation', with its historic overtones of Royalists and Roundheads. Even the questioning afterwards had been relatively benign – much even laudatory. The carefully-organised event had paid dividends, and the political value of previously-Remain Manchester being seen as increasingly pro-British and anti-EU was a masterstroke. The only hostile moments had apparently happened outside, when a large column of Remainers – following an intimidating European Army personnel carrier festooned with EU flags - had slowly moved forward, trying to create a passage through the thousands of Leavers who had not been able to get into the hall and were watching the event on large screens outside. Whether it was leading up to an assault by further European units stationed nearby, no-one knew, because the infiltrators had been stopped in their tracks by a regiment of loyal British soldiers gently but forcibly barring them - and resolutely seen to be part of the much larger assembly of Leavers. The Remain crowd had been mainly boisterous rather than violent and only one soldier had been hit - by a piece of hurled paving-stone – but he was not in a serious condition.

It was propitious that there were so many Leavers who had assembled: on news footage, the Remain demonstration looked miniscule amongst the sea of Leavers, and the British soldiers looked an even tinier fraction of the supporters, so the event did not look like an army coup but an uprising of the people – which it surely was. Once the crowd had been dispersed and no further repercussions seemed likely, Michael and Jemima slipped away from the hall together and got into Michael's car to return to London.

As they travelled, they were in high spirits: they discussed how well the convention had gone and that even the BBC had put out a fairly balanced report; things must have started moving their way. It was then that Michael noticed, in his mirror, an armed personnel carrier coming up fast behind them, exhibiting EU army insignia: this was not unusual as, despite rising popularity for Restoration, the area was nonetheless outside the Swathe and there would still be a larger number of deniers in the area. They knew that the EU army presence would eventually diminish as they approached more friendly territory in the Swathe around the Midlands, before becoming more prevalent again as they neared London, but the speed of the vehicle was frightening. "What's the matter?" asked Jemima, noting his suddenly worried expression.

"We're being followed by an EU army vehicle."

"Oh, shit."

"Get down – I'm going to try to outpace him and see if there's any reaction." He floored the accelerator and glided a long way ahead, then let the car slow down: he did not want to be headline news the next day for another politician caught speeding.

"Perhaps I'm becoming paranoid," Michael joked, as he pulled back into the inside lane and they ceased to be concerned. They continued to talk about the rally and what they would do next - when suddenly the APC was overtaking them on the middle lane: then it violently veered in front of them and braked abruptly. Michael was about to hit it; yet he managed to swerve inwards across the hard shoulder and the back of the car on his side crunched into the rear of the vehicle, slewing the car around as metal scraped on metal: yet he managed to keep going and pulled ahead. But the car's rear wheel alignment had been disturbed and the car was travelling in a slightly crab-like way, with the smell of rubber becoming more noticeable as it scorched the road surface. Michael was not going to stop, though: he was still just managing to outpace the carrier despite his untrue direction and pulled back onto the main carriageway. He noticed Jemima furiously texting on her mobile. "What are you doing?" he enquired in the mayhem.

"Texting all our colleagues – especially the PM: we're being targeted – so might they be. They must be made aware."

Michael was due to pull off the motorway onto a more minor road but decided that this would be dangerous for both them and civilians if they got caught at junctions, roundabouts and in towns – so he sped on. "You've just missed the turning," Jemima protested.

"I know – safer."

She did not argue, then started to dial a number. After a moment, she said, "Is that Major-General Cummings' office? Great; could I speak to him urgently, please? It's Jemima Grice, MP for Wiltshire East here…. Good afternoon, Sir. Yes, we're being attacked in our car by an EU Army forces APC on the M6. Any chance you can get a fast armed loyal British army vehicle to intercept this EU one? Yes, the M6 heading south, between junctions 20 and 19…. Thank God for that. We can turn off at the Knutsford Services and drive around the carpark until you arrive and then you can intercept them…. We're about eight miles away from it – but our car's been hit so we're a bit slower than we might be…. So are there any brigades or regiments nearby you can call on? Bit stretched due to loyalty issues… OK…Too many to deploy in such a short time? – Yes, I understand…" she sounded concerned again as Michael noticed the APC was slightly nearer than before. "Might be better if we can go off at junction 18?... OK, but I think he's gaining on us and I don't know how long our skewed tyre can hold out… Best chance of getting to us in time? OK… A54 to Congleton… pub on left after a mile, The Splendid… Left down farm track immediately after – go up there and keep going as far as we can – you'll try to get a chopper there with anyone you can spare? And nail him from behind from the air? Thank God for that, no chance of civilian casualties – but hurry, please – thanks." She gave Cummings the car details and then rang off as she turned to Michael: "There's a loyal regiment around here near Congleton that can intercept the bastards using a helicopter and a small force. Cummings is optimistic." The motorway started up a long incline.

"Good, this'll slow him up," whispered Michael hoarsely. "Do you think this has Cash's authority?"

"What – to try and take out prominent Restoration people?" Michael nodded. "Mm. Could be 'The 48%', though, too."

He nodded again. "Yup," he concurred, grimly.

"Might be Cash… if he's been found, that is," she countered. "Or Gatting?"

Michael shook his head. "Doubt it. More likely Cash: perhaps it's all a bluff and he's already president of Europe. Perhaps he and his mob never left Brussels and he's just been looking for an excuse to use force and impose EU hegemony more harshly. Our Restoration rally is just the excuse he's been looking for."

"And keeping himself safe in Brussels at the same time," she sneered. "Well, he's got a fight on his hands now, then." She paused to reflect, then said: "But I think we'd know if he was back – either in control here or running things from Brussels. He values the sound of his own importance too much not to be on the airwaves, wherever he might be. No, I think our boys took him so we could have our counter-revolution. Don't forget, we're being supported by the Americans so perhaps he's hoping they'll change their minds if he can create a reason to do so and they'll change sides or push off."

"Hmm. No," Michael rejoined. "I think Gold's

determined to put the people first – like Laporte – so there's little chance of his suddenly changing his mind over Cash. And Brexit was the catalyst for his unexpected win, remember."

"Perhaps… but don't forget that a lot of Americans hate Gold and generally still think Cash's wonderful for some reason. Beats me, but…"

"They didn't have to live through his governments," Mike retorted acidly, noting that their assailants were now a long way behind.

"Although," Jemima continued, "if the Americans are fearful of this escalating into a full-on war between what's left of the EU and Britain, with American support, then it could be they're just keeping a low profile. Although Russia seems to be cosying up to them at the moment - but that could change overnight."

Michael contemplated what she had just said. "No, perhaps, on second thoughts, you're right and it's Gatting. He was roundly defeated by Cash in 1997 because he still thinks it was due to his 'cabinet bastards' as he called them: those that were – and still are, if they're still living – anti-EU. Tradition dies hard with the British – even if they are on the wrong side. But actually I think it's a one-off. Perhaps it's even just an EU army vehicle that's been hijacked by people bankrolling the challenges to Brexit. Like 'The 48%', as you said. They're becoming ever-more desperate and angry."

At the moment he said this, just before they passed under a bridge, a bullet tore into the roof of their car. Michael just saw the man aiming at him, leaning over the handrail, but he had had an involuntarily reaction and swerved slightly: the car went into swinging convulsions as he tried to right its course against its skewed shape. But then the bridge was behind them and the car righted itself. "Christ," shouted Jemima.

"I'm turning off as soon as I can," said Michael. "I don't think we'll make the A54."

"But what about Cummings and the chopper?"

"Too bad – we'll have to take our chances," shouted Michael.

"It's the Knutsford Services," she observed. "Look, the exit's coming up."

And so it was: Michael steered his crippled vehicle off the motorway and onto the acres of concrete, sticking to the furthest perimeter of the car park he could manage, as they kept their eyes peeled for another assailant. After a few minutes of aimlessly but worriedly driving around, Jemima's phone rang. "Cummings here. Change of plan." Jemima's heart sank. "We've got an off-duty soldier who's about to leave a service station: been given compassionate leave to be with his dying mother and was having a cuppa in the restaurant. He's closest to you."

"Which services?" screamed Jemima.

"Erm, hang on, he's on the other line…" Jemima bit her lip as the seconds ticked away and the car slewed uncertainly around the motley ranks of vehicles. Then he replied: "Knutsford Southbound."

"We're there already," she screamed with relief. "We had to turn off – we were shot at from a bridge."

"Jesus – really? Hang on." Again, a long pause, then: "He thinks he's seen you – black Alfa with a stoved-in offside rear wheel – that's what you told me, isn't it?"

"Yes! We haven't had a chance to look at the damage but it's certainly black and certainly an Alfa."

"Good. He's in his own car but is armed – for obvious reasons these days."

"Oh, my God," Jemima burst out. "I can see the Army carrier – it's a hundred yards behind – must have caught us up. But how did the driver know we were in the Services area? He was too far away."

"Accomplices, probably," stated Michael loudly so Cummings would hear.

"Get away from him and park up, then get out and get down," Cummings shouted – but Jemima had put her phone on speaker and Michael heard him clearly anyway: he did as he was told as the EU army vehicle passed in the adjacent parking lane but in the opposite direction. He screeched to a halt in an empty space between two vans and switched off the engine as they cowered down. Then there was a long pause – only seconds but what seemed like minutes. Then Cummings' voice on Jemima's phone punctured the silence: "Our boy's seen it – says he's going to take him out now." The EU army carrier was coming back down the lane behind and towards them but they also saw a fit-looking man in casual clothes stepping out to the rear of their car with a rifle at his shoulder in classic military pose. There was a screeching of tyres as the APC came to an emergency stop but it skidded and there was a crunch and grinding of metal as it ploughed into cars only three away from them, pushing the vehicles into theirs like a concertina, crushing the other rear side so that their car could not now move. Michael and Jemima could just see the kerb-side door opening and a soldier with a pistol aiming through the open space between the windscreen and the passenger door's window: then there was a sharp crack and the man fell out the door onto the tarmac, a perfect round red hole puncturing his forehead. The driver was trapped and the British soldier rushed around and pumped three bullets into him: he fell across the wheel, his unseeing eyes staring through the windscreen. After the noise of gunfire, screams suddenly became apparent as people tried to run away.

"Any more inside?" the soldier shouted at Michael and Jemima, without taking his eye off the vehicle.

"We don't know," Michael called back to him.

"Right – get down everybody – EVERYBODY, GET DOWN and try to take cover. There's going to be a bit of a bang – and some metal flying around." He went around to the back of the carrier and they saw him throw a rear door open – a second later it was slammed shut. A long pause ensued before he re-appeared around the front of the carrier and ran to hide behind Michael's door. There was a loud muffled bang and the sides of the carrier heaved out like an expanding balloon – but did not burst. The soldier stood up and opened Michael's door. "I've always wanted an excuse to do that," he said, smiling but without emotion. "Four of 'em in the back. Were, anyway. Good bit of kit, that carrier – sadly, it's French-built – a BMX-01. But better than your average French car." He smiled briefly, then went serious again as he continued: "The buggers inside must have been British, though, despite their poxy flags. Playing for the other side. Bastards. Better off without them. Probably all hoping for promotion after all this was over. Well, they won't get it now. OK, let's get you out of here before we're either attacked ourselves or people start asking too many questions. Leave your car, but get your stuff out and come with me." They did as he said, and soon they were heading back towards London. They could not thank him enough – but knew they were now marked.

No other members of the Restoration had had similar encounters. Which seemed unusual. Someone was out to get them specifically, it seemed.

Chapter Twenty-Nine

Kate was in the Boulevard shopping centre in the EU's Berlaymont complex. She was troubled: Guifford had been aloof for a few days and, although he had a lot on his mind, she felt he thought she had betrayed him – and it was the BBC interview which was to blame. Yet why could he not see that she was only doing her job? The element of surprise was part of her trade and made good television: she could not be seen to be under his influence, either. She stopped in front of a shop window, which was full of expensive things, except they were indistinct - all a blur. Had she gone into all this relationship with her eyes closed? Did Guifford really only offer her the world – or Europe, anyway – just for his own political game? She knew she was attractive – not because she was arrogant enough to say so but because everyone always told her. Including Guifford. And Michael. Ah, Michael: she had not heard from him for a long while now. Did he have a lover yet? No, probably not – he was too involved with Restoration. And then she wondered, with a chill of unpredicted revelation, if she had only gone with Guifford to spite Michael for having a different view to hers? She had seen his

Restoration speech – it been all over the news and had gone viral. He had seemed in high spirits and was obviously itching for a positive resolution to the impasse which had descended on Britain and, indeed, Europe. His optimism was in stark contrast to Guifford's, who now looked even more drawn and haggard than he usually did. Perhaps she should have stayed with Michael… but their political differences were now too great. And then the thought struck her: was she becoming like her old friend Xenia, with whom Michael had so vocally disagreed a few years ago? Xenia was a socialist snob – that contradictory, strange state of mind where people support the masses yet disdain everything about them: that was what all the legal challenges to Brexit were about, to be honest. Xenia was just like them: intransigent, patronising and an inverted racist in that she seemed to prefer anyone from other lands in preference to her own, whatever their views or actions. She shuddered as she realised it had been Laporte who had said that – she wasn't becoming like her, was she?

Yet another thing which puzzled her was that there had been demonstrations against the democratically-elected President Gold, yet no other international dictators and autocrats. Why? Xenia was, indeed, a bleeding-heart socialist who would support any cause other than those of her own country – or America or Israel. Was she, Kate, becoming compromised, embittered, unable to see other people's points of view and – more importantly – beg to differ, argue and discuss rather than scream and harangue, like her erstwhile friend? She could feel that this was the way the European Union was going and yet she was part of it, supporting it. Or – as she continually wondered – was she just happy to follow any man as long as he had power, influence and money? Michael now had all those attributes and, if she had stayed with him, they would be hers, too. But then again, if they had not had the differences of opinion he would possibly not have had the drive to follow his very different but successful path. She sighed: she missed England and her friends. Did she really want it to become just another bland piece of land within a huge mass of people, with all the same rules, laws, houses, signs, foods, drinks, attitudes and clothes? She was realising that the Nation State was possibly the most important thing that had ever evolved just because it championed difference and debate, stimulation and creativity. Yet the Nation State was the epitome of everything Guifford wanted to destroy: 'ever more Europe' was like a daily mantra branded onto his brain. And as she eyed up all the expensive jewellery in the shop window she had stopped outside when her reverie began, she realised with a bump that 'Europe' was a sham.

*

James Gatting received Julia Reeve back into Downing Street with the news that she had been sacked. He accused her of disloyalty and treachery, making his diatribe against her sound like a Tudor court in that she deserved to be beheaded for what she had done. She just stood there for the full two minutes he shouted at her: yet all it made her realise was that he was afraid – afraid for what had happened to Cash, what could happen to him, and angry that the carefully-constructed edifice of the European Union was in the act of being demolished: and all whilst he was at the helm. Julia stood her ground and then just responded: "Dear Sir James; I understand you are angry but you are wrong to say that it is I who have betrayed you. It is you who have betrayed your country. You only got the Maastricht Treaty through as part of the journey to subjugate your country – of which you were then Prime Minister – under an undemocratic and essentially unelected un-British yoke; and despite all you did, and all the coercion and now forceful invasion by a foreign country – or group of states, if you prefer, but amounting to the same thing – you exhorted your countrymen to be 'patriotic' to defer their parliament and laws to people who have no interest in us other than our money and our downfall. You are the traitor, not I. What you have done has been a terrible betrayal – a historic mistake." Then she turned on her heel and walked out, pausing at the door only to turn to him and say, "And I will soon be back here at the head of a British government, but you will not. Thank you and goodbye – it was good to know you in the old days – but I have seen the light. It's only a pity that you did not." And she was gone.

*

Terry Cash had been busy. Not in government in Brussels as Michael and Jemima had theorised, because he was still under Russian house arrest in a remote and unknown location in Latvia. But he was rich. Very rich. And money can buy people. The person he picked on was a simple man of good humour and impeccable manners who brought him his food and had his clothes laundered. But Cash felt he was fallible, so he would try and exploit him with the bribe of lots of money if this man could get a note out to international sources to let them know where he and his Cabinet were being held.

This man's name was Emek Gundars, born in 1979; he was a family man from the north of the country who could speak Russian, which his father had taught him during the previous Soviet occupation in the 1980s; never believing that Latvia would gain independence in 1990, he was pragmatic enough to ensure his son would improve this capability. After that event, though, the need for Russian became of no use and so he learned English. He had had a variety of jobs and had most recently been working in Riga on a tourist magazine. Cash had picked up that he knew the country well as a result, even if Emek was always adamant that he did not know where they were, having been brought to this place in a van without windows for that very purpose. Yet Cash felt he knew more than he let on, and within days had had a conversation with him.

"Emek, would you like to be back under Russian dominance or back under the European Union?"

"Of course, Europe," he uttered quietly.

"Well, you know who I am, don't you?" asked Cash.

"I have seen your face," he said, "but I have not been told who you are. Except you're important."

Cash was slightly annoyed at this response – he thought everyone knew who he was. Putting the slight aside, he continued: "I am – was – the Prime Minister of Great Britain, elected by the council of the European Union." He knew that was a lie, as he had been imposed, but there must have been an election there somewhere for the EU to impose him. Anyway, it suited his argument. "I – and my colleagues here – all need to get back to Britain very soon," he continued. "There is a crisis in Britain and I need to get back to stop a very silly thing that is happening there. The European Union is being replaced by people who don't know what they're doing and taking my country down the path of ruination." He paused as Emek digested this. Then: "You want to get back into the EU, they want us to get out. We can help each other. You help to get me – us - out and I'll help you to get back in when I'm restored to control in London. And I'll make sure you'll be very well paid – you'll be rich."

Emek looked down, pondered for a moment, and then said: "If you can get me and my family to London too, that would be best thing. Money important but London… that would be best thing."

"I can do that – no problem. I brought thousands to Britain when I was Prime Minister before – and I can do it again. As long as we're still members of the EU, of course. And so it would help you and me if you assist me to escape from here so I can ensure we stay in the Union: all you have to do is find out exactly where we are and then tell the world. International diplomacy can do the rest."

"I see what I can do," Emek replied, and left.

Cash felt more optimistic than he had done for quite a few weeks.

Chapter Thirty

Michael and Jemima had been given army protection. The minders they had expected after his Manchester speech had not materialised, even though each of their homes were in the middle of Remain areas in London. Michael's house, being more secure than hers, meant that, whenever possible, Jemima stayed with him. It was good having a woman back in the house and he really cherished their time together: yet there was much to be done, as they were helping to organise the final push that would liberate their country on a wave of popular feeling – a very British revolution. As was usual, the Scottish Parliament was causing difficulties, pledging undying allegiance to the European Union and a second independence referendum if England, Wales and Northern Ireland left. What they were not willing to contemplate – or admit – was that the feelings for the EU in Scotland had shifted dramatically since the European Army invasion, and although Scottish regiments had not joined their English and Welsh counterparts in resisting it – nor assisting the Restoration - there were an increasing number of Scots who wished to do so. It was also becoming apparent that the Swathe was, so to speak, 'moving' towards Scotland, rather in the manner of Great Birnam Wood to Dunsinane, which was proving to be a spiritual barrier, if not a physical one. And with Scotland's closest spiritual ally, France, now also on the point of leaving, common sense and pragmatism were starting to erode the SNP's domination. Michael had realised that the influence of The Swathe was now consuming almost the whole of England with the exception, still, of London and the south-east: but even this was diminishing, and London was starting to be seen as the last bastion to fall.

*

And so it was that a secret date was drawn up within the Restoration movement to organise a Grand Restoration March to descend on London from the north, east and west – the centre of the Swathe: it would be planned for October 21st – Trafalgar Day – which would henceforward be a new national holiday to mark the return of elective democracy to Britain. It would be called Restoration Day. In addition, June 23rd would also be made a national holiday, to be officially named Independence Day, to mark when the people rose up to break away from the shackles of the European Union. And the remains of the occupying army would be sent back to France and Germany – by force, if necessary.

Then, a day later, providence intervened to help the mood of Restoration: Laporte announced that the French army contingents would be taken out of Britain immediately. They were flying in the face of history by extending a helping hand to the British to seek self-determination – something she wished to demonstrate to the French, too. What was less proclaimed but no less true was that she needed her troops back in France to stop the rioting which always accompanied huge shifts of power in that country. James Gatting was powerless to stop them: with his control ebbing away in the face of popular revolt, the British Army against him and the mood for a return of sovereignty becoming unstoppable, he knew he was fighting a rearguard action – unless he could make London a separate country. Almost as a last roll of the dice, and in concert with Seidel in Germany and those countries who had not yet left the bloc, he ordered all the remaining German EU Army units around the country to move immediately to barracks in and around London. And without betraying any of his intentions to the EU, he secretly asked the Spanish prime minister if he would consider sending some units to London, too. It was a desperate ploy, and one which would ultimately help to bring the opposite result to which he had intended.

With the situation changing so rapidly, and loyalties welling up behind Restoration, it was not long before a mole in Downing Street leaked the perfidy to the BBC and social media. Within moments, British Army units, supported by American forces, were alerted and started the process of surrounding any German EU army and air force divisions so that they could not move. Tanks were parked on runways so planes could not take off, and the uneasy co-habitation of areas with German units close to loyalist British ones was quietly resolved: the Germans could sense what was happening and that they would be routed if they tried any attack. It was a sign of changing realisations too that many were unhappy at being forced to fight a country which had exercised its sovereign right and many Germans secretly agreed with them. It was not for no reason that the AfD was doing well in Germany, and many could see that they were on the wrong side of history if they had intervened. Not a shot was fired.

In defiance of Gatting's edict, too, Restoration announced that – pending the imminence of their expected reclamation of British rule - any units arriving from Spain would be regarded as an anti-sovereign act and would be shot down or sunk: any Armada would suffer the same fate as the one in 1588. It was a spectacular success and the Spanish backed down immediately. Gatting was on his own.

When Trausch heard this news and had digested the response, he felt he could not let the situation get out of hand any more: events had gone too far now. He had to do something dramatic in order to 'save' Britain from itself and the European Union generally. And the proper subjugation of Britain was now the top priority: if 'punishing' Britain for leaving would not work, then he could not risk any more departures and Britain still held the key to European Union success. As Europe's second largest economy, he had to have it back in the fold to deter the others at any cost. Weighing up his dwindling options, he had been courting Poland assiduously because, for historical reasons mostly associated with the Second World War, he realised the Poles were closer to Britain ideologically and temperamentally than most other states outside the Visegrad group. If he could get them onside and they could supply EU troops to Britain to sustain Gatting's government, he hoped they would encourage the other Visegrad states to join them, and any would be less disliked than the French and Germans and could organise a benign coup. Then the European Union could start to re-assert itself - and the inclusion of a 'willing' Britain might tempt others which had left back into the bloc. It was a last-ditch plan, and he would have to act quickly as the French were already back in France and the vacuum they left could not be filled by German troops alone. Worse, he had just heard they were trapped in their billets in Britain. Within hours, he and his team were leaving Brussels for Warsaw – with one exception: Guifford Neveu. He had disappeared and Trausch had no clue as to where he was. Neither had anyone else.

*

In fact, Neveu had left a little later than his colleagues but was on his way to the airport too – not to catch a plane to Warsaw, but to London. He had not told Kate he was going and was ostensibly travelling to see if he could be an arch-appeaser by finding out how the EU could best help Gatting. He felt nervous at entering the lion's den but reasoned that he could knock some sense into a situation which was spiralling hopelessly out of control. And he would become a European hero as a result. He had some other business to settle, too: but that was private.

He arrived at the airport and waved away his driver after telling him when he expected to be back. He was traversing the check-in hall when a long-bearded man pushing a luggage trolley and dressed in long white robes and sandals accosted him. "Excuse me," he said, in a heavily Middle-Eastern accent. "I am going to Stuttgart and I cannot see my flight – can you help me?"

Guifford was not in the habit of talking to anyone outside his gilded circle but looked at the man's ticket and then up at the flight-board. "I don't think it's been posted yet," he said, slightly contemptuously. "Sorry – ask someone else later."

"Ah, I think I recognise you – are you Guifford Neveu from the EU?"

"Well, er, yes, I am, actually," he confided, then said, "I really must go – flight to catch."

"Allahu akbar!" the man suddenly shouted and, in the moment before the explosion, Guifford noticed his black-gloved hand press a concealed button on the trolley. It was the last thing he saw as the terminal was ripped apart by a huge fireball; screams and body-parts, mangled metal and possessions were dispersed across the hall in a profusion of smoke, carnage and rubble.

Chapter Thirty-One

At the moment the bomb went off, Michael was crossing the arrivals lounge on the floor below. He heard the explosion above and the screams but, realising what it must have been, decided it would be better for him to get out of the way and continue. He was on his way to see Kate. He had received a call from her the night before and, although he was needed in Britain to help with the uprising to free his country, the tone of her call had made him wish to meet her briefly, which had been well received. She had sounded confused and unhappy and he still loved her enough to care for her, despite the fact that she had left him for Guifford. He suspected that all was not well there, but his other mission was to explain his own blossoming relationship with Jemima and that he wanted a divorce. Being a gentleman, though, he wanted to tell her face to face: he was no cad and desired to do it properly. He managed to get a taxi before the emergency services arrived and proceeded to the centre of Brussels. He rang the doorbell to her flat and waited for the reply. None came.

*

Emek knocked on the door of Terry Cash's

sumptuous apartment and entered when answered. He closed the door quietly behind him and then furtively approached Cash. Leaning close to him, he whispered: "I may be able to help you, sir, but as is, I shall say, dangerous for me, I need lot of money in advance. You see, I will have to 'disappear' if I tell people where you are and I need lot, lot of money to escape to other country with my family."

Cash was visibly irritated by this. "But, Emek," he countered, "how can I get you your money now when I'm stuck in isolation here and have no contact with the outside world? You'll just have to trust me." Emek looked concerned at that statement. "Why don't you believe me?" Cash added, noting with increasing tetchiness his expression of doubt.

Emek avoided that question and stated: "I can no escape myself as I have no money for bribe people."

"But I'm internationally famous: of course I'll be able to get you your money – and British citizenship for you and your family, when I get back to London. I'll make you famous, too, if you like, as the man who helped the legitimate Prime Minister of Britain to return to rule his country. You'll have fame, fortune if you want it. I just cannot give you the money now."

Emek looked down at his highly-polished black shoes, then back at Cash. He dropped his voice and whispered to Cash: "There are forces here, who will kill me if I help you. That why I must have money now. Big risk for me."

Cash turned and looked at the view outside the window which, although spectacular, nonetheless constituted a prison. Then he turned back to Emek and said: "Are there any phones here in the building?"

"I think so – but they are in locked room."

"And computers?"

"Probably – I don't know."

"And you can't find out?"

"As I say – is difficult… and dangerous."

"Do *you* have a mobile phone?" Emek nodded. "Can you lend it to me?"

There was a pause. "It no work here – no signal. And dangerous."

"Can you get me mine back? Even just for a few minutes? There might be a signal – perhaps they're just blocking yours. If they think mine's under lock and key then they might not have blocked it. And you *will* get your money – I promise."

Emek looked into Cash's eyes, as if searching for some missing proof, then left the room. Cash was exasperated and angry at his impotence: he, a respected politician with global contacts reduced to living under clandestine house arrest somewhere in Latvia under the control of an occupying army. It was a disgrace. And when he got out of here… His inner fulminations were interrupted by Emek returning and carefully closing the door. He put his hand in his pocket and surreptitiously drew out a small purple bag with Cash's name on it. His mobile was inside. "Good luck," he whispered, "but I return soon or they will see is no there. I don't know if it work or no." With that, he left.

Like a schoolboy with an unopened bag of sweets, Cash took it out of the bag and powered it up. There was only a small amount of charge left and it took ages to find anything. Then, finally, a weak signal appeared; trembling with excitement, he dialled the number for his wife and pressed 'call'. He waited. After what seemed an age, he heard it ringing. Then the inevitable voicemail message. It wasn't Coralie's personal message, but he put that down to international connections. He whispered at the tone: "Darling, it's me. I'm OK but under Russian house arrest in a beautiful, huge white ornate house miles away from anywhere in Latvia. Oh, yes – and in the bend of a small river – that might help with aerial location. We need rescuing as soon as you get this. Don't phone back or the guy who got me my phone to make this call will be in trouble." After he rang off, he tried to phone the switchboard at Downing Street. Again, the same voicemail message. This was strange. The switchboard there was always manned and it was not a mobile signal but a landline. His fears grew. He left a message anyway in the same vein as to his wife, switched the phone off and returned it to the bag; then he hid it, ready for Emek's return.

An hour later, he heard people coming down the hall and the door opened without being knocked upon. Two men with earpieces and sharp suits entered and he could see that there were two armed soldiers behind them. "We're leaving," stated one of the suits. Cash was instantly nervous; had his call got through but also been intercepted?

Before he could answer, the other said, "Now. Your things will be brought on later." He wished he had kept the phone on his person, but there was nothing he could do now as he was manhandled out of the room, down the corridor and into the huge hallway, where his other colleagues were also being assembled. Each was in a different stage of indignant protestation. They were given heavy winter coats to put on and then marched outside to where the same flotilla of black limousines which had brought them there were just pulling up. They were bundled in unceremoniously and they moved off. As they got to the end of the long driveway, Cash noticed a very tall, slim archway in front of them which he had not noticed driving through when they arrived. And then his blood ran cold as he saw a body hanging from its topmost arc, suspended by a rope around its neck. As they passed underneath it, the cars' movements making it swing slightly, he could see that the throat had been cut. It was Emek. He felt sick – not just because he realised his plan had failed, but because now they would treat them more harshly somewhere else. The fact that it was Emek was annoying, too.

*

Michael waited outside Kate's flat for nearly an hour, ringing her phone every ten minutes or so, asking where she might be. But it was always the same result – voicemail. He was about to leave to catch the last flight back to London when two police cars screamed to a halt outside and four officers jumped out, each pointing a pistol at him. Instinctively, he raised his hands as they rushed up the steps. Another man in plain clothes got out the car, came up to him and said tersely: "Michael Hope?" He nodded, bewildered. "We are arresting you on the suspected involvement in the assassination of Guifford Neveu at Brussels Airport two hours ago."

As Michael was being driven away, his mind was jumbled with conflicting reasons for his arrest. The officers would not speak to him and he suspected did not speak English anyway. When he had tried French, they just ignored him. But where was Kate? Why had she arranged to meet and then jilted him? Was she all right? Or was the prospect of seeing him after such a while - and when so much had happened to both of them - suddenly too much for her? Then he wondered if Guifford had put her up to it to get him to Brussels so he could kidnap him – or even kill him? His blood ran cold... the slush funds, the connection to 'The 48%'... It was possible. Or was it just that the reported assassination of Guifford made Kate believe he might be involved – so she would not dare answer him? It was so unlike her just to ignore him, though.

They soon arrived at the main police station and he was bundled into a small, airless room with tiny windows, two chairs and a table with recording equipment on it. A moment or two later, a sweaty, balding and somewhat unfit-looking man walked in with a new file in his hand already showing signs of greasy thumbprints. "My name is Detective-Inspector Louis Bejart," he announced, as he started the recording and then deliberately spoke clearly into it. "Michael Owen Hope: you are charged with being complicit in the terrorist murder of EU Commissioner Guifford Neveu. Anything you say - "

"Yes, yes," Michael interrupted. "I know the spiel. Let's just get on with it."

The man continued: "If you want a lawyer, you can have one, but I think for now it would be better, as you say, to get on with things. If you want one later, that is no problem." Michael nodded: he wanted to get this finished, too. "Now, as you know, there was a terrorist bomb attack at Brussels Airport this afternoon and we know from your flight details and passport that you were in the building at the moment the bomb went off."

Michael was astonished. "I didn't even know Guifford Neveu had been killed until your policemen arrested me. Is this what all this is about? he asked.

"It is."

"But why on earth would I want to kill Guifford Neveu – apart from our completely different positions on democracy?"

"Exactly," he replied, "and perhaps his rumoured links to the '48%'?" He paused and looked intently at the incredulous Michael, then went on: "Although I suspect the main reason may be that you have only recently heard your wife was having an affair with him."

"I've known that for a long time. And anyway, I'm now quite reconciled to that – in fact, I've found someone else anyway, which was actually the main reason for my coming to Brussels - to tell her. And it was a terrorist bomb, I should imagine, wasn't it? Do you honestly think I was caught up in something like that? It's against every principle in my body."

"Or a good front," the detective said, almost sneeringly. Through the two-way mirror, Kate put her already wet handkerchief to her face and wept some more. But even she was unsure whether it was for the loss of her lover and all the promise it held, or the confirmation she had just heard and dreaded - that

Michael was now with someone else, too.

"But what motive would I have to kill him apart from that? This is ridiculous. Yes, I heard an explosion as I left the airport and feared it was a suicide bomb but I'm short of time and wanted to see my wife as soon as possible before I returned."

"I never said it was a suicide bomb."

"Oh, for goodness' sake... They usually are in those environments. The last one in Brussels was – it's not unusual."

"But you knew."

"No, I didn't. Of course I didn't."

"So why did your wife tell us you might have been involved?" At this, Michael was speechless. He could not believe his once-dear wife would ever do that, whatever the situation. Hell hath no fury, and all that, but it was she who started an affair first. Michael told the detective that.

"So jealousy could be even more of a motive, then?"

Michael realised he was getting nowhere with this man. "Look, if anyone should be angry it's me. I'm very fond of my wife - whatever she's done to me and however we've fallen out politically – but I'm as concerned as to where she is as you are. Remember, I came here to see *her*, and this stupid concoction that I had something to do with Neveu's death is bonkers."

"So you had no idea that he was on his way to England?" Michael shook his head. "Possibly to kill you...?" Michael's mouth fell open in amazement. In the observation room, even Kate burst out with a cry of disbelief and horror. "We managed to salvage his wallet and inside it were all your details - address, phone, and a list of likely places he might be able to attack you... and the contact details of three well-known hitmen. Useful, actually; Europol has been after one of them for years. Oh, and £20,000 euros in cash."

Michael just sat there motionless. Would someone he did not know seriously try to kill him just because this person disliked him for trying to overturn Britain's enforced membership of the EU? Did it really mean so much to Neveu and – possibly by definition, the European Union - that Restoration was on the cusp of reclaiming its country from an illegal invasion? Or was he, Michael, just a focus for all the bile that Britain's temerity to wish to leave the bloc had thrown up?

Bejart continued, his voice a little softer and more forgiving, now: "He was either very jealous or desperately wanted to ensure you were out of the way so he had no competition. Or, of course, the other thing - regarding Brexit and the Restoration movement, which we understand you are a leading light in." Then, with a completely different, almost normal tone, he said, "Anyway, to put your mind at rest, your wife's here. I'll go and get her." He turned at the door, saying, "And, no, she didn't say you were going to try to kill Neveu. That was my way of trying to shock you into a confession - if it had been true. And you quite obviously didn't, so you're free to go. Sorry for the tactics but we have to follow all leads. There are possible motives, as I've explained."

Suddenly, the chase down the M6 and the bullet

through the roof seemed to make sense: it must have been Neveu's first attempt at killing him. He could not tell Kate of his suspicions, though: he was certain she would have known nothing about it, even if it was his doing.

A moment later, Kate came in and threw her arms round him, still sobbing. Michael caressed her back as his face became flooded with her tears. "I'm so sorry this has happened to you," he said comfortingly.

"I didn't know you were having an affair, too," she sobbed. "And I don't blame you, either. I had a feeling you were, but that – and all this… in one horrible evening…"

After they left, they went back to her flat: it was too late to catch a flight and the airport was closed anyway. Forty-seven people had been killed but, of course, the main news story was that one of them was Guifford Neveu, European Commissioner.

In time, the terrorist would eventually be identified as an illegal immigrant from Syria who had been radicalised and crossed Europe with no checks at all after passing through the border into Hungary with countless others. He had benefited from Seidel's open-door refugee policy and had struck lucky by stumbling across one of the most perfect representations of all he hated and wanted to destroy: a European politician.

Chapter Thirty-Two

Terry Cash now rued his attempt at trying to bribe his way out of captivity. And with delayed remorse, he felt sorry for Emek and his family, too, whom he had so compromised. Poor man: Emek did not have any wealth or influence like he did but he had made him a pawn in the global game of politics, avarice and power. As for his colleagues, he felt bad about keeping the truth of Emek's demise from them: but he could not risk them chastising him. One MP had realised that the murdered man was obviously strung up there as a warning to them, but fortunately had not realised who it was nor made any connection.

They were now in a much smaller building with tiny windows and a huge surrounding wall over forty feet high. Nothing like the previous place: it was possibly a small barracks, but to them it was just another closed, concrete and even more claustrophobic prison. There were no facilities as there had been before, either, and the food was poor. As for the wine… well, there wasn't any. And worst of all, no television news feed: they were isolated and in the dark. Their captors were making them pay dearly for their bid at freedom.

*

In the aftermath of Guifford's death, Kate had received a surprise: he had made a will and left half his possessions to her - and half to a wife and daughter she never knew existed. He had obviously loved her and would have left his wife – or so she supposed. The people in the Commission had been kind to Kate and would allow her to stay in the grace-and-favour flat she had shared with him forever if she wanted to. She knew this was wrong in principle, as it was these freebies for the elites which had put so many people off the EU, but why look a gift-horse in the mouth? In her current state she was happy to accept the benefits, despite her conscience niggling her as she knew the money could be better spent trying to alleviate youth unemployment or reduce taxes to stimulate growth. Her Commission friends had also said that if she left the BBC she could have a job as the next Commissioner's assistant if she wanted it, and hoped she would. Yet deep down, she had already started to wonder whether the EU would last that much longer; it was, she could see, corrupt: the cracks could be seen everywhere. If she did accept a full-time job rather than the unofficial one she had enjoyed under Guifford then she would, if it collapsed, receive a huge pay-off – like all the others working there. That was the way it worked. Yet did she want to stay in a sinking ship? She had still not made up her mind.

The BBC gave her some time off to recover, and so she collected herself by looking around the cultural pleasures of Brussels for a few days, which she had not had time to do since she arrived and events had whisked her off her feet so irrevocably. She went to concerts and art galleries but was upset that so many beautiful 19th century terraces in the city had been blighted by poor planning, noting that this sort of visual violence would not have been allowed in London. She thought of Michael a lot and hoped he would be happy with Jemima: they seemed better suited to each other with their similar politics and, now she knew more about her from Michael, she rather warmed to her - despite the emotional complications.

She had to admit, though, that, deep down, she was miffed that her husband was with someone else: even though she had not a leg to stand on.

Chapter Thirty-Three

It was October 20th – the day before Restoration would take back control and re-open Parliament. It would also be the day that millions of people would start marching from all corners of the country – even many from Scotland and Northern Ireland – to ensure the Remainers acceded to the will of the people and gave them back their voice and their Parliament. The loyal British troops, whose numbers had been swelled further by many soldiers initially fearful of court-martial, were adding their voices and souls to the rest of the people daily. Penitent influential Remainers – the so-called 'elites' - had been outed and made to swear an oath of allegiance to the new regime; many judges, military chiefs, bankers, scientists, teachers, economists and other 'experts' who had come around to being 'in the wrong' – for whatever reasons – now proclaimed themselves as adherents and supporters of Restoration with the zeal of born-again Christians. The unyielding die-hards, however, had their details and locations logged and volunteers ensured that they could speak their minds if they wished to but would be barred from public duty after the takeover. It was harsh, but administered kindly – unlike under the invasion. Under Restoration, free speech and diversity of opinion would be encouraged, not proscribed. This was emphasised and proclaimed as being in direct contrast to what the previous administration had demanded, ideas which had spread like a plague across the nation, stifling innovation, discussion and innovative, free thought. The liberal elites had been the bedrock of this groupthink for too long, where every opinion had to comply with the prevailing 'correct' opinions, or one was finished for life.

Needless to say, this mindset still featured in Brussels.

As the day dawned, the spread of Restoration people across the country to drum up support for the re-taking of Parliament were inevitably nervous; there were departure points in the centres of towns and cities close to London, Manchester, Birmingham, Cardiff and Edinburgh, but most would descend on London by whatever means possible in a protest against those who had tried to suppress democracy in its own name. Yet acting Prime Minister James Gatting had been on television the night before in a haughty last-ditch attempt to deter people from travelling to London to retake and open Parliament. He used again his phrase that they would be exercising 'the tyranny of the majority' and the actions were 'unpatriotic'; he maintained that the action was also against the wishes of the state and the European Court of Justice, who had condemned it from Brussels. But this only encouraged even more to show their feelings; many had already started their journey on foot - as a reminder of the Jarrow crusaders – so his appeal had come too late anyway. Indeed, they had purposely decided to pass specifically through Remain strongholds such as Cambridge and Oxford which, even now, were still wedded to the idea of EU hegemony. Resistance from militant Remainers was still a big possibility, and clashes were deemed to be inevitable, so British Army loyalists were joined by supporters from right across the other armed services; those on naval manoeuvres had ignored any commanders who had ordered them to stay on their vessels if they were moored in British ports. The whole event was assuming the spirit of a benign anarchy, and the beautiful sunny day that blessed the country implied that the gods were sympathetic to this re-affirmation of Democracy. The people wanted their country back, with their own sovereign laws, their own controls on immigration and policies - and the right to elect their own Parliament. And they were determined to get it.

Chapter Thirty-Four

In Downing Street, an increasingly nervous James Gatting could see the writing on the wall and – observing the crowds amassing from an early hour outside Downing Street – he and his wife fled to Brussels on a German army helicopter, allowed to leave by special dispensation provided neither it – nor they - returned. To ensure this, it was escorted out of British airspace by two Royal Navy Chinooks.

As the capital filled up, the mass of people converging severally on Parliament Square were like tributaries forming solid rivers of humanity. Most were led by loyalist British Army men and women – just to reassure the people that their will would finally be implemented and to snuff out any trouble. A European Union flag on a building near Whitehall was wrenched from its horizontal post by a troupe of acrobats who stepped one upon the other to rip it down, accompanied by great cheers from the crowd. Nervous Remainers in pubs and offices kept their thoughts to themselves as the crowd moved resolutely, slowly past: they knew that, for once, it was best to keep their thoughts to themselves. As for the few Asian and South American tourists who had come to London to see the sights, they looked on helplessly. Many had travelled to Britain lured by the weak pound and the attractions of an invaded but resurgent nation, but had not expected to be caught up in such a spirited national event as this. There were few European tourists, but Americans and Commonwealth cousins had arrived in large numbers, perhaps with the idea of witnessing what would turn out to be a historic moment in the life of their Mother nation. The tide had turned fast, and they were now involved in the joy it promised.

*

There was a knock on the door and Studd entered. "God, I'm so bloody bored," he announced.

Cash nodded. "Me, too."

"Heard any news from England, by any chance? Any titbits to get happy or angry about?" Cash shook his head. "Then I'll just stay angry," he confided. "Mind you... My Russian's patchy but I may have heard something one of the suits was discussing - a rumour that there's a General Election in Britain sometime soon. May even be today. Who knows?" He shrugged his shoulders.

The effect of his words was like a power spike through Cash, who looked up and said, "Where did you hear that? Have you got someone telling you things they haven't told me?" The hint of annoyance was palpable – that someone here might know more than he did.

"No, as I said – I *may* have understood that there was... but I may have *mis*understood it, too," Studd replied, slightly miffed. He *had* been a Deputy Prime

Minister, so it was possible he might have been told something…

At that moment, Little came in. "Hi. Either of you know anything new?"

Cash replied, "Well, Studd thinks he may have heard the Russians talking about a British election any time now. If there is, we bloody well ought to be there." They all looked shocked, but agreed.

"Mind you, if that's the case, then once it's all over, I think we'll be released," opined Cash.

"What makes you suspect that?" asked Studd.

"Well, they haven't disposed of us yet," Cash observed, "and I think we're being held as hostages in case Rastov needs some leverage."

"Rastov… You still think it's him, do you?" Little blurted. "Why?"

"For the simple reason it wouldn't be the Latvians, Estonians, Timbuctooians or wherever we are who'd have the balls to kidnap us, that's why. We're big people in a big game. We're just not being allowed to play now until the time is right. My guess is that sometime soon the doors will just be opened and we'll get turned out into the street, with strict instructions to say nothing to anyone - or else. You know how they work. I'd agree now and say nothing – I want to have a happy retirement, not be poisoned by polonium or shot."

The others looked at him almost pityingly. "Well, I won't compromise my principles," said Little eventually. "They'd have to shoot me to shut me up."

Cash was indicating the ceiling as Little said this,

intimating the almost certain probability that every word was being recorded and listened to. "Then you will be," he said without feeling: "I have to say that I just can't be bothered any more – I only want to go home."

Little looked somewhat abashed and slunk out of the room. Studd just looked at Cash and, giving him a withering look, walked out.

*

A podium had been erected on St Stephen's Green opposite the Houses of Parliament, festooned with Union Jacks and various posters and slogans representing those factions which had inspired and energised the votes of those who had wished sovereignty be returned to Britain – Leave.EU, Vote Leave, Grassroots Out, UKIP, Economists For Britain, Business for Britain and many, many more. At 12 o'clock, a bevy of Leave-supporting MPs made their way through the throng on the way to the podium. The acclaim was deafening, with whistling, cheering and shouting: it was Independence Day, and it was going to be remembered. The MPs were joined by industrialists, economists and even one or two media personalities who had either previously been too afraid to reveal their views or had realised they needed now to be seen as supporters for their professional futures. The television news crews and reporters had been especially picked to show the gathering in its best light – a tactic usually deployed by media in reverse when trying to bend viewers' minds to the 'stupidity' of the Leave cause. This time, it would be different. Then Michael, Jemima, Borya, Lafargue, Griselda and other leading lights of the campaign made their way through the crowd to huge applause – led by the incumbent and previously deposed Prime Minister, Tessa Lewis. They stood together on the podium, surrounded by Services personnel – not just around them on the ground but also on rooftops and in windows. Lewis stood up to speak to a massive cheer, which cascaded down myriad streets in disparate waves as people watching on their phones saw her appear. Then the crowd fell silent in an expectant hush.

"My Friends," she started, which drew another huge cheer – but she waved a hand to quieten them. "Today really IS our Independence Day!" The crowd erupted. "It's also Trafalgar Day, a historic day in our nation's history when Lord Nelson," and she waved a hand in the direction of his column in nearby Trafalgar Square, "defeated European forces at the Battle of Trafalgar in 1805. Today, on that anniversary, we are celebrating the defeat of an assault on our democracy. We voted to leave the European Union and yet – helped by those people who felt they were too important or powerful to accept the democratic result," ("Shame, shame!"), "we were invaded by our supposed friends and allies for the first time since 1066. And yet here we are, about to take back our sovereign Parliament from those who would wrest it from us. Perhaps I was too naïve in not triggering Article 50 the moment I came to power, and it would have been easier if my predecessor had included in the Referendum wording that the outcome was irrefutable and enshrined as a full Act of Parliament. Yet he did not, and what we have seen over the past few months has been the result. And yet you, the wonderful British people, would not lie down and take it, and our loyal members of the armed forces have been particularly amazing by listening to the voice of democracy rather than the dictates of those in our land who believe it is only legitimate if it's what they themselves believe in. But the British spirit has prevailed once more! In a few minutes, I will walk into the Palace of Westminster behind me and – for the first time in many long weeks – take my place at the despatch box. All other elected MPs will be joining me there as if nothing had happened. However, some of those who did – and still would - resist the will of the people have decided not to join us there, and so I will be announcing in the chamber a Bill to call a General Election. But this will take place within three weeks as we cannot go on without a democratically-elected Parliament for any longer. I therefore ask you all to vote for us or any prospective MP who will vote to leave the EU immediately, with all the trade deals we were implementing before this annoying 'interruption' to our history."

Laughter stopped her for a few moments, then she continued: "As some continental newspapers have tried to pour scorn on our endeavours and called us 'Little Britain', I say 'Get ready for *Great* Britain' once more! We are not Little Englanders but Big Englanders – and Big Welsh, Big Northern Irish and, Big Scots, too. And with the vote you will now soon have, you can proclaim that you also want to be a United Kingdom once again. Then we can ensure that we build on our four nations' combined strengths and friendships; with what has recently happened in mind you can make that point forcefully across our newly-united group of nations. And now, after a few words from our supporters behind me, I am going to cross that road and open Parliament again!" The applause was deafening and, again, the waves of clapping and unmitigated joy swept in torrents up the streets, across the capital and out into the countryside and cities beyond.

Chapter Thirty-Five

Kate, watching in the BBC newsroom in Brussels, found – despite herself - a surge of pride. 'Freedom of movement' for a start, should never have meant the invasion of another state. There was no doubt in her mind now that if the European Union was to continue, it would have to reform from the ground up. She would support that... although witnessing the abject gloom around her from assembled colleagues, she wondered if they would ever countenance it for fear of getting something worse. Then Michael came onto the screen and she had to listen again, her 'heretical' thoughts – in this media environment and city, at least – being brought back into sharp focus. How happy he looked! And behind him was Jemima Grice. It was the first time she had seen her in close-up or knowing exactly who she was and she looked nice, Kate thought. Michael's poise and performance, supplemented by frequent looks and smiles to the lady, made her realise that they were deeply in love. Far more than he had ever been in love with her, perhaps - although theirs had been motivated by expectation, not empathy. Michael and Jemima's mutual adulation, she could see, was spontaneous, honest and real. As he spoke, she thought of Guifford; would she really have been happy with him? She would never know, now. She had been asked out by two other MEPs over the short time he had been gone, yet he was not even buried yet: how like this elitist class, quickly glossing over her emotions for the sake of satisfying theirs! Did they have no soul? Or was it just the perpetuation of the machine and its outward appearances that were most important in this bureaucratic, administrative city?

Michael was now finishing his speech and it was obvious he was popular – far more so than Guifford had been; Guifford had respect because of his position and resolute support for the institution that was the EU – but was he loved, except by her? Michael had the crowd in the palm of his hand, and he was obviously enjoying it. A huge cheer from the television indicated that the true Prime Minister was about to open Parliament again, and the poor cameraman was desperately trying to keep up with her as they approached the entrance. Then, she disappeared into its voluminous halls and the cameraman was left outside, barred by a policeman and soldiers. Soldiers. Some things would take a few months to change.

In all this, it was quietly made known that the Queen would also attend Parliament as an observer, to see the will of the people enacted; she was careful not to show any bias, but her radiance betrayed her innermost feelings. And she was aware that she was the first reigning monarch to have suffered an invasion of her country since 1066 – and it clearly rankled.

Some hours later, all that the Prime Minister had

announced outside the House had been delivered inside it, and the election was called. Very few had dared to obstruct the Bill to dissolve Parliament as the feeling outside for them to do so was palpable and intense; the MPs were surrounded by a populace which wanted sovereignty back, and running the gauntlet of a resolute crowd which would have known of any MP who had voted against that was not an option many relished. As the Liberal Democrat leadership was still incarcerated somewhere in Latvia with Cash, there were only four of their MPs left in the Commons, so the vote was even more emphatic. There were seventy-six abstentions to the vote and only twenty-one against: also one Conservative who was retiring anyway, and twenty Scottish Nationalists. On leaving the House as a group after the vote, the deniers were grateful for police and army protection as they were loudly booed and abused. However, when the crowd heard that the election had been called for three weeks' time, the feeling was one of thankfulness and satisfaction: the occupation was over.

The statement delivered, most started to return to their towns, cities and villages around the country. The mood of those who had travelled to ensure that they were there on Independence Day was euphoric, especially as their presence had emphatically made it clear to any Remain-supporting MPs that they would not be voted for in areas of high Leave support.

*

It was true that some EU nationals who had previously worked in Britain had decided to leave – especially Italian and French; yet, rather than using Brexit as an excuse, they now had their own sovereign countries to return to, which were both now doing well - with global trade deals secured in weeks rather than the customary years. British nationals in France and Italy were allowed to stay: it was important for their economies as so many British lived and worked there. Spain, although still a member of the EU, had quickly agreed the same deal, much to the fury of the EU elites who threatened them with expulsion: but they were hobbled, and the Spanish knew it – and also that British expatriates brought much-needed cash into their still-beleaguered economy, still suffering with almost 50% youth unemployment.

Tessa Lewis had also – in direct defiance of EU dictates – secretly started discussing global trade deals with the United States and Canada, India, Switzerland, Singapore, South Korea, Australia, New Zealand, China and many more: the desire for this was astonishing. Yet they had to swear their potential partners to silence as, although officially against EU rules, Restoration had secretly been working on this outcome for a long time, knowing that the EU had no competence over Britain's post-Brexit trade policies. It had been the biggest and best-kept secret since long before the election as they had estimated the EU would challenge it, if not out of legality, then of pique. Yet if they *had* known about it, the EU also realised the feelings their abortive invasion had caused, and that the more they castigated Britain, the more likely it would be that others might join in their desire to leave. Indeed, the Czech Republic mooted a separate trade deal with Britain because its prime minister knew any deal with the EU would take years. He wanted continued trade with Britain *and* the rest of the world - without any interruptions or delays.

Underlining the growing feeling of resentment towards the European Union and its increasing powerlessness, Poland and Hungary took the brave step, too, of defying EU law and made overtures to Britain about reciprocal trade between the two countries. Realising that they could get better tariffs, cheaper deals and faster co-operation outside the EU, they also discussed a bespoke deal to allow selective immigration between them and Britain, the second-biggest pre-Leave stumbling block after sovereignty. With Britain now actively helping developing nations which were not shut out of the EU Customs Union, Britain's food bills had plummeted – which also had the benefit of helping these nations develop and thrive: Poland and Hungary were keen to expand this mutually beneficial development. It would become of huge importance to all their economies, as British expertise in medicine, aero-technology and life sciences were areas in which Poland needed help to expand, as did the Czech Republic.

The irony of these developments was not lost on Trausch and, like so many of the elites, it had been their sense of innate superiority and hubris which had motivated them to try and deter the Czech Republic, Poland and Hungary from leaving – and to help quell Britain again. They knew it was desperation, but this was why he and his five Presidents were in deep discussion on the plane as it headed to Warsaw, then Prague and Budapest; as they flew, they decided to give these countries almost anything they wanted if it made them reconsider. Yet it was not lost on them that their plan to punish Britain for leaving – and the subsequent abortive invasion – had changed the public mood towards the EU forever. And so this last-ditch attempt to stop history would probably be abortive, too. And they were still unaware of what had befallen Guifford Neveu, too.

But their feeling of helpless indignation and anger would not be enough to arrest what would happen next ...

*

Amidst the collapse of support for the crumbling bloc, Ireland, too, had finally decided to leave the EU: whilst many still supported the ideal, a sense of realism – and the promise of more investment from America and trade with Britain than the country had ever had with the EU – had ensured their exit. It was telling that the EU was now powerless to stop them: the Taoiseach just announced they were leaving without invoking Article 50. They just left, and stopped paying into the EU immediately without 'divorce' payments or demur – except for angry words from the fragmented economic wilderness that the EU had now become.

*

Michael and Jemima were assessing what had been achieved. They needed to catch up – events had happened at an unprecedented speed. In the media, the news was open and unquestioning, the battle for Britain seemingly won for a generation. The election campaign was already going well and Michael and Leslie Caxton could hardly keep up with the avalanche of requests for trade deals with Britain from around the world. Indeed, they had been covertly pushing hard for them even when they were 'in exile' - and more so since the departure of EU forces. This had meant the enlarging of the Department for International Trade, and they were frequently having to jet all over the world: the number of slightly embarrassed enquiries from former EU countries were the ones they liked most, as it confirmed what they had always suspected – that the EU would miss Britain rather than the other way around.

This higher profile engendered more media exposure for Michael, who was now, with Borya, the go-to person for interviews wherever possible. To his concern, he was now being labelled as a future Prime Minister, which was something he played down as much as he could – he would brook no speculation. He just wished to make a success of the job he was in. And to see Britain globally successful again as a trading and manufacturing nation, as it had been in its 19th century heyday.

His relationship with Jemima was becoming ever better and stronger, and they began to be known as 'a golden couple'. Yet there was no sarcasm or hostility to them – they were universally described by that elusive yet cosy epithet, a dual 'national treasure'. They were often interviewed together if it was a 'sofa' discussion, and their joint views and happy demeanour were a welcome distraction to the daily grind of intense politics.

In Brussels, Kate often caught the interviews and felt a begrudging pride tinged with remorse: what a pity she and Michael had never actually shared that innate and spontaneous rapport – even if they thought they had possessed it at the beginning. She was aware that her situation without Guifford was probably making her feel more lonely and vulnerable, but that would change in time when she met someone else. At least, she hoped so.

Chapter Thirty-Six

In Germany, James Gatting looked out over the city of Berlin, the new Reichstag in the distance looming out of a grey, misty morning. Everything seemed so normal here, so ordered; yet viewing it from his sumptuous, eighth-storey flat, he was wracked with anger, despair and disbelief. Only a few days ago he had been Prime Minister again, yet his tenure was now over and Tessa Lewis would be sitting in his office at that precise moment, countermanding all the laws he had been preparing and those he had already enacted. Julia Reeve would be back in there, too, and she knew all the people he trusted and had worked with: they would have been fired by now, which was a pity, as many were in the media posing as Leavers but actually sympathetic to Remain, who would now be exposed.

The Single Market would now not be any more, although it was fragmenting anyway: an increasing number of countries – even within the EU - were now talking of creating their own deals with Britain and the world, almost as if the European Union had never existed. This distressed him: he had met some highly intelligent, cultured people in Europe and would miss their sense of shared sovereignty, even if he was secretly all too aware that the uncontrolled influx of people from other lands had driven a wedge through the consciousness of his once-beloved England. Perhaps if he had not opted out of the Schengen Agreement in 1993 it would have been a different story, with so many more immigrants there now that a coup would have been both impossible and unnecessary. It made him wonder where Cash was, and whether the man was safe. Was this all, essentially, his recent colleague's fault, allowing virtually unfettered immigration to Britain without any safety clauses or time-delays? He was unsure. That issue's roots were mired in the mists of time: the British were a mongrel race, yet they had assumed a common dignity, stoicism and perception which was priceless. But then, that was the point: they were a proud race who cherished their history and traditions which, even he had to admit, had been compromised and eroded. He realised he was already starting to miss the British sense of humour and tolerance for diverse thought, fused with the ability to disagree openly and yet stay friends: perhaps his 'cabinet bastards' had been more prescient than him and he should have been 'less European'. Whatever the reasons, though, he was missing Britain greatly ... Well, it was all too late now.

On the bright side, Germany was clean, functional and efficient – but it lacked warmth, he felt, and the dirigiste nature of its hierarchy was in stark contrast to the more open and discursive characteristics of the British. The people just obeyed, without question. No cricket here, either, that wonderful, open leveller... With a sudden flash of clarity, like a lightning-bolt illuminating an unseen intruder, he wondered whether he was now the old guard, a dinosaur - and that the re-birth of globally-integrated nation-states was indeed, perhaps, the way forward. He sighed: he was out of touch. But he would never admit it to anyone. Not even his dear wife sleeping next door. With a huge sigh, he poured himself a drink and wondered whether his return into front-line politics for the kind of government he had striven for had been futile; he was out of his time and perhaps Julia Reeve, quoting his line back at him, had been right: he had become a historic mistake.

*

In Latvia, Cash was wondering how Gatting was getting on and what was happening. Since their removal from the first prison they had now been forfeited any news or communication and the only people they came into contact with were guards or soldiers, none of whom spoke English. Or the other language he spoke, French. Or Spanish, which Studd spoke. There was nothing they could do. Their enforced removal from Britain had made them permanently angry, although due to this enforced situation, in Cash's more thoughtful moments he was beginning to better understand how other people lived. Perhaps he had not helped them enough as he chased personal wealth and domination... But then his inner sense of pride kicked in and his indignation intensified — he was a chosen one, a Messiah, and he shouted at the guards when they brought him his meals. To no avail. He was an international prisoner and no-one except the occupying government here knew where he and Studd, Smithers, Little and the rest of his entourage were. Perhaps even the Latvians did not know. Or were they, perhaps, now in Estonia? With no EU borders, it was difficult to know where they had ended up. This suited the Russian occupiers, of course, because they could easily invade borders without frontiers. And did. They were exploiting it well.

The door was unexpectedly opened and a diplomat he had not met before brought him a piece of paper. On it was some news, written in good English and which came straight to the point. The Restoration government had taken power in Britain and elections were imminent. Once these were over, the secret terms of a tacit agreement between Russia and America would be imposed. As Rastov and the Russians now had such a good rapport with the new American President, Cash and his colleagues would be returned to England. And the Russians – with no substantial European force against them - would melt back into the Motherland as if nothing had ever happened. A new NATO/Russia non-aggression pact would see to that.

Cash digested this with horror. An agreement between Gold and Rastov? A benign takeover of the Baltic states now reversed, and a NATO/Russia non-aggression pact? That was more than even he had ever managed. He could not go back to England now – he would be lynched. He hoped that his wife, Coralie, had gone already, although stark questions kept coming back to him: what of all his properties there? Would he ever be allowed to sell them? Had she sold them already? Where could they go, and with how much of his fortune? And, most importantly, if he could sell them, would he be able to repatriate the proceeds to somewhere else without penalty? Or had they been requisitioned, as had happened to those deemed as traitors in the past? Restoration! It sounded like a huge leap backwards in time to him. He had never understood the lure and resonance of history in Britain: it had happened, so what was the point in re-visiting it all the time when it all took place so long ago? What did it matter? Did history really have the capacity to repeat itself? Of course not – the parameters and influences were always different. Then the thought struck him: was that not what he was now trying to do, returning Britain to a model which the people had rejected, and was, indeed, now history? His indignation swelled up, but the fact he had even questioned himself astonished him.

Chapter Thirty-Seven

Tessa Lewis was, indeed, doing just what James Gatting had feared. With a phrase borrowed from the new American President, she was attacking legislation from 'Day One'. The sense of doing what the country's majority wanted was a liberating and inspiring tonic, and she felt invigorated. She felt like Cash must have done in 1997 when he swept to power with such a huge majority. It was heady stuff. Yet look how that all turned out, she warned herself: humility had been trampled under the yoke of becoming a supplicant nation and hubris took over from rational debate. She would not allow that to happen to her.

Julia Reeve came in and gave her yet another file to look at. "As it's PMQ's tomorrow," she said, "this is what we think will come up: the by-elections you instigated to replace the MP's whose constituencies were represented by those who aren't here any more," and a smile crossed her face, "when we thought the elections would take longer to call, is a prime expectation. As you say, the general election will sort out that anomaly anyway, but someone's still bound to raise it. The date has been confirmed – November

10th. It seems that most of the government controls to implement it are still in position, which is good: perhaps the rogue government hadn't got around to meddling with election processes as they weren't planning to use them anytime soon."

"Especially if the EU had gone the way of China or Russia," Tessa Lewis added with a similar smile to Julia's.

"I thought they already had!" Julia quipped back. They both laughed. "Anyway, we're firing on all cylinders and ready to go."

"Excellent – well done," replied the Prime Minister. "Now we're not in that monster any more, Leslie Caxton, Michael and I have been in direct touch with any countries we'd started setting up trade deals with which haven't rushed to us like most others have. So I'd like a huge trade meeting, here in London, a week or so before the election, which will underline people's realisation that Britain is open for global business. Let Borya know about this fast, will you? I know he's in America but he'll need to apply his usual jovial imprimatur onto the facts so the people know we're all in this together."

"Yes, Prime Minister. And what's our policy on the Americans? Their ambassador wants to know if you want them to stay until after the election, in case there's another invasion or coup."

"Yes, I think we ask them to stay discreetly here until after it," she replied. "For, whilst I don't think even the most militant Remainers can do anything now, some of the Forces Chiefs may have another go, so best to keep them here, I think. The good thing is that we now have history on our side, as well as just about everything else. The Americans have been wonderful – quietly supporting us without anyone really noticing them. More than can be said for the other lot. Anyway, you organised a call with President Gold later this morning, didn't you?" Julia nodded. "Good. I'll tell him to get his delegates fired up for the trade meeting – and we want to hear of no protectionist instincts. I think us Brits may just be on the cusp of liberating world trade again."

"The Germans won't like it," Julia smiled.

"And?" the Prime Minister beamed back. "Actually, make sure that Italy, France, Ireland and the Visegrad states are offered high-profile invitations, too. And, as the Russians are tacitly helping us – thanks to the influence of our American friends, of course - it may be a good idea to invite them and the Baltic States, too, as well as the usual: China, India, Commonwealth countries, of course… Anyway, we'll discuss it all in Cabinet later. If you could just get the ball rolling…"

"Of course, Prime Minister," and Julia left. When she had gone, Tessa Lewis wondered when – if ever - they should all let the world know that the Russians, under their secret deal with the Americans, were indeed holding the arch-Remainers in Latvia and that it was a covert deal to help Presidents Gold and Rastov. It was dependent on the latter keeping his side of the bargain and actually withdrawing from the Baltic States, of course, something he would instinctively not like doing, especially with his adventures in Crimea and Ukraine. Yet, to leave would be good news for both of them. The

NATO/Russia non-aggression pact was a huge milestone, although how often it was stretched would be interesting. She decided that it would be best to let things be for now; after the general election would be a better time – then, when Cash and his cronies were released, it would be too late for them to make any difference anyway. No, she would have to ensure that the world would never know she had known about the plot to remove them. Complicit, even. Behind the smiles, politics was a dirty game.

*

As Trausch's airliner was about to commence its descent into Prague, there was suddenly a bump, as if the jet had hit something in mid-air; for an instant, there was a moment for them all to register fear: then, a moment later, a blinding flash of white light and smoke engulfed the aircraft, the noise of the explosion being left miles behind as it fragmented into thousands of pieces and plummeted to the earth. Fortunately, it had taken place over a remote and sparsely inhabited area, so only one tiny village was affected. Yet the debris was in such tiny pieces as to indicate the intensity of the explosion: no-one was hurt badly or killed on the ground, but everyone on the aircraft had inevitably perished.

Later, when the news went global, nobody could understand why the aeroplane had suddenly disintegrated: it was only when, a day later, that the flight recorder was unexpectedly recovered intact from a forest north of Kosewko, that theories began to excite imaginations. Some said they had seen a trail of fire in the sky before the explosion, which would have indicated a missile; yet no-one claimed responsibility. Isil was in retreat due to the determination of the new American President and Russian President Rastov... As such, it looked increasingly as if the only country to benefit might be the latter's, and it was likely that the missile – if it was such – had been fired from Belarus, which had once been part of the Soviet empire. And Rastov was known to want to have it completely back under his control... No-one accused him, for fear of jeopardising the tacit agreement: but his swift and uncompromising denial spoke volumes.

*

In Brussels, Kate was being entertained by people with whom she had been unofficially working when with Guifford. They had just scattered his ashes in a forest in Bavaria, and she had seen his wife for the first time. Although she seemed pleasant enough to others, she obviously knew who Kate was and the frost was palpable - after one glance at Kate she had looked away; Kate did not blame her and had done her best to stay a discreet distance apart as the final service was performed. She wondered now whether any that might dislike her would expose her and try to get her out. That would be ironic: the BBC knew of their relationship and had turned a blind eye because it had helped them. Yet with the changing mood and circumstances at home and here in Brussels, one never could foretell which way the wind would blow. BBC journalistic teams had received instructions from the incoming news boss, who had obviously been told by the putative new government to show a more balanced line; yet for dyed-in-the-wool journos who only knew how to finish what might have appeared a reasonably balanced item with a hint of questioning distrust, it was proving difficult. She realised it herself. And she found she was stuck between a newly-balanced BBC and a smug and bullying institution which could not accept any criticism at all. Yet she was part of both.

She knew deep down, too, that the whole confection would collapse eventually; only a day ago there had even been huge co-ordinated riots across Greece and Spain, with so-called 'populist' parties in the ascendant. And a new wave of sexual attacks on women in German cities had been reported by a media previously told not to do so for fear of making race relations worse - and giving more ammunition to the AfD party, which wanted to stop immigration completely. People had also witnessed what had happened in France: after the usual burning of cars and rioting, even the French Left had fallen in behind Laporte's edicts and any Muslim wishing to leave the country was given a bountiful financial package to do so – provided they went to their mother countries and never came back. Thousands had taken the money and returned to find their countries more peaceful, which had happened when the new American President's promise to crush Isil had been supported by Laporte and their countries of origin: most were now enjoying an unusual state of uneasy calm. Throughout France, tensions were easing and the vacating of accommodation had resulted in a dramatic lowering of property prices; because there was less benefits support coming out of the public coffers, too, there was more money for the new government to spend on social programmes that would benefit the native French. Needless to say, this had proved popular and was being espoused by the AfD in Germany, too.

Italy had changed, as well: liberated from EU diktats, its economy was continuing to soar and the resulting money from an expanding economy had allowed the government to invest more in border control. Around its coastline and land borders with former EU countries, migrants had been stopped wherever they arrived and were sent back; if the booming economy needed migrants, they had to come in officially, but this would not happen any time soon with Italy still having 41% youth unemployment to conquer. Yet its new ability to dramatically drive down unemployment without any interference from Brussels had also been well noted by populist parties. As for the Visegrad countries, they had more or less decided, after Trausch's demise, to go it alone together as a kind of union within the union – which had already proved beneficial. Previous inward investment from Europe – made possible by subsidies for factories which the EU had closed in areas such as Wales, Scotland and Portugal - had been wisely used. That the money was not forthcoming any more was of little matter to them now: Lewis had enticed them with special terms which would ensure good trade with Britain after the election, and the response had been mutual, warm and positive. As for Bulgaria and Romania, they did not know who to side with, and continued in a state of studied indifference.

Essentially, the European Union was but a shadow of its former pomp. Brexit – and then the election of a populist American President, followed by the new French revolution and the earlier secession of Italy -

had seen other nations question the European Dream of 'ever-closer union'. Through dogma, bullying, high tariffs, a patronising lack of democracy, corruption, unaccountability and unrealistic goals – compounded by the disaster that was the euro pushing people into austerity and poverty - Europe had created the perfect storm to defeat itself. And it was unravelling fast.

PART THREE

AFTERMATH

Chapter Thirty-Eight

It was the day of Britain's General Election. The polls had put Tessa Lewis's government out of sight, yet she knew how wrong they could be, and only admitted to a sense of 'cautious optimism'. For Labour, the omens were dire: an ineffectual, confused and hard-Left leader, a squabbling front bench who could agree on nothing, constituencies which had previously voted half Remain and half Leave, MPs who were mainly for thwarting Brexit but who would not reflect their constituents' wishes… these were all causing a predicted collapse of the party's vote. In many more affluent areas, the Lib-Dems were expected to pick up Labour seats where the voters preferred Remain; yet in those areas where Labour had been strong before due to working-class solidarity and middle-class inverted snobbery, they appeared to be in trouble. In those areas, UKIP seemed to be in the ascendant.

The fall-out from Trausch's apparent assassination

had produced conflicting arguments with what was left of the EU: although America and Britain kept a discreet silence on the matter, the global and European press were increasingly adamant that the plane had been shot down by a Russian missile fired from Belarus. For the few that knew the truth of the American/Russian agreement, they were worrying times, as each wanted Rastov onside to fulfil his promise. Rastov vehemently denied any accusation, which had caused diplomatic incidents: he privately knew President Gold and Tessa Lewis had not rocked the boat but publicly had to pretend that they too were part of the chorus of accusation. Any more, and there would be no deal on leaving the Baltic states. Or releasing a certain coterie of British politicians. As this would have had the effect of causing a crisis around the election and implied complicity, the interested parties did all they could to pacify those pressing for further Russian sanctions. The accusations abruptly ceased. Rastov had appeared to get away with it once again, whatever the truth of the matter.

As for Cash and his colleagues, the world was still in the dark as to where they were; indeed, with the magnitude of other events going on in Europe, Britain and America, the topic was seldom raised. There were occasional supposed reported sightings, but these carried little credence as the man would never have avoided the limelight voluntarily. As for him, the fury with himself for allowing his self-importance to believe he could escape from the prison by bribing his factotum was constant and uncharacteristic: if he had not done so, they would still be in that much more pleasant place and might have been released by now. He might even be

President of Europe, too.

*

It was mid-afternoon and the exit poll predictions were looking correct, for once: it generally seemed that those constituencies who had voted Leave before the judicial shenanigans and then the EU invasion were voting for the Conservatives or for UKIP, and those with a predominant Remain catchment were voting either Labour or Lib Dem. This was good news for those wishing to give anyone trying to thwart Brexit a bloody nose, for 450 constituencies had voted Leave, whatever each MP's thoughts; and Remain-leaning constituencies only amounted to 150. If the figures were borne out, then Lewis would have a majority of almost dictatorial proportions.

As it happened, it was looking as if she would win around 390 seats, UKIP 75, the Lib Dems 30 and Labour just 62, with the SNP losing 40 seats. A few independents and the DUP were predicted to make up the rest.

In his constituency, Michael was surfing that wave and, like the others in his party, was becoming more certain by the moment that a historic momentum was being turned into an extraordinary mandate – a clear rebuttal of those who had tried to deny the sovereign will of the people. He was receiving frequent updates from Jemima, who was also on course to expand her majority, and he felt elated, proud and excited. In contrast, the hastily-appointed new President of the European Commission, Klaus Behrens, was sitting alone in his Brussels office. He was aware of several camera crews awaiting him outside but adamantly refused to go and talk to them. Amongst them, Kate was listening on talkback to the BBC response in London, which was one of shock and despair. The pundits in the studio were visibly horrified at the result, unlike most people around the country who now knew beyond doubt that there was zero chance of their being taken back into a united Europe. In Paris, Marine Laporte was hailing the result as a great leap forward for the British people; in America, President Gold was ecstatic – and when Nick Lafargue won his seat in Clacton, he was immediately chosen by the President to be his British spokesperson and confidante. In Russia, Rastov told one of his aides to start the process of releasing the hostages as part of his pre-arranged plan. Across the Commonwealth, there were scenes of acute joy – no more so than in Canada, India, Australia and New Zealand, who could now look forward to huge trade deals with Britain and a restoration of those Commonwealth ties so brutally and rudely severed when Britain first joined the European Union in 1973.

Only those in the rump of the EU were despairing and angry: for now their dream of ever-closer union was completely shattered.

In the run-up to the election, Tessa Lewis had proclaimed that, if she won a majority, the process for choosing judges would be changed to the American system. No more would legal technicalities be used to thwart the will of the people – whatever the legal and historical precedents: democracy was democracy, and it would never again be allowed to be blocked by skilful re-interpretations of Acts of Parliament, as the Referendum result had been. She had also made it clear that Britain would never again be subject to the European Court of Justice, which had so stymied many of Britain's laws on statute since 1215. It appeared that the Restoration agenda was about to be implemented.

Chapter Thirty-Nine

When the polls finally closed, the government majority was almost exactly as predicted, and Tessa Lewis was supremely prepared for it. Aware of not being ready to implement Brexit immediately after the Referendum, she had ensured that intended legislation was ready to immediately enact; and when the House of Lords threatened to vote against the proceedings – as she knew the over-representation of Remain-supporting members and others in the chamber would do - she revealed a surprise Bill. The Lords, she said, would be reduced to a maximum of six hundred: also, that they would still be appointed – not elected - as they had been in times past. But the make-up would be a percentage of a party's seats in the House of Commons. In one stroke, she would ensure that over-representation of one party in the Lords could not wreck Bills; it also meant that Hereditary Peers would not be replaced when they retired. It would assume a huge importance for truly representative democracy in the decades to come.

At around the same time, the Queen let it be known that there would be a national holiday from that day forth on June 23rd, which had been agreed with Tessa Lewis before the election, should she prevail with a large enough majority to implement it. It was a masterstroke – and the sovereign would announce it in due course at the State Opening of Parliament.

*

Cash, Smithers, Studd and the others were being told by some gruff Russian security men to don coats and warm clothing for a journey. Their questions as to where they were going remained unanswered, yet the fact that they were accompanied by a dozen soldiers was not without its menace. They were put into a large windowless van with hard slatted seats down the insides and told to get in, their protests being ignored.

"Now I know what it's like being an illegal immigrant," Studd observed, as the door clanged shut and was locked from the outside.

"But we haven't paid for this," said Smithers with a sardonic attempt at a joke.

"Perhaps we shall," Cash summed up, and silence descended on them all as the engine started and they moved off; then they heard the huge iron gates of their prison opening and they were bumping down what seemed like narrow side streets. After a while, the different resonances told them they were in open country and the roads became bumpier still.

"Where the hell are they taking us now?" posited Cash.

"Siberia, probably," Smithers replied flatly.

After several hours of travelling, cold, bruised

from the movements of the spartan van and wondering what they would see when they got out, the van suddenly stopped. They heard the two front doors of their van open, people getting out, and the doors being slammed shut. Then a car started up a few feet away, there were some shouts and laughs which had a metallic ring in their small vehicle, and they heard four doors clumped closed. Then the car drove off. After it had left, there was an oppressive and claustrophobic silence. No-one spoke: no-one dared to presume where they were or what they might see – nor did they feel confident enough to want to.

"They're not just going to leave us here, are they?" said Studd, a tremor of fear in his voice augmented by the cold.

"Let's wait a moment," suggested Cash. They did. Then one of the assistants stood up and went to the door. Gingerly and as quietly as possible, he pressed down on the handle. It opened, a tiny breeze of cold, fresh air blowing into the space. "It wasn't locked," he proclaimed with surprise. "But I heard them do it." The others all leaned forward to peer through the crack. What they saw surprised them.

*

Michael was with Tessa Lewis in her Downing Street office. She had congratulated him on his organisational work which had helped so much to smooth the stunning election result, and she also praised his articles and television appearances which, she was sure, had resulted in thousands more votes across the country. She was also impressed by the fact that his sorties to Scotland, underlining that the country sold more goods to the rest of Britain than the entire EU put together, had made those wishing to stay in the United Kingdom there less fearful of the SNP's determined and vocal propaganda. Indeed, SNP numbers had dropped from 56 to just 16, and the other Scottish seats were now split between the Conservatives and UKIP. The Scottish leader had just held on to her seat, but despite her shrieking protestations, there would be no chance of a second independence referendum now. So pleased was Lewis with Michael that she offered him promotion as Under-Secretary of State for International Trade, which would help Leslie Caxton enormously. Michael was honoured and accepted on the spot. Outside the office, Leslie was waiting for him and congratulated him warmly – then informed him that they were off to Brussels that evening for a trade fair appearance. "Talk about going into the lions' den," he quipped. Yet the truth was that, whatever was left of the EU, it now needed Britain much more than Britain needed it. As Michael already knew, within days, trade deals between Commonwealth countries, the ASEAN states, the USA, China, Japan and India would be announced. With such a huge mandate, the conclusion of these deals as soon as possible for the benefit of the country and global trade was an imperative. And Michael was going to be even more instrumental in helping Leslie Caxton deliver them.

Michael instantly told Jemima his news, and they decided to celebrate by going for a brief but good lunch before he departed with Leslie for Brussels. Over the main course, she suddenly looked at him and enquired: "Have you told Kate your news, yet?" For a second he was stumped by the question, coming out of the blue like this, and he struggled for an answer for two reasons: the first was that they had never talked about Kate before, except in the vaguest of terms; secondly, because he realised he had not given her a thought for the past few days.

"Er, no, I haven't, actually. Why do you ask?"

"Just wondered."

"Hmm." He paused, then: "Look, darling, I'm not with her any more. I'm with you. But I don't want to see her anyway. She left me. I'm sorry she hasn't got Guifford any more, because obviously what he could offer her in terms of power, influence and a future was more important than me or what I could offer."

"Not any more. You're famous, now. And powerful; influential. She may come running back."

Michael was aware she was probing him, but he did not mind. "Look," he said, leaning closer to her and taking her hand, "I realise now – more and more every day - that what I thought I had with Kate we didn't. And her actions not only revealed those but then confirmed them. I know now we weren't right for each other. Anyway, she's probably got her eye on someone else in the EU hierarchy."

"It's becoming a much smaller pond!" she exclaimed, "She'll have to work fast."

He laughed. "I'm letting her get over her grief and embarrassment, then I'll talk to her."

"That's one of the things I really love about you," she said quietly, after looking deep into his eyes for a moment. "You're so kind."

Michael felt a thrill of pleasure surge through his body when she said this, and he realised once again how he had never really known what true love was before he met Jemima; but at this precise moment it was being revealed anew with a tantalising piquancy that added a delicate mystique. He was happier than he had ever been before. "I will ask you, in time," he said, after a moment.

"Ask me what?" Jemima retorted with mock surprise.

"Ask you to marry me," he said. She went pink, then looked at him, moved closer and planted a kiss on his lips.

"And when you do, I'll say 'Yes'."

Later that evening, during the journey to Brussels, it wasn't only the plane that was in the air: Michael was flying, too.

*

They opened the door fully, which squeaked with a rubbery sound as it did so, and looked out. They were in the middle of what seemed like a huge industrial area, with pylons, silos and pipes everywhere. The concrete stretched beneath them and as far as the eye could see, yet it was deserted, silent. Whatever it was, they were right in the middle of it.

"It's not a nuclear power station, is it?" asked Studd.

"Dunno," retorted Little. "Hope not."

"Well, what are we supposed to do now?" demanded Cash, with panic in his eyes.

"Dunno," said Little again.

"Did they give anyone their mobile phone back?" asked Little. They all shook their heads. "Then we're stuffed," he concluded.

No sooner had he said that, however, than a dirty, old and decrepit maintenance van came out slowly from around a distant silo, meandering slightly across the wide aisle as it approached them. About a hundred yards from them, as if only suddenly just grasping the reality of this unexpected, large scruffy van with eighteen or so well-attired people in front of it, the driver abruptly stopped, unsure whether to continue or turn around and make a hasty exit. The former might entail a lot of paperwork, so perhaps escape was the better option... Then, Cash started waving his arms – as did the others, shouting at him – and he reluctantly started off again and drove slowly towards them. From behind the dirty and scratched windscreen, Cash and his entourage could hardly make out the person driving: when the man got out, they saw he was short, overweight, balding, unshaven and scruffy. Yet, to them, he was like a messiah.

The man, Dimitri, spoke not a word of English but had recognised Cash and surmised he would now be famous for finding the British politician who had disappeared some months before – he had seen and heard it on the news. Later, these people, dumped unceremoniously in the centre of this huge expanse of metalwork, learned it had been a showcase chemical complex built in the pre-Glasnost era to 'prove' that Russia was ahead of the West in terms of chemical prowess: it had never been operational, never used. His job was to ensure that no-one would occupy the site or take anything from it. The authorities had told him it was a Soviet secret and that, one day, it might be fully equipped and put into production again. If the Russian economy ever recovered from its sanctions, of course.

So they were in Russia, not Latvia.

Chapter Forty

As Michael and Leslie Caxton arrived at the Berlaymont building, the hostility was palpable. They were not met by any ministers, presidents or attachés but functionaries who were brisk, polite but unapproachable. Leslie gave Michael a wry raised eyebrow – which was picked up by a cameraman, the clip featuring extensively across news bulletins and front pages of global newspapers the next morning.

In the Council meeting-room, the frost was no less obvious: Guifford Neveu's replacement, Hans Trøngen, conveyed no more than a cold smile, and the others treated Michael and Leslie as if they had brought a nasty smell into a small room. Yet Leslie was used to this from many appearances on *Newsnight*, and Michael had been expecting it anyway. Yet Leslie was in an ebullient, unstoppable mood, and it was infectious: it did not make the admonishments any easier to listen to, but this was not the case of the responses. Leslie had done the trade deals bar some final details, the election had cleared away any British hurdles, the Lords had been revised and would pass any legislation – and what could the EU do about it anyway? It was crushed, fragmented, irrelevant and virtually powerless. "So come on," he said, "and let's get on with helping you that are left and create an Anglo-EU trade deal of benefit to all parties. You have to get your economies trading again: even Germany's caught a cold, and now Greece is coming after you all for damages under the imposed austerity drive which you failed to stop Germany imposing. So it's time to stop wondering what might have been and start trading with us under our conditions so we can all be friends again. We wanted out of the EU, not Europe, so let's get on with it. Anyway, to be blunt, we don't need you any more – we can get anything we need from other countries with lower tariffs, no contributions, no CAP, no customs union and no hassle. So you should be able to see which side your bread is buttered." Things immediately went very smoothly indeed.

That evening, as they left the building in high spirits, there were many camera crews outside. A pretty woman smiled and gave a forlorn wave to Michael, as if trying to attract his attention. It took him a moment to realise that it was Kate. Sensing the awkwardness, Leslie went over to her and offered an interview, whilst Michael was interviewed by others. Yet he could not help but throw a glance every so often to his wife. Yes, she was still his wife, even if events and emotions had changed beyond all recognition.

After thanking Leslie for his honourable intervention, Michael returned with him to their hotel in a slightly chastened mood; having seen Kate there so unexpectedly – no, how could it have been unexpected? that was her job – he felt sad. Against his better judgement, he rang her.

"Hello, Michael," she said. "I'm glad you phoned. I expected it." Michael felt a little piqued by this: was he that soft, that predictable? Everything had changed since he had last seen her just after Guifford's assassination. He had hardly spoken to her, let alone thought about her.

Pulling himself together – he was stronger and more important than he had been that last time – he just said: "Well, it was nice to see you. I thought you looked sad. That's why I phoned."

"Oh. I thought it was because you suddenly realised you still loved me." This hit him hard. Did he? Or was she trying to twist him around her little finger? And if so, why? Was it because he was now powerful and famous, a household name, which he had not been before? Or that she knew now that the chance of a plum job in a rapidly-crumbling EU was becoming daily less probable? "Are you still there?" she asked, as he mulled over his thoughts.

"Yeah. Erm… have you found a nice replacement for Guifford?" was all he could think of asking.

"'Replacement'? That's a cold word." Then, when she got no response, just continued: "There are a couple of people chasing me. But no-one special or permanent."

"No-one with the prospects that Guifford had, then?" A palpable frost was apparent down the line.

"Is that all you think it was?" she responded eventually. He did not reply. "Oh, I see. Well, in that case - "

"No, sorry. Sorry. I just didn't expect this."

"Then why did you ring me?"

"You've already explained that to me. You women always know what we're thinking better than us men do." She smiled to herself. "Where are you?" he asked after a long pause.

"Downstairs in your hotel foyer."

"Ah. So... Erm, I see. Well... Do you want to come up?"

"I'm on my way." After she rang off, Michael wondered what on earth he was doing. She had left him; they were estranged; they were politically and emotionally miles apart now; they had found other lovers... and Jemima was 'the one', he knew. They were so compatible, and he found her so much easier, less prickly, more intellectual, less grasping. Or was she just like Kate, in fact? She had 'promoted' Michael, helped him, been at his side as his career progressed and made him forget Kate to all intents and purposes. He suddenly felt vulnerable: were all women like this? And were all men like him, so easily confused emotionally? One wink from a pretty girl and they were capable of all sorts of emotional and physical treachery. He must ring Jemima, he thought, before... what? No, not now, you fool. He would be tongue-tied. And anyway....

The doorbell rang: when he opened the door and he saw her just standing there, radiant in a flowery dress and silk stockings, high heels and a subtle make-up, he knew he would be even more confused. She came in and walked past him, a hint of perfume wafting around him as she did so, then turned back and nonchalantly gave him a peck on the cheek –

which sent an involuntary thrill down his entire body.

Right on cue, his phone rang. It was Jemima's ringtone. Seeing his confusion, she intimated the bathroom and slipped into it, closing the door quietly as he answered. "Hello, darling," he said softly.

In London, Jemima noticed his hushed tones and asked: "Sorry, is this a bad moment?"

He was glad she had offered an excuse: "Yes, it is, darling – sorry. Just discussing events today – haven't finished yet. Can I call you later?"

"Yes, of course. You ring me."

"Will do. By the way, it's all good news regarding trade deals, whatever."

"Excellent. Tell me all about it later. Love you."

"Love you too," he whispered, and rang off as the bathroom door opened and Kate stepped out. Apart from her heels and stockings, she was completely naked.

Chapter Forty-One

Cash and his colleagues had been correct in suspecting they had been incarcerated in Latvia, but had then been driven East, across the Latvian border, into a sparsely-populated area of western Russia, near to the town of Pustoshka. Needless to say, after the driver had taken them to his local village town hall, from where he had phoned the nearest major police station some one-hundred-and twenty-miles away in Pskov, the Russian authorities had made a huge point of having 'discovered' the missing ex-Prime Minister of Great Britain and putative President of the European Union. Suddenly, the world's press descended on the tiny town, and Cash was back in his element – in front of the cameras. Yet he had been quietly taken aside beforehand by a group of sharp-suited security agents who had made him acutely 'aware' that he had not been taken by Russian forces but Latvian ones. He knew that they knew that this was untrue, of course – he had seen the Russian fighter jets with his own eyes – but was fully aware of the subterfuge and was happy to go along with it if it secured his freedom: he had played similar games himself many times when he had been in power.

The story was that the Latvians would have used him as a bargaining-chip if Russia did not leave the Baltic States as promised after the re-imposition of a democratically-elected British government and the near-collapse of the European Union. He was painfully aware, though, that any deal between Rastov and Gold was nothing he could do anything about: he was now completely powerless. This he realised even more acutely when he was at last availed of what he had been kept in the dark about when under arrest all those weeks in the second prison. Purposely, of course: events regarding the EU and the takeover by the new Restoration government, the clandestine deal between the two presidents, the collusion which would strengthen Britain, America and Russia at the expense of his beloved EU. It angered and depressed him: all the money he had spent trying to thwart the will of the people over Brexit had been wasted - and now Britain was forging ahead in the world as the EU fragmented into bitterness, blame and infighting. And over all this, Rastov would officially be seen as the diplomatic victor.

After a couple of hours of intense interviews, he and his colleagues were plucked from the town by an army helicopter and flown to Ostrov, a more substantial town which had a small airport. From there, they were flown to Saint Petersburg; more interviews and a good night's sleep in a sumptuous hotel later, they were on their way back to Heathrow airport and a Britain which looked exactly the same as when he had left it… but which was now a very different country indeed.

*

Kate walked past Michael again and sat on the bed, facing him. She crossed her legs, then leant back on her arms, which made her breasts even more beautiful as she did so, and smiled. "Well, here we are," she said simply.

"Yes. Here we are. Look, I don't think - "

"Don't worry. It's not permanent – just a hark back to old times – happier times. Anyway, what's the problem? It's not as if it's the first time, is it?"

And perhaps not the last, Michael thought, observing her superb body, which he had hitherto perhaps always taken for granted. But Jemima was stunning as well, so he blurted out, "Look, I'm with someone else, Kate - "

Kate looked at him with a coy smile. "Yes, I know – Jemima. And very nice she looks, too. You seem well-matched. But I'm still your wife."

Michael had not been so bewildered for months. He could not think straight and his sense of what was right and wrong was tying him in knots; and yet, his nether regions were combating his doubts and making any polemic impossible. He knew any resort back to what had gone before would be stupid and dangerous, yet he had suddenly been reminded of all the reasons he had fallen for her in the first place – and not just her beauty, but her *self-assurance*, her impudence. It was compelling, devastating and irresistible.

He sat on the bed. "This isn't right. I'm not going to jeopardise my relationship with - "

She had sprung up and stopped Jemima's name being emitted by thrusting her tongue into his mouth and was swirling it around. His instincts were in chaos as she pulled him onto her whilst tugging at his shirt and tie, the tearing sound almost unheard as they started rolling and groaning on the bed. Then she kicked off her shoes and found his being pulled roughly off, too; her vagina was wet and inviting as his underwear disappeared across the room and he was inside her, the pulsing of his loins in perfect harmony with hers. It had never, ever been like this before with her – the expectation of their eventual marriage had almost circumnavigated the joy of emotion, but here it was – at the wrong moment – making an unwelcome introduction. What had Guifford done to her, he wondered, to make her so irrepressibly sexual, animal and yet harshly feminine? And then he realised that Jemima, too, had made him a better lover – so now he could enjoy the physical side with no inhibitions, worries or cares: they could be rationalised when the moment was over. But it would be a very long moment. All night, in fact.

*

The next day, things progressed well with the EU. Despite some barbs, wrangling and points of order, Leslie and Michael soon got onto the basic terms of a trade deal with the rump of the EU. It would not take two years: based on a loose interpretation of WTO rules, the elements were put before the EU Council. And ratified a week later.

*

In those interim days, Michael had seen Kate every night; and when Jemima had rung to ask why he had not called her back on the first evening he had lied, explaining he had fallen asleep when he got back to his room. From then on, he called her frequently so she would suspect nothing; deep down, too, he was certain that any resurgent feelings for Kate would not stand the test of time. It was a mutual expression of unfinished business and a lust for the past which they now both knew had never quite materialised properly. He was privately proud that he could have had a lady in two cities but knew that, if this came out, his career would be blown wide open – and all three would be hurt by the fallout. Reluctantly, then, he told Kate the night prior to his return to London and Parliament that it would have to end. As always, she understood and was sympathetic, accepting; she made the point that, now Britain was out of the EU, they had nothing to divide them. Michael, though, suspected old rivalries and differences would recur anyway. But they would still be friends, he hoped; and she agreed. He was relieved: for he still felt bad about being disloyal to Jemima but forced himself to believe that the episode with Kate would make their relationship even happier together in the long term - once the dust had settled.

Chapter Forty-Two

Before being released from Russian captivity, Cash and his colleagues had been lectured by one of Rastov's closest advisors to ensure they understood what the parameters were going to be from then on; any evidence they found, suspected or had been disseminated - that Gold and Rastov had colluded to 'escort' them away from Britain and the EU - would be fiercely denied and cause a massive diplomatic incident. In addition, Cash had been saved from ignominy and a possibly unpleasant end if he had continued his undemocratic and unlawful assumption of power against the elected will of the British people, even if he felt he had been compromised by the unholy alliance of Russia and the USA. When he pointed out that this was rich coming from an authoritarian country which allegedly interfered in the politics of other countries, the stark and immutable response was that it was worse to betray your own country than someone else's – and that he risked everything by causing any disturbance. In fact, if he did, then all his houses, assets and foundations would 'unexpectedly' be found to be illegally procured or linked to proscribed terrorist organisations, which would ruin him forever – and disgrace him in the eyes of the world.

His reaction – and that of the others - had been to accept: what else could they do? He had to think of Coralie and the children, and was now in no position to rock the boat. He could now enjoy life almost anywhere in the world and hobnob with old presidents and ministers, and discuss his impact on the world in a glow of international warmth.

All this passed through his mind as he touched down at Heathrow and stood on the aircraft steps to wave to the crowd. But there was none – just a couple of cameramen and reporters. He realised he and his colleagues had become non-people in their own country, and they were old news. Time had moved on. This was highlighted further after he passed through customs and found the bright lights and cameras were waiting. Again, he smiled and waved – but they were pointing in a different direction and the focus, plaudits and questions were being directed at Leslie Caxton and Michael, who had just arrived back from Brussels. Cash and his colleagues were photographed by a few well-wishers and subjected to not a few boos: the writing was on the wall and they quietly dispersed into the crowd.

Later in Downing Street, Leslie and Michael were briefing the Cabinet on what they had achieved, and were lauded all round. The deal with the EU was better than anything the previous hostile diplomacy would have foretold, and it looked now as if Germany's closet hopes of ruling Europe economically through the imposed beneficial value of the euro at the expense of everyone else's economies would soon be a broken dream. Since Britain's markets were taking off spectacularly – and Leslie and Michael's news had ensured the pound and FTSE soared further – hostility was cast aside as they all wanted a share of it. The former EU countries which had left the euro each had their own bespoke trade deals with Britain now, and even the Scots had officially accepted they were better off within the UK than the EU. And these economic developments meant that any rancour with Ireland over borders with an EU and a non-EU country were superfluous: under covert pressure from Gold, a quick referendum was taken in Ireland on whether that country should join the British Isles economically but not politically. It was carried by a huge majority, which was augmented by the fact that President Gold had also openly promised huge further investment in Ireland should they decide to join Britain.

*

Kate was waiting outside the Berlaymont building in Brussels with a now very small clique of media. The heads of the only countries left in the European Union were about to arrive, and the BBC – still steadfastly enamoured with the EU project – was still doing its best to perpetuate the idea that the EU was important to Britain: hence Kate's continuing presence there. Yet the building had a haunted and empty demeanour now, and the once-vibrant and colourful array of flags had been depleted to such an extent that even the ones that still fluttered limply between now-empty flagpoles seemed isolated, sad and alone.

Then suddenly a number of international news

crews were turning up, arriving from all corners of the city, and the numbers swelled to perhaps three or four times what they had been. At first, there was an air of bemusement, but Kate quickly realised that something big – very big – was about to be announced, and news crews were racing to get to the building. It was the busiest she had seen it for many months, the drip-drip of countries leaving making the institution less newsworthy with each passing day. But something was up – and she felt she knew what it might be. Indeed, despite having sated her old feelings for Michael recently – and secretly realising that perhaps she should not have been so hot-headed and ambitious, especially as he was now more powerful than her previous lover – she was now linked to a rich Luxembourg MEP who would leave his wife shortly. Possibly for her, if she played her cards right. She had been with him the night before, but he had said nothing to her about a possible big announcement: yet he would have known about it, but had said nor implied nothing.

The crews were soon overwhelming the front of the building, yet there was no podium: that must mean that the announcement – whatever it was – would take place inside, in the giant assembly hall used for such grandstanding events. Sure enough, the crews were suddenly being given security checks and invited into that main area: this, beyond doubt, was going to be something huge, and Kate made sure she was at the front of the horde with her cameraman. The new European Commission President, Klaus Behrens, was already there, as were all the other leaders of the remaining European States. They were trying to show an indignant and united front: so much so that Kate instinctively had the feeling that they were about to announce that the European Union was now finished.

And she was right. As President Behrens walked solemnly to the podium, the mood was leaden but the air vibrant with anticipation. "My friends and supporters," he began, "today marks a very sad and depressing day in the history of our great continent, Europe. As you all know, we started a great project in Rome in 1957 to unite and protect, care for, enhance and bring together from the brink of war and poverty the lives of millions of people from a diversity of nations. We made great strides and ever since have been uniting people with different histories, cultures and beliefs into one great race – Europeans. We believed that, despite our diversities, we had the will to forge a race of different identities into one great nation. We broke down barriers, supported failing industries, improved the health and hopes of millions, allowing the four freedoms - movement of goods, people, services and capital across our continent to benefit our peoples. We have had huge successes – the euro, for example," someone sniggered loudly, "and we had two of the greatest races on our planet – Germany and France – working together rather than against each other for the betterment of the rest of the lands. Yes, we made mistakes… but these should never have been allowed to lead to the decision we are taking today. I – we – do not intend to be angry, or to blame anyone or anything, but it is certainly relevant that the failure of Great Britain to vote to remain in the European Union caused a cataclysmic rupture - "

"Rubbish! It was your invasion of a sovereign

member state and the disaster of the euro that caused that!" shouted a British journalist to a mix of applause, boos, cheers and cat-calls.

Behrens waited, then continued: "Past events have aroused a number of passions," he stated simply, "but we did what we did for the best outcome as we believed it."

"Fascists!" shouted the man, who was then told to be quiet or he would be escorted from the hall. Again, Behrens continued: "The rupture had deep consequences. And perhaps our will to prevail was hasty and extreme, but we always felt that the end justified the means."

"Trotsky said that!" shouted a Hungarian journalist. "So you are communists after all!"

"I should have chosen my words more carefully," admitted Behrens. "Actually, though, it was Machiavelli."

"Even worse!" exclaimed the man.

"Well, whoever said it," Behrens continued dispassionately, "the result is that today, sadly, I am instructed by the European Commission to state that the European Union, as it currently exists, will now cease to continue as from this moment forward."

A hush descended on the gathering, as a sense of disbelief and astonishment cloaked the hall. Then some started shouting, "No, no!" as others applauded and cheered: yet whichever the faction, the announcement confected a feeling of hollowness and failure.

After a moment, as the noise died down, Behrens then said resolutely and with vigour: "However…

there will be a *new* union, consisting of Germany, Belgium, Luxembourg, Austria, Spain and Portugal. Six nations, as there were at the beginning of this noble concept."

"Conquest, more like," shouted the same British journalist, who was then escorted from the proceedings. 'He'll get the first scoop now,' thought Kate.

President Behrens continued. "We will call this new union 'The Democratic Union of European States', or DUES. It will be represented from this building and takes effect from now, with its constitution and framework to be developed over the coming months. The Strasbourg building will be mothballed until or unless the union grows to a comparative size in the future. The DUES will be fundamentally different from the EU in that all states will have equal parity, whatever their size. There will also, from the outset, be associate members who wish to proceed to this new destination in a manner more suited to their situations. Currently, these will include Greece, Norway, Sweden, Denmark and Finland. The Visegrad countries – Poland, the Czech Republic, Hungary, Slovakia, and also the Baltic states – Latvia, Estonia and Lithuania – have decided to leave from this moment to pursue their own destinies."

"What about the euro?" a Spanish journalist shouted.

"I was just coming to that. For now, while the upheaval on currency markets takes stock of what I have just announced, the euro will exist for the foreseeable future, but with a major difference. It will start at the same rate across all the DUES, but each state will float its euro as if it was a national currency so, for example, there will be a Spanish euro, a German euro, etc. If states wish to revert to their own currencies in future, this is something which will be discussed at the appropriate time. What this will do is allow each state to find its own natural level and to be able to devalue if necessary, so helping their national economies. The whole construct will be overseen, as now, by the ECB."

Kate was astonished at this: the euro had been created so Germany would reign supreme at its preferential rate forever – the reason why Italy, Greece, France, Spain and Portugal, in particular, had suffered; this was a huge climbdown from them. Now Germany would have to compete with other countries within their own bloc on equal terms, which could only be a good thing.

A hand squeezed her shoulder: looking around, she saw it was Christoph, her new lover. He looked grave but resolute, and he smiled coyly. "If you want an interview, they want you to do it, as they wish the BBC to be first. So if you want to talk to Behrens, you have an exclusive. Be ready to go in fifteen minutes. In my office. It's all arranged."

"But we're not finished here yet," she protested.

"There is little more – believe me," he said. "But isn't *this*," – and he waved a hand to imply the room and its historic announcement – "big enough for you?" He smiled again: he was nice, she thought. Yes, he'll do. And he's good-looking, too. He continued: "Behrens wants you to do the interview and will answer any questions you wish to ask. I've ensured that." 'Influence, too,' thought Kate. She would do well to stay with him.

"OK," she agreed. "Thanks, Christoph." And she rose and went to tell her cameraman to get lit and set up as soon as possible in Christoph's office.

Chapter Forty-Three

The news inevitably caused enormous see-saws of capital and stock markets across the world: after sixty years of such a powerful bloc, what else could happen? The biggest story was generally agreed to be the humbling of Germany – as it was most often interpreted – and the fact that from now on they would have to abide by consensual rules rather than creating and rigidly applying them. After a few days, the markets started to settle: when they did, Greece was the first to devalue its euro – to such an extent that investment started to pour into the country and holiday bookings there soared. It was good for Greece – as it would turn out to be for many other nations as well, whether inside or outside the DUES…

Even Kate was not as despairing as she thought she would have been, and despite her overall upset at the demise of what could have been a great project if it had been handled more sensitively and democratically, even she found herself thinking that the European gravy-train had crashed into the slough of its own smug self-importance, corruption and undemocratic, bullying practices. Deep inside, she realised that Michael had been right, and for both reasons – if tinged with a slight regret – she felt intensely happy.

*

Michael's return to Britain in triumph with Leslie had also helped his relationship with Jemima: she was so proud of him. His unexpected dalliance with his wife was quickly not so much forgotten as dismissed. Whilst he privately berated himself for his weak behaviour it was his secret and so he could contain it. Also, he realised that it was the perfect full-stop to an imperfect relationship. It had ended in fire and passion on a high note that was appreciated by both parties – and it proved to him that although the marriage had not lasted a lifetime, it had been good before the tumult of Brexit. He knew several friends and relatives who had split, walked out, shouted and abused each other over the issue and, whilst this had happened to him too, his emotional and then geographical distance from Kate had at least not been too hostile, if not completely cordial either. It had been instrumental in making his career take off in such a big way, too, and for that he would always be grateful. Gains and losses – they were both huge.

That weekend he and Jemima spent together. They had much the same tastes – music, literature, art films – and an innate understanding. The fact that they were both so committed to the same goal – of making Britain sovereign, democratic, successful and free again – was a fundamental part of their chemical make-up: if there were any disagreements, they were only minor ones and never developed into full-blown rows. Their friends, too, all seemed to be drawn from the same milieu but that never fostered complacency or boredom: they came from a wide network of professions and backgrounds and none ever looked down on anyone as Kate's friend Xenia had done.

A few days later, Michael received a text from Kate which said she needed an urgent meeting with him. He had heard that she had been seeing Christoph, a wealthy Luxembourg MEP and banker, from a friend who was an MEP herself. Apparently, it was no secret in Brussels that they had started a relationship and it appeared Kate wanted a divorce, wanting to marry Christoph as quickly as possible. Yet the speed of the proposed settlement troubled him: why the hurry?

He told Jemima and, as always, she was understanding and co-operative, saying that he should see Kate as soon as he could. Two days later, they met in an Oxford Street department store and had tea. She came straight to the point.

"Michael, I know you've heard that Christoph wants to marry me, and I've accepted in principle."

"That's marvellous, Kate. I'm so pleased for you."

Yet she seemed anything but happy, and obviously had something of pressing importance on her mind. "I know it's over between us," she continued, "but I hope we can still be friends after we divorce."

"I don't see why not. Jemima's very understanding and - "

"There's more. The point is... well, you remember our last wonderful few nights together?"

"I could hardly forget. They were the most beautiful and explosive final moments a couple could ever have had."

She looked down and he could see she was trying to hold back the tears. "The point is," she said again, "I want to get this all done and settled quickly."

"OK. But why the rush?"

She looked down again and a tear dropped onto her dress. "Bugger," she said, trying to dab it dry with a napkin. Then she looked up at him and her whole face was wet, the small amount of mascara she needed running into tiny rivulets down her cheeks. "You see, Michael, you're going to be a father… and I'd like Christoph to think it's his, because – well, he didn't know that you and I were – you know – at the time we were… So, for his sake and mine – and yours, of course, I'd like to get it all done as soon as possible. Jemima need never know… and Christoph is nice… very wealthy… and I don't want to lose him, so…"

Michael put an arm around her and kissed her wet lips. The news had completely floored him – he had not expected this. "Well, that's fine by me," he said heroically. "We'd better get cracking, then. But are you sure you wouldn't rather… you know…?"

"Get rid of it? Certainly not! It's our little secret and it would be so nice to have something of you to grow up with me. Because we were happy once, weren't we? Christoph and I can have another in time… but I just don't want to risk losing him if he got to know. It would be so unfair on him."

Michael was both flattered and perturbed. This woman he once loved, who had become estranged through mutual dissent due to an issue bigger than both of them, wanted to divorce him yet have his child for past emotional reasons - but quickly, so that her current lover would not suspect anything. It was bizarre.

"I don't think either Christoph or Jemima should ever know," he said at length. "As you say, it'll be our little secret. I'll ring the solicitor tomorrow and let you know the details. But no complications – we split everything. If we don't, it'll drag on for ages."

She nodded and smiled. "That's fine," she said. "And don't worry about me – I shan't be short of a few bob."

So there it was. She had reverted to type – the girl he never thought she was but had become, primarily wanting power and money. With the demise of Guifford, though, she had decided to accept just the money, with the emotional prop of having his child. At least, though, she had just about conceded that Christoph was nice – that was some respite... He was suddenly very keen indeed to get back to Jemima. They both soon parted and he did just that. He never saw her again.

Chapter Forty-Four

The fallout from recent political events eventually settled into a nervous balancing act between nations. Britain's unofficial new-found leadership of the post-EU and global trade – situated so perfectly between Europe and the United States – meant that if there were headwinds in one hemisphere they could be counteracted in the other. From being an invaded country a few months before, it was Britain which was suddenly seen again as a world leader in diplomacy, trade, law and innovation, as it had been from the eighteenth century until its relative demise just before – and then during – its membership of the European Union. Those Remainers who had seen only doom and collapse were ever more frustrated and annoyed as Britain rose from the ashes once more, the shackles of laws irrelevant to its existence no longer a hindrance. Without the CAP or billions of pounds of contributions every year, the spark of innovation made the country richer again, too. A new relationship with almost every other country in the world was now a reality, and the Commonwealth was becoming relevant and powerful once more, with many who had left in the 1970s and 1980s re-joining as full or associate members. Britain's global past was now reaping dividends again as food costs plummeted due to cheaper food from Africa and India – and seasonal foods and cheaper wines from far-flung Commonwealth friends such as Australia and New Zealand. The east coast started its fishing industry again, giving a boost to the whole of the east and south of the country from Aberdeen around to Cornwall, and the dream of virtually full employment again became a tangible probability. With control of its borders, too, Britain could choose the best people from around the world, without being forced to accept workers it did not need. And when the Chancellor suddenly slashed taxes, employment and wages increased: soon, more British people than ever were in work, lured by the prospect of a better life with more money than had ever been possible on benefits.

*

And yet the Remainers griped: unwilling to believe or accept they had ever been proved wrong, they still grasped at any tiny slowdown of growth, GDP, or failed international deal as justification of their superior understanding of how the world works. Yet the facts were stark: Britain – and the EU states which had left the EU – were booming again in a spirit of mutual self-reliance with friends, rather than resented and untrusted antagonists in the same bloc. The newly-invigorated Commonwealth, too, was doing wonders for their countries – and economies. Even environmental problems were sorted quickly and amicably across nations: the use of plastics and over-packaging was restricted dramatically by mutual consent, not diktat, and bio-degradable technology was enforced globally. The seas, in time, started to recover as a result: what had been the cusp of an environmental disaster had been circumvented by countries pooling resources for the betterment of the planet rather than narrow competitive instincts, rivalries and jealousies between unwieldy and self-important blocs. It was testament to a world – not just Europe – which had been set free.

But it would take another ten years – and the resurgence of a freed, nation-loving but global new generation – before these obstructionist and selfish Luddites would pass into their dotage, outplayed but unbroken. Most of them, despite the fire and idealism – and self-importance – soon faded into the twilight, most forgotten footnotes in history. The only one who was occasionally discussed and interviewed was Terry Cash, who had gone to live in Geneva. He had made it too clear after his removal that he did not like Britain any more, which was generally interpreted as spite for Britain not liking him. He was forever tainted with his support for the EU's invasion but still resolutely spent his life justifying it. Yet he and his colleagues would forever be known as the people representing 'The Age of the Elites'. In contrast, it was quietly recognised that it had not been them with the vision of a free, sovereign country, but the working people of Britain: it was they who had determined to vote for it through Brexit and it was they who had halted a corrupt, egotistical and self-satisfied status quo. And the whole world would be the better for it.

Best of all, Britain was Great Britain again – and daily becoming greater still.

EPILOGUE

Some years later, when the upheavals of Brexit and the consequent invasion of Britain were but a distant memory, Michael sat down to write his memoirs. He had done well: Tessa Lewis had won a further landslide election and he had succeeded her as Prime Minister, serving two terms as a very popular and clever administrator. He had married Jemima soon after his divorce from Kate and they produced two children, both of whom became successful and well-known. How could they not, in a country which had re-found its confidence and direction, and whose laws, trade expertise, innovation and traditions had become foundation benchmarks for so many global countries?

There had been crises and difficult times, of course: that was life, politics… The rest of Europe had become a series of nation-states and the people in each generally found they preferred that condition to being part of a bland, homogenous mass, where local colour, customs, opinions and traditions were seen as something to cherish rather than subdue. All the threats of visas, punishments, tariffs and barriers had vanished as countries re-adjusted in an adult way to the realities of what people felt happiest with, and the products and services they needed in a global world. Poverty had become confined to only a few parts of the world, and environmental crises had provoked intelligent and far-reaching solutions – most notably the development of capture technology which meant that power generated from renewable sources could be used even when there was no wind or light. And thorium power had made a huge contribution to energy needs, its small footprint allowing the creation of hundreds of mini-power plants around the world, minimising pylons and cables as the power could be placed exactly where it was needed.

One day, sitting in his study in his house in Wiltshire, there was a ring on Michael's doorbell. His children were living in London and Jemima was out, so it was he who answered the door.

In front of him stood a beautiful girl, tall, lissom and long-haired, who seemed to look familiar, yet whom he was sure he had never met before. "Hello," she said, flicking her hair from her face as the light caught an impeccable pair of white teeth. "Are you Michael?"

"Er, yes…"

"Hello, Daddy," she said simply, looking slightly coy and embarrassed. "I'm Lucy."

"Lucy? You mean…?"

"Yes," she replied with a disarming laugh. "I'm you daughter by Kate. May I come in?"

Michael could hardly speak, so waved her into the sitting-room. He was relieved that Jemima was not there, as it would have caused some awkward explanations.

"I hope I'm not inconveniencing you," she said, then, seeing the astonishment on his face, added, "or have I shocked you too much? Mummy said you'd be surprised."

Michael replied that it was, indeed, a shock and, yes, a surprise too; in her looks and movements he could see Kate's features, which was both unnerving and fascinating, and why he instinctively felt he had known her. Then she suddenly came up with a direct statement, which he also recognised as a trait of Kate's.

"Well, this is just to let you know that sadly Mummy died last week and so I'm here to tell you the news – but to introduce myself at the same time."

"Died?" Michael eventually managed to say. "But why did I not know?"

"You never kept in touch," was the slightly admonishing reply.

"But that was the deal – it was what your mother wanted. I'd have kept in touch if - "

"It doesn't matter. But she wanted me to be the one to tell you. She'd been suffering with depression for a while, which led to cancer, which… eventually led to what happened last week. But she didn't tell you because she didn't want to embarrass you or rake up the past."

Michael was speechless, heartbroken and confused. "I never saw her after she said she wanted to marry Christoph."

"She often talked about you – in private of course. Christoph left her after a few years but kept her in the manner she had come to expect. I was always told I was your child, not his – when I was old enough to understand and not tell Christoph, that is. But you always seemed to be, well, 'there', even if I never met you. He was distant. Perhaps he knew I wasn't his – but he never said anything."

So Kate had been secretly harbouring Michael's memory ever since she left him. And he had never told Jemima, as they had agreed. "I'm delighted you've come here," he said after a few moments' reflection, "but you'd better go now. It's all a bit too much for me at the moment." He was aware that tears were welling up, but managed to continue. "I'm glad my wife's not here… You see, as I say, I never told her and, after all this time, I don't really want to bring it all up now – especially under the sad circumstances. I don't think I could cope."

Lucy put a hand on his knee. "I understand," she said simply. "That's why I waited for her to leave. She always goes out on Tuesdays – I knew that."

Smart girl, he thought. And kind, too. Just like her mother. "But you must give me your details – we'll meet up again," he said.

"I'd like that. Daddy."

And she left. When Jemima returned some hours later, she found her husband in a strange, subdued and introverted mood, which she had never seen before.

Like Brexit, the past had become the present – but in completely different ways.

AUTHOR BIOGRAPHY

RICHARD SIMON was born in London to an actor/writer and actress. He studied at schools in London and Sussex and spent his career in broadcast and corporate television, writing many scripts and treatments and making documentaries, business programmes and dramas. His interest in global politics began when he became concerned at former Prime Minister Edward Heath's statement that joining the European Economic Community (forerunner to the EU) would "involve no essential loss of sovereignty". "The word 'essential' always stuck in my mind as weasel words and ones which could in time betray our nation," he says, "and I was not proved wrong." He has despaired for years at the erosion of Britain's influence and ability to enact its own laws and priorities, and when the Referendum was announced became an avid Brexiteer, playing a prominent part in urging people to vote to Leave. With that unbounded joy realised, he started to see how vested interests and illiberal forces would try to thwart the result and bend the word 'democracy' to an untrue and wilfully misrepresented end. This novel is the result.

Richard and his wife have no children which is, in their view, 'the best thing they never did' and live in London and Wiltshire.

Printed in Great Britain
by Amazon